VOLUME EIGHT OF THE

YALE EDITION OF THE

UNPUBLISHED WRITINGS OF

GERTRUDE STEIN

under the general editorship of

Carl Van Vechten

with an advisory committee of

Donald Gallup,

Donald Sutherland,

and Thornton Wilder

THE YALE EDITION OF THE

UNPUBLISHED WRITINGS OF GERTRUDE STEIN

Two: Gertrude Stein and Her Brother

Mrs. Reynolds and Five Earlier Novelettes

Bee Time Vine and Other Pieces (1913–1927)

As Fine as Melanctha (1914–1930)

Painted Lace and Other Pieces (1914–1937)

Stanzas in Meditation and Other Poems (1929–1933)

Alphabets and Birthdays

A Novel of Thank You

A NOVEL

OF THANK YOU

BY GERTRUDE STEIN

with an Introduction by Carl Van Vechten

Select Bibliographies Reprint Series

BOOKS FOR LIBRARIES PRESS
FREEPORT, NEW YORK

PS
3537
.T323
A6
1969
V. 8

S 8192 m

M

STANDARD BOOK NUMBER:

8369-5164-6

LIBRARY OF CONGRESS CATALOG CARD NUMBER:

73-103664

PRINTED IN THE UNITED STATES OF AMERICA

CONTENTS

Introduction by Carl Van Vechten   vii

A Novel of Thank You (1925–26)   3

Three Moral Tales (1920–21)   243

Prudence Caution and Foresight, A Story of Avignon
   (1922)   253

A Little Novel (1926)   261

A FEW NOTES À PROPOS OF A
"Little" Novel of Thank You

by Carl Van Vechten

NOBODY was more surprised than I to read in the *New York Times* of August 11, 1946, shortly after Gertrude Stein's death, that she had made me, in some of her last conscious moments, her literary executor, with instructions to publish what material of hers still remained unpublished, for which purpose she instructed her attorney to provide me with the essential sums of money. My initial feeling was that Gertrude had bitten off more than I could easily chew, a feeling greatly intensified after I had inquired of certain publishing friends of mine how much it would cost to print and bind the vast pile of manuscript still unpublished. The sums mentioned were so enormous that my heart sank at the thought of the project ahead of me.

Gradually, however, the prospect became brighter. In several institutions of learning Gertrude was advanced to the required-reading category, and drama groups in many parts of the country were glad to pay royalties to produce her plays. Her operas, of which Virgil Thomson was the principal composer, were heard on the radio. Rinehart and Company issued her *Last Operas and Plays*, many of which had not yet appeared on the printed page. The Banyan Press (was she known as Gismonda or Theodora?) published a short detective story, *Blood on the Dining-Room Floor*, without any notable degree of success, but when later this Press published "Q. E. D." (issued under the substituted title of *Things as They Are*) and when, at some subsequent period, Edmund Wilson wrote a flaming review of this book for the *New Yorker*, the whole edition sold out within a week at ten dollars a copy! Much of Gertrude was heard on the radio and the dramatic version of *Brewsie and Willie* was presented over television.

I cannot recall the exact date, but it was probably around 1950, that Donald Gallup wrote me, or told me, that we could make a reasonable arrangement with the Yale University Press (which had published *Four in America* in 1947) to undertake the publication of what unpublished material still remained, all of it lodged in the Yale University Library. From the initial production, *Two: Gertrude Stein and Her Brother, and Other Early Portraits* (1951), until the last, this volume of *A Novel of Thank You*, the Yale Press has continued to print one volume a year.

There are several references in Gertrude's letters to "A Novel of Thank You," apparently written at Bilignin in 1925–26. In a letter to me, postmarked December 4, 1926, she wrote: "I have just finished a longish novel. I rather like it." In *The Autobiography of Alice B. Toklas*, Gertrude wrote:

> Brewer was interested in the work of Gertrude Stein and though he promised nothing he and she talked over the possibilities of his firm printing something of hers. She had just written a short novel called A Novel of Thank You.

Joseph Brewer's letters to Gertrude do not mention this conversation and, as he himself remembers nothing of it, it is quite likely that this transaction never went very far, if indeed it actually was begun at all. What, eventually, Joseph Brewer published was not "A Novel of Thank You," but *Useful Knowledge*, a volume of short pieces. There was, however, an earlier attempt than the present one toward the publication of "A Novel of Thank You," made by an Englishman named Edward W. Titus who controlled a Paris book store. His letters to Gertrude (the first one dated March 9, 1927) are fortunately preserved in the Yale Collection. Hers to him, unfortunately, are still unavailable. Titus' letters, particularly the final·one, are sufficiently acrimonious to suggest that hers to him must have been burning.

Titus actually began to print the novel and he also issued a prospectus for it. Unfortunately, Yale does not possess a copy of this prospectus and I have been unable to locate one in any other assortment of source material. The letter to me in which Gertrude indicates that she has finally finished the novel is dated December 4, 1926. Titus' letter announcing his terms for the publication of the book is dated May 3, 1927, and his final letter, which seems to have ended the correspondence, is dated November 9, 1927. According to Miss Toklas' recollection, Gertrude broke with Mr. Titus because she disapproved of the American publicity. But the American publicity, brought about by Mr. Titus' prospectus, occurred in late December 1927 and early January 1928, a fact which makes it difficult to explain why, after Mr. Titus' letter dated early in November there should have been publicity in America later in 1927 and early in 1928.

According to Gertrude Stein's letters, "A Novel of Thank You" was written in 1925 and 1926, not very prolific years for our author. It was some time during the middle twenties that Gertrude announced her intention to write in a more obscure vein than she had employed hitherto in her career. Certainly, "A Novel of Thank You" is one of her most hermetic books and one about which very little has been written, even by Gertrude, or remembered, even by Alice Toklas. Remy de Gourmont's comment on Villiers de l'Isle Adam has something to tell us about Gertrude at this epoch: "L'Idéalisme de Villiers était un véritable idéalisme verbal, c'est-à-dire qu'il croyait vraiment à la puissance evocative des mots, à leur vertu magique." And George Moore actually may have had Gertrude Stein in mind when he said to me: "There are no such things as thoughts, only words." A few lines glow with intensity out of "A Novel of Thank You." For instance, "Before the flowers of friendship faded, friendship faded" makes its witty début. Actual names are scattered through the text, together with invented ones: Elmer Harden, Allen Tanner, Robert Coates, Mrs. (*sic*) Clermont-Tonnerre (*née* de Gramont), (Henry) McBride, (Virgil)

Thomson, (William Aspenwall) Bradley, Emily Chadbourne, Beverly Nichols, and Avery Hopwood.

Many of the following comments were made by Alice Toklas on rereading the manuscript. The page numbers refer the reader to the present volume. Page 29: Mr. and Mrs. Pernollet, of the Hôtel Pernollet at Belley, where Gertrude and Alice summered before they discovered the adjacent Bilignin. Skylarks appear just above this passage, mention of which caused Alice to comment: "Skylarks should not be here; Bilignin had nightingales"; page 31: Lindo Webb, English vice-consul at Mallorca, 1915; page 40: Etienne (Pernollet); page 47: "They felt an anxious moment coming" is the title of a short piece by Gertrude; page 58: Zenobie, Marie Jeanne, and Hélène were waitresses at the Hôtel Pernollet; page 63: Emily Dawson was a cousin of the first Mrs. Berenson, the first Mrs. Bertrand Russell, and Logan Pearsall Smith; she said of Mrs. Michael Stein that she was something between a Luini and a carpet-sweeper; page 65: Madame Mont-Blanc was so called by Gertrude when seen on a clear day from a spot near Belley, to which she drove frequently; page 65: Thérèse-Josephine and Louise were maids at the Hôtel Pernollet; page 71: pansies were Gertrude's favorite flowers; page 76: Ethel Mars, American painter and the original of Miss Furr in Gertrude's story, "Miss Furr and Miss Skeene"; page 77: "In the course of conversation" was Leo Stein's explanation when Gertrude scolded him for repeating something she had asked him *not* to repeat; page 77: Julia Ford was Ford Madox Ford's daughter; page 78: Gabrielle de Manzie, Doctor Claribel Cone, and Dora and Minnie Meiningen, Gertrude had known as a young girl in California; page 90: Janet Scudder, an American sculptor, a school friend of my sister Emma, who was living in Paris at this period; page 90: Paul Chalfin, American painter, also a friend of mine living in Paris before World War I; page 95: Célestine, another of the servants; "I can feel the Beauty" was the title of another short piece by Gertrude; page 97: Pritchard, friend of Emily Chadbourne, later a well-known professor at Oxford; page 98: Josephine Baker—Caroline Regan brought the Harlem group to Paris as the Revue Nègre; her sister, Katherine Dudley made the costumes for the revue;

page 105: Nellie and Frank Jacott, California friends of Gertrude Stein and Alice Toklas; René Crevel, Gertrude's favorite of his generation; page 130: Allen Tanner, an American accompanist; page 135: Romaine Brooks, an American painter, who painted an excellent portrait of me, gave it to me, and later asked for it back; Constance Fletcher, English writer; page 140: Robert Coates, whose first book Gertrude liked a lot, is now a contributor to the *New Yorker*; page 151: "Nice and quiet, I thank you!" was said by an uncle of Alice Toklas during the collapse of a boom to a banker who had inquired how his mining stocks were; page 154: the third of February was Gertrude Stein's birthday; page 161: Georgiana Goddard King was an old friend of Gertrude, professor of belles-lettres at Bryn Mawr; page 161: Neith (Boyce) Hapgood, wife of Hutchins Hapgood, an early friend of Gertrude; page 170: Bernardine Szold, at this period a partner of Schiaparelli, also a friend of Fania Marinoff; page 176: "Believe me, it is not only for my pleasure that I do it," was said in the early Nevada days by a man when presenting his fiancée; page 196: Sophie Regan and her mother (*née* Dudley, now Mrs. Joseph Delteil); Grace Lewellyn Janes, a beautiful San Francisco girl; page 229: Beverly Nichols, English writer; page 230: Mildred Aldrich, a dear friend of Gertrude, author of *A Hilltop on the Marne;* page 237: "Jews do not like the country," observation of a doughboy—overheard by Gertrude—who gave this as an explanation of why he did not marry his fiancée.

As is usual in any book by Gertrude Stein, there are passages of wit and beauty. Such passages, indeed, abound in "A Novel of Thank You"; for example (page 44):

It is to be asked does he do it because he prefers country to country or does he do it because he prefers morning to afternoon. Does he do it because he prefers pieces to pieces or does he do it because he prefers one to one. Does he do it because he prefers smaller to larger or does he do it for the purpose of not yet. Does he do it because it is at least as well or does he do it because he is delighted. Does he do it because five is satisfactory when it is when it has been added or does he do it because he is remembered as well. Does he do it because he is able to do it or does he do it because he hears it as well. Does he do it because he is placed beside it or does he do it because it is arranged so well. Does he do it because it is as well divided or does he do it because it is followed as well. Does he do it because if it is done now or if it is done now does he do it as what has meant to reach to the day when afterwards when time as it shall have to arrange that in the meantime fortunately by this and that of course.

The following passage (page 104) is just as typically Steinese:

There can be two kinds of ladies and cakes two kinds of children and bread two kinds of men and rice. There can be two kinds of birds and weights two kinds of dolls and Simons two kinds of losses and cups. There can be two kinds of change and changes two kinds of miles and mingling two kinds of settling and their. There they are.

Here is another peculiarly Steinian paragraph (page 117):

There is no difference between at that time and at that time there is no difference between how do you do and how do you do there is no difference between every little while and every little while there is no difference between singling them out and singling them out there is no difference between charming and charming there is no difference between relating it to it and relating it to it there is no difference between they made it more nearly the same and they made it more nearly the same there is no difference between not more than there is and not more than there is there is no difference between what is more used and what is more used there is no difference between nearly as many and nearly as many there is no difference between as many as that in all and as many as that in all there is no difference between when there can be no thought of why they had no further need of that and when there can be no thought of why they had no further need of that there is no difference between as they went there very often it made no difference to them as they might just as well be praised and as they went there very often it made no difference to them as they might just as well be praised and there is no difference between they had leaned forward not to see but to be comfortable and they had leaned forward not to see but to be comfortable. It might just as well have been in a minute.

In the above passage, Gertrude becomes delightfully inconsistent ("Do I contradict myself? Well, then I contradict myself") because elsewhere she protests that a phrase repeated is never the same as the original phrase, that every repetition changes the meaning.

Now I will quote for you what she herself says about "A Novel of Thank You":

A Novel of Thank You means that at any time they are as much when it is widened by its being worn out worn and less worn then and everybody can say should it be what they came to do.

At the end of the novel, "Three Moral Tales," "Prudence Caution and Foresight," and "A Little Novel" are given their initial printing.

This volume eight concludes the publication of Gertrude Stein's hitherto unpublished work, an undertaking that has taken eight years to achieve. The accomplishment of this duty has been a labor of love for all those concerned, even a little more than that to Donald Gallup and me! What a pleasure it is to conclude this task so successfully! I wish to thank everyone who has been kind enough to contribute a preface to one of these volumes; particularly, I want to thank Donald Gallup, always on hand when a problem arose, for his cooperation in their preparation. With this final paragraph I end my stewardship of Gertrude Stein's literary affairs. The task is by no means at an end. Doubtless, many more individuals and groups will want to print selections from Gertrude's work, to perform one of her plays, to sing one of her operas, or desire to question an authority in regard to the whereabouts of a certain passage in her work. I have only witnessed the ending of one decade since your death, dear Gertrude, but with my advancing years I am quite ready to relinquish my stewardship of your literary affairs, shouting Salve atque Vale from my garret window, as I appoint Donald Gallup, Curator of the Gertrude Stein Collection in the Yale University Library, as my more-than-adequate successor.

CARL VAN VECHTEN

New York
February 4, 1958

A NOVEL OF THANK YOU

1925–26

How many more than two are there. If they heard it at once and at once was as afterward whom would they have to mention. And leaves. This makes them wish.

A LONGER CHAPTER.

This makes them wish and afterwards this makes them leave and afterwards this makes them leave and wish and this makes them leave and leaves and wish and afterward, this makes them wish and leave and leaves and afterward.

DESCRIBED

In the rest of all eighty of all eighty and of all eighty, of all eighty and of all eighty and in the rest, the rest of all of eighty.

COUNTRY

The country is at once and left left of it, to the left of it to the right of it and at once. We have decided to leave for the country at once.

New York Boston Paris and English.

Fourteen cities are larger there than here. Fourteen cities are larger here than there. Fourteen cities and that is where she said she would stay. Fourteen cities very likely she said she would stay.

CHAPTER HEAD. FOURTEEN CITIES.

Led and leading. She had the advantage of that. There is more advantage in that. There is more and more advantage in that. She has this advantage.

CHAPTER
MEETING

She met to expect she expected to say, the month of May. The month of May was next month.

Busily and busily, is it more, is it as easily is it easier to have to have and to directly and indirectly fasten and unfasten and liberate and liberally and inclined to be inclined to take it.

CHAPTER

He is not the same as the other one. This one is happy and contented. He does not insist equally if one sees three dogs to whom do two of them belong.

There are different denominations in currency.

CHAPTER

She said just as easy and he said generally. He said easily and she said finally. She said as much. And he said he said as much. She said equally and walking and he said and an advantage. Eagerly and is made as well. An announcement. She said begin again and he said having begun.

After a little time, a little time makes it coming at first at once.

CHAPTER FORTY-NINE.

How to explain numbers. All numbers, every number every number and a number. A number at once. She said and united. He said and united. She said united reunited. He said united reunited. She said united, reunited. She said united reunited united at once reunited at once. She said at once. He said at once. He said united reunited he said reunited at once he said united at once. She said both at once and he said both at once.

A novelty.

A novelty is something that is new especially delivered and attractive and fairly well announced also something that in exchange is received more than usually. Introductions to them to them and introductions.

Furtively.

CHAPTER FORTUNE.

He made his fortune by by and by by by and by he made his fortune by and by by and by he made his fortune.

CHAPTER

If he fell again and yet would it show.

She said that looking and looking, looked like, and looking like, and liking and if ten times ten make a hundred how many more are there in one hundred and fifty and forty more. She knew and she knew. This makes them return.

CHAPTER FOR CHAPTER.

Very likely.

It is easily thought and just as easily bought. It is just as easily carried carried for them. Are they grateful for at this end and that end.

It can be used.

CHAPTER

They knew all about wood.

If it is redder marriage is all right, if it is browner it is as well to have it known, if it is as much as much of it as is wanted, she

said that she could with a good deal and she could not she could
not she could and she could not follow this and that about, this
and that about this and that and would they fix it up. It is remarkable that fix it up is forgotten.

CHAPTER

To seriously say to a son to seriously say to a son, and to seriously say to him and to seriously say to a son.

Kindly enquire about it.

Understood as understanding. Can a son be a father. Can a
father be a son. She said can a father be a son. She said can a son
be a father. She said he can and he will.

When you buy by and by.

When you sell very well.

When you come come and come.

When you have it have it for them. All this makes them live in
a larger in as large a house. After that. Michael. Michael can be
the name of everything connected with at most. At most.

CHAPTERS BEGINNING HERE

Changes change and they intend to go where he has come from.

CHAPTER OF ANNOUNCEMENTS

He delivers it. She delivers it. He has four names for it. She
has four names for it. There is this difference. Differently. Or
so slowly. All so also all so slowly.

Edible mushrooms are easily found.

INTRODUCING A CHAPTER HERE

Did she kill a child. Had she killed a child. Had she had had
she had she had to have parts a part of hereditary if in direct
descendant. All children one or one another and so wondering
if at once. Did he like it and percentage.

CHAPTERS IN THE MIDDLE

She found it quite as useful to finish later.
Please quote more.

CHAPTER X

Fat and fire. The fire burns very well. This depends largely on whether he has or he has not determined to have it to do. So they say in the South.

CHAPTER XI

There are many changes at once.

Sometimes even a stone has been displaced and placed where it could be can be seen. Sometimes all at once as fortunately as ever.

If she sent it, and if she received an answer, and if she received an answer and if she received an answer and sent it, sent it sooner. Follow and following them.

CHAPTER XII

All who have hilly places to see to will please see to the places and after that every one is practically built.

An instance of at night and in the evening and as if in the morning. To introduce a name, William Edwin Harden, they all thought so, to introduce a name, they all thought so. She said is it not astonishing the known introduction to know that as introducing introducing anything introducing as naming as a name in delineation. All the more or so and not for this to end.

Coming made a cook.

Did the reason for and before did the reason before and for, never to make a difference before and for and to make a difference for and before.

Before it.

To begin a story of little riches.

The modest sum.

And the modest sum.

And the modest sum.

And the modest sum.

To begin the story of arrangements.

Arrangements of pears and not apples of oranges and not pears of pears and not fruit. Who considers fruit from the point of view of obstacles and this is religious.

To begin a little story of at once for them.

She had intended to feel as astonished, astonished too.

And requests.

CHAPTER XV

Chapter for chapter and larger for larger, at once larger.

Can charms be charms.

In the middle they did use she did use, they were used to names.

Let one imagine forty.

Who knew that it was.

Supposing Henry Harper had a mother who had been added to at once by having heard and had allowed it to be used to it. Supposing afterward they almost attracted it to them so much for it by that and by and by and by and by. He knew Bianco and called it fairly at once and exciting, find it as they have last and at last and in the added houses. If they said that they were no longer building were they longer building longer. Always and she said one of the two.

A longer way to have it pay.

For himself he believes that it would be better if he used it most.

She agreed with me.

At last.

Very well.

At last.

When five is the fifth how many is eight. The eighth.

Does it make it follow it at once.

She has to hear it and to be to be at once for once and by pleasure at her pleasure.

Forward and back and back to back, back to back and further back.

In that direction.

CHAPTER XXV

Jane Addington Hilda Baker, Irene Alice and Cora Elliot. This is satisfactory.

When it began again.

Blanche Gay Josephine Blucher Ida Israel and Ernestine Elizabeth when it comes sooner. After that.

Let us know the difference.

If she had not had three advantages if she had not had three advantages. An advantage. If she had had three advantages. If she had had all three all three as advantages. Now is the day daylight and now.

So much makes willingness to go.

Behind their mistake now and then.

She came to William.

He came to Helen.

He came to Helen and she came to William.

In no other way are reasons stated.

To keep Edith and Ida out.

Henry Clay Harden.

After that she returned some more.

CHAPTER XXVI

No. Everybody's little love and lovely.

First, apt to be.

Second apt and to be.

Third the reason why they have given it is either that they wished it to be here that they hoped to have held it in place or that there was an opportunity.

The story of a preparation for and because of a disturbance. I think it very likely that she is going out this evening. What is the reason for this supposition. That she is not only occupied but also that she has succeeded in adding prestige.

What did they mean by it.

Not more than heard and had and headed headed this way.

In the first place, she and he, he and she both he and both she were actually were really applying for registration. Registration does make indiscriminate addresses useful. Are three addresses sinister. Are four addresses to be followed by four addresses or indeed might they have meant everything. No one is inclined to be obliging any more.

A useful purpose.

He thought of bread.

So did he.

He thought of evening and morning.

So did he.

He thought of afterwards and before.

So did he.

He thought of it.

So did he.

This makes it easy to account for the number that were carefully explained as afterwards pleased.

Pleases.

He pleases and if he pleases. All of it makes an especial and speculated he speculated about it. Can early and in general, left and a harvest, politeness and is easily meaning, and this is all in the way. Can one decide that they will please go.

Conversations as arranged.

Will you think about it. Yes I will think about it. Do think about it. I do think about it. And in thinking about it. Yes and in thinking about it. It is very easy to be molested.

Conversations as prearranged. In adding to it whom do you please. I please just as I please, just as I please I please. I did not wish as long an answer I wished only to know what was added to it. I have replied that it was added to it. No one causes it at all.

If he said and sat and saw saw to it, if he said and sat and saw to it, perhaps it is. Very many have silent fancies.

CHAPTER XXVII

All the left left left I had a good job and I left. He knew.
He knew that at one time, he knew that, at one time.

Supposing seven thousand supposing fifteen thousand supposing four thousand supposing four thousand less seven thousand
less fifteen thousand less supposing four thousand more supposing seven thousand more supposing fifteen thousand more, supposing more than four thousand more supposing more than
seven thousand more supposing more than seven thousand more.

CHAPTER XVI

We very nearly said as much we very nearly did we very
nearly said as much.

She is to have it happen she is to introduce into it into it she
is to introduce it into it and after the business is all over he is
said to say that in appreciating he has had no more than at once
and also in this way. One can hesitate between this and in.

Having had it before from door to door. Pits and fits. She
saw me write it.

To ask to know to see to it and so, this is why they added me.
When this you see you added me.

To what.

To a lovely Odilly.

This is the first time I have mentioned that and that does not
mean mispronounced or mispronouncing. Was she very amused.

Now then all for Johnson.

He was born and raised and lived and had and would and sofa
and seen, where, here, where there is wood on wood and all the
rest. Wood makes if you like objected.

After that and nobody knew their voice her voice her voice
their voice was not at all disguised. This made them mean to be
very likely. All of it is kind, kind to be, kind Miss Agnes had
better have had two children after she married and became Mrs.
Christopher Harriet.

Stop and begin. Was she a love. Yes. Stop and begin and coming. Was she a love. Yes.

Almost enough.

They were they said they were.

They said they were they said they were. To find it more disturbing.

Twenty-four have twenty-four. He did want a long time. How many are there here.

Longer than those and opposite.

CHAPTER XXIX

Little leaves it leaves very little. How is he.

They do not at all say that it is for them. A little slower afterwards.

She has changed her name to Henry she was twenty-two at that she was well and well and very well and then then they had a change from it for them. Count daisies. Do you count daisies open or closed. Both. And do you count jellies open or closed. Both. And do you count houses open or closed. Both.

CHAPTER XXX

How funny.

Can she very well can she.

Very well can she very well.

In this way a mountain has happened to have had to have a top.

All who sit upon a seat and save it save it, all who sit upon a seat and save it.

After that and have forgotten.

Change it to more.

Have sent.

Which is which yesterday.

If a little of it as when it is as well as seen when they have and fasten for for it tore it she is mean. I mean I mean.

Now then Harry's room.

When Miss Todd came to see, us, when Miss Todd came to see, us, when Miss Todd came to see, us.

When Miss Todd came to see us.

Who need never be mentioned.

CHAPTER XXXI

And one.

What is a surprise. A continued story is a surprise. This is a continued story, this is a surprise this is a continued story. What is a surprise, a continued story is a surprise. This is a continued story, a surprise a continued story is a surprise.

Now they mention men, now they mention men now they mention now they mention now they mention when they mention and they mention or they mention and they mentioned mentioned, who sees days of days of it.

Let three be stupid.

How stupid.

Let three be how stupid.

One says about pearls that she prefers it. The other says about lists that she prefers it. The third says about it that she prefers it.

And so they never meet each other. They never have.

After that no one is destroyed. To be destroyed makes eating easier. Eating is quite all the time. And so she enjoys pearls. And so she enjoys lists and so she enjoys it.

Never meeting of course never meeting, of course never meeting and why, why because one is never meeting and the other is never meeting and the third is never meeting. Never meeting of course never meeting, not at all at one time.

Letting love to have a mother. Letting love to have letting love to have a mother letting love to have.

In plenty of time.

CHAPTER XXXII

If he never said he would.

Kitty Carnegie makes you laugh.

Does she want to sell a letter for five dollars does she want to sell a letter my letter the letter any letter a letter for five dollars and if she does will she. This is the way the tenth of May the tenth of May the tenth of May this is the way the tenth of May and Kitty Carnegie may. May she, may she be as may she be and change it. To change it from may she be to as may she be. A part of a long and a part of along. It is easy to find twenty maps and go there.

And she heard me say it just as much.

If all the best of all, if all even even all, if all if all if all all to say so.

Differently and different.

A choice of four differences.

The first difference is a tree as a place.

The second difference is a tree as a place. The third difference is a difference. The fourth difference makes it look well and be well. After this they were satisfied. They said that they had arranged for it all very well.

The little little little boat perhaps. Perhaps she meant to tell her story too and it was this. When she went away she went away not alone no indeed accompanied to Russia to America and to Indo China. This does astonish you and you. After that upon her return she had very prettily arranged to dress and to be careful. More than that was expected. After that she often re-arranged and replaced and attended to it. This made her entirely returned. After that she did and added to it from the rest.

This is as moderate as ever.

Not to change from him to them.

Nicely nearly it is a very easy thing when every time she writes she writes and every time she talks she talks and every time she eats she eats and every time she does not she does not. Every time she does not. Carrie is Carrie.

Oh do they see the half the half they bring it there and prettily.

A paper makes a line.

Two papers make two lines.

She smiled to see Robert see and did he see to see and season. How can more please her.

CHAPTER XXXII

It is very satisfactory to engage to go.
Are they willing to see Edward.
Are they willing to see so.
And now for the first time to speak of it. If it had not happened that she spoke it would not have been possible to know how it sounded. And having heard it and entirely agreed. Agreeable and not agreeable agreed. This comes about with an addition. Confused by cheerfulness.

It is very easy for her to remember Ida but it is not as easy for me to remember Ida. I remember Carry and Edith and Helen and Charles and everybody.

All who make a half of it have this conversation. "How do you how do you print white on white paper." "I am very sorry but I do not do it any more. I now print it as well as ever." "Who makes the most of it." "They make more of it and as they are very patient it is very pretty when it is well done." "It is well done every once in a while." "Naturally as each one in his way is very attracted." "Finally he knows all about what has been called for it has been called for just in that way."

CHAPTER XXXVIII

It is usually ahead of time a time and ahead of time. Ahead of time and attracted by their calling for them so very soon. As soon as ever.

They nicely make that their mistake and so as they are behind them and behind them and that entirely newly.

Miss Alice Toklas wishes to engage someone who will be reliable courteous and efficient.

CHAPTER XXXIX

Shall she tell me what she said. As much.
Seriously recommending her.

Has any one any of it.

And as they have do they have to be advised.

He said how do you do.

She said I was here with her and she did not recognise us. And he said. In the meantime. And she said it was because she was there with me. And he said he felt it very much. He also was and he was very nearly turning it so that it could be seen.

After that it was not told twice and at once.

This makes a mistake.

A second time.

When he was not well and well well what do you want. I want you to have it. And what do you want. I want you to have it. And what do you want. I want you to have it.

Can many of them arrange it differently at once.

Farther and father.

Interrupted and conversation.

Who loves me loves me.

He said that for several days he did not.

CHAPTER XL

At all.

He was.

By themselves.

He was.

He did not care.

Find it around and say two things.

First to have to have her write it for me. Second to have to have a road. A little later and a little better. She made an attachment.

To really make a story true this must be you.

What did she do for me.

She thought of arranging something so that I asked and so it came about that it was nearly at last and afterwards it meant more.

What else did she do for me. She suggested that it would be just as well as many more have held it. It held very well.

What did I do for her.

I arranged that she had a friend and that that friend would show to advantage. What else did I do for her. I planted roses in such a way that if she took ordinary precautions and showed determination there would be presently an additional enjoyment confidence and pleasure and this might be at a distance and intelligence.

Please say it soon.

Why do they remember the name of a street. Why do they remember to name the street. Why do they.

Wonderfully thoughtful.

He knew it better than ever.

I asked her never to mention that.

CHAPTER XLI

As she was as much as that and happened to have it.

I do not know why I think of that I think of that to-day. It is this somewhere in that part of the day and later at once we went and often when they met carts and there were stones not thrown but carted and in meeting them it might be inconvenient. More having had a corner and around it for nearly that and some space and not more than twice. Twice at once. This way. Often and always later. How can hours make that difference.

Come back to me Fanny and have a little lace. There is a great deal of difference between lace and lace making. What suggested this. Her desire to be incapable of their help. So much help. Help him help her, help her how help her help him help him how how to help him how to help her now.

This made obstacles. Obstacles may be a seat.

She said read, read it, that is she said do not and have not and had not read it. No confusion. Pretty little plants are here. There are some kind of them that need what they have and finally not three not any three are three. We hope therefore.

And now to tell her who they were.

Who they are to be is as much an answer as ever.

Next time some time.

The only thing that we remember is that she was not told by word of mouth never to let it go farther.

Let it go.
Let it go so.

CHAPTER XLII

Union.
A conversation between them.
They came every day.
They came every other day. They came every other day.
Virtually.
And now extra merriment and meant.
This is introducing and this is arranging and this is returning and this is resembling this is resembling too.
He was immensely interested.

CHAPTER XLIII

Any longer longer than that and not a change and not a change and not any longer than that and not a change. Not a change and not any longer than that and not a change.

Many preferably are precious and a mistake it is a mistake to like to go. After that she smiled for them. And now I wish to talk about Rosalie. Rosalie has no intention to lag behind and she recognises us and so she will come to-morrow just in time to make it more nearly exact. Someone said.

Let me hear it in there. Hat head, rings ears, beads neck, and hands heard. Heard as yet.

She does intend to have at least that. This makes a novel sooner. What is the difference between a novel and a story, no one said it.

Butter and better and she was very glad to be as sad as that indeed and who said misses.

Better and curtains. The next time that there were objections she would stop at once.

Having heard everything.

If in Dorothy than Lorna.

If in Henry than Robert.

If in she changed it from Lena than Eva.
Must it be yet.
It is easily remembered that once in a while is added.
This makes it matter a matter or for that matter.
He needed which.
Could two syllables make three.

CHAPTER XLIV

All girls call.

CHAPTER XLV

She had a habit of erasing and letting it go. So do I. She has
a habit of easily mine, mine is it mine. She had a habit of almost
as soon. And so was this. A kiss is one.

CHAPTER XLVI

Forty-six and fifty-one, one one and two have not it at first.
This makes it show there. Everyone knows what is meant
does everyone know what is meant and how does everyone
know what is meant.

CHAPTER XLVII

To be almost as uncomfortable too.
From six to three candy. There is a great difference between
having had and having heard and having and having. Having to
have hinges. Supposing it happened that and without it it was
put where it was seen. Then no one would dismiss it as an account of it would they. But indeed and perhaps if in the meantime and not as once only, one might say once in a while, it
would happen and not at all particularly, but the result excellent.
Can you see how oceans are oceans.
When you see either way either way.
Attend to all and perhaps.

CHAPTER XLVIII

She never knew numerals.

It is easy to look and see.

About to be numbers of them about to be numbers of them.

Consider a novel a novel of it.

Indicated and indicating so easily aroused.

There is a great difference between start and startle.

To rest and the rest and all of that related to an interval during which no satisfaction at all is expressed.

Michael and Alexander.

A widen and widen a widened and widened a widened and widened a widen and widen.

Two down there and one up here. What is it.

In a little she knew three three that had not been there before two in one two women two candles and two weights, the other one one one horse one horse and one glass, and the third about the third one one cannot be certain.

Does she come down as she went meant lent, or went. She went she said she went to bed.

After that if awakened can it be easily more a gratification more a gratification.

To have almost paused to mean, I mean I mean, am I in it. Changed to mind.

It is well to tell it is just as well to tell what was what and while and while it and while it is and while it is while worth while.

To be mistaken about having heard walking and talking.

CHAPTER XLVII

Yet and Henriette and where are they placed they are placed before and next to two, one steady and stayed the other easy and jointed and all all three just as you see excellently used to be here. Here here.

Rosy rhymes with cosy and posy rhymes with rosy and rosy

rhymes with rosy and posy rhymes with posy with cosy with rosy and with an effort. It is easy to say knitted.

Everything I need to-day is here. Have it here.

Everything one thing.

She began. What did she begin. She began eating. What did she begin eating she began eating what she began eating and it was given to her that is to say it had been given to her and it had been given to her for this because if partly and more than partly, if more than partly then indeed who has it. They have it. At once. Twice at once. Better four.

He makes a finer wider hat than she. Does he.

She said not to say.

CHAPTER XLIX

We would very much rather that she felt very well.

How many can be carried here and there. Those who correctly attach themselves to ribbons ribbons are really awfully long and all.

Who can hear her say so. She can be awfully very well placed for it advantageously.

And this makes that around.

Parted by the way by the way they came by the way parted by the way. They came by the way. Parted by the way.

Nearly knew the time they may have to have it by themselves. By themselves too.

How very nearly and a while. A while can be very fond of it.

At first, more.

At first, there.

At first, how.

At first, why at first, why at first.

Soon they get used soon you get used soon you get used to it and this shows conclusively that he was right and that she did not have a sound separate.

A sound separates soon.

Distanced too, Julian Julius Julia, Julian Julia Julius, Julius Julian Julia, Julius Julia Julian. Its a favor.

Was it well and just as well was it just as well as that was it just as well as that and well was it just as well.

Hear this as they have this as they have all of this. Disappointment. No. Reunion. No. Not easily explained no. Having heard an announcement. No. No and yes.

Was he what was he, was he a manager and not in there while they while they were while they were in there while they were there in there. Nobody knew when she withdrew.

Withdrawing.

CHAPTER L

It is not often that they soften, it is not often that they soften this. She is needed in a minute, and if he said he did not mind being called that but he did mind having been collected as at once what should have been said. Very often and to soften. She did not soften very often. He did not soften very often he did not soften. He objected to being additionally reserved for it at once. Very early and as often, very often and to soften.

Prepare a novel.

This is the way that they can pay that he can pay that she can pay this is the way that they can pay that they can pave the way.

Preparing a novel.

Preparing a novel and preparing away.

Preparing a novel prepared to stay.

Preparing a novel.

She is preparing a novel.

Preparing a novel.

He is preparing a novel.

Preparing a novel, preparing it as it is best as is the best as is the best or most prepared way.

Preparing a novel to-day.

In preparing a novel this is in the way. In preparing a novel he knew that he had a fairly nearly and returned to in preparing a novel and returned to. She prepared the novel. He prepared the novel. She prepared the novel.

CHAPTER LI

Three to four men and a woman. A house and houses and trees. As likely to be placed where they are within reach of those of these of their places and described by it. They looked up at it as if it was to be nearer than it was when it was actually in sight. How many ladies have their hats and how many are with them. Fascinating.

CHAPTER LII

Have to have a hat to fit the head my baby said, and I said too I said it too to you.

Have to have it held my baby said and have to have it too and I said it too I said to have it held to have to have it held I said it too. And then I said I have to have it too I said and have to have it too my baby said and have to have it too and have it held and have to have it held and have it too my baby said and have to have it held I said to you.

Quickly as a stretch, stretches it so that when it has useful and ought to be able to have minutes minutes later did they want do they want to do they want to did they want to did they want to have to do it have it to do or you. You know. You know we know, we know how do we know. We know that whoever opened it before did not open it so that as a door as a door before. And this makes two of them bother. Like a little like a little.

CHAPTER LII

She went away and cried a little. He was as much as that as much as that and so we so we so we.

All three made four.

What is it for regretfully.

Can easily be and a house and in front and so mistaken. He was mistaken and regretted it.

Then quietly having had a minute in which to decide he decided wrongly and at once it was very well and an advantage. I do not wish to appear so.

Then cups are available and fish eggs and always afterwards it happens that there was no and not a privilege. Thank them intermittently.

Introducing what is done.

When is a salad not Russian, when it is made of tomatoes lettuce and oil and not as directed. In that way he never asks why and she never asks why and he never asks why and she never asks why and he never asks why is it, and she never asks why is it and he never asks why is it and nearly all at once. They liked it.

Right right it, right and right it, who is right and who is righting it. At a glance.

Can it have a settled seat and saddened too, I quote it.

To Emily and Elmer both begin with e and easy and expected.

Can it have settled it all as easily and can it have it settled as easy and expected and can it have and settled and as easy and expected and begin.

There is no use in ever again mentioning that it can begin.

After that she mentioned that we after that she mentioned she mentioned that she that she we mentioned that she that we had very much better not begin and not begin and begin and not again and begin. No one ever changes begin to begun not in directions not in giving directions not in placing houses. Houses and houses and house. As a friend. A friend of when a friend and when has she had a happy idea of saying if I have been asked to return it then I ask to return it. This shows that she was right and not easy and expected as again and for this having had a refusal a refusal to accede. Suddenly it has to be to them.

CHAPTER LIII

Mrs. George Allen and I will not use her name.

Beside what.

And not and not to really have to go and not to have really to go by there. And who was it she said. She said she was the daughter she was the mother and not one who was as old as her sister. In this way and at once.

It is not often that everything that has been seen is neglected. And not much. As much. Please point it out. Does a pitcher look like the one we use or like the one we would use.

That's all darling.

CHAPTER LIV

She wishes me to describe statuary statuary of a woman sitting by a seat and leaning on a pedestal and handling a vase and she wishes me to describe the elegance of her form the grace of her position and the flow of her dress and she wishes me also to describe the color of the material and the lightness of the rock which imitated in marble which is clay resembles milk which is used and so we have before us what we have left behind us. After this there is no less pleasure in what altogether has made two and different in color. One green and if a head then a head on it and the other of a different color and the one chosen is the one in use. Certainly we have spent an afternoon.

CHAPTER LV

Fifty-five is always restful it is restful in Italian in German in French and in Spanish, it is also restful in everything else at least it is to be hoped and at first and no curiosity no curiosity about Mrs. George Allen because she makes Maria as angry as that Maria as angry as that oh yes.

And as I have said yes as I have said.

Forgetting a name.

Yes as I have said and as I have said.

Forgetting a name.

One two three all out but she.

Forgetting a name.

One two three all out but she and as I have said yes as I have said.

Forgetting a name.

All out but she.

One two three all out but she forgetting a name and as I have
said yes as I have said.

CHAPTER LVI

Who would prefer one to the other. She would prefer one to
the other. Which would she prefer. She would prefer the one
she had chosen, and which one did she prefer she did prefer one.
Of what advantage was that to her. It was of no advantage to
her because it was decided that it was preferable that it would
be advantageous that as she had preferred and as she had had a
preference there was of necessity a great obligation in actually
and being well adapted to this as an activity would she actually
authorise and be authorised. It has been admirably said and with
the air of some complaint that only a wife who brings with her
a sufficient income to authorise such habits can when she is
habitually busy industrious successful and observing can and
does remain as she has found it best and most acceptable not to
rise before nine o'clock. This may make a difference to those
who change not their last names but their first names, their first
or Christian names not their last or surnames.

She said different and older and he said different and older and
he said is it different and she said it is different and she said it is
different and as different and he said it was as different and in
a way they remained at once. At once always means twice and
now three days. The first day at her house and not more than
fifty present the second day at another house and a hundred
present and the third day at her house and a large number present. And what it was it was a wedding and she married him
after having been more or less in love with someone else. The
man with whom she was more or less in love was one who would
always be what he was as he was and the one whom she married
had a father and mother who would naturally prefer to rest.
Could they be easily representative and a failure. Not she. Not
he. Not they and not their friends or their acquaintances or at
first. It is a great pleasure to be absolutely certain that everything
that she hears has a name and that she knows the name. It is a
great comfort to those who are fond of memory.

As fond of memory.

CHAPTER LVII

It comes too easily it comes to me too easily it comes too easily to me too easily to me too easily. Yes sir.

CHAPTER LVIII

He would have had a chance to say that nearer and at least as well how many things have been seen. Sixteen. First, would they need wood. Second would two push or shove well if neither one was strong. Third is there likely to be a way to point it out to him. Fourth when they are out they are one and two and not a wife. Fifth it might be that a year ago white a year ago and white when above. Sixth when it fell a few fell and later he asked them to be very good now. Seventh it was raining. Eighth ask how many times women wash for them for her. Ninth on account of wild flowers. Tenth was she ready to like silver in a pitcher. Eleventh pansies and so so. Twelfth undoubtedly as late. Thirteenth does it make a difference if all there dress differently. Fourteenth cannot see Lucy. Fifteenth two vegetables. Sixteenth and all the same.

CHAPTER LIX

When it went again and now now and now. Now and now too.

To remember very well where nuns left and monks came. Monks are brothers nuns are sisters. To remember very well where sisters left and brothers came. Brothers that are monks and sisters that are nuns. To remember very well where nuns left and monks came. To remember very well where sisters left and brothers came. To remember very well where nuns left and monks came.

He employed him to get up earlier.

She employed them in the same way.

They employed all of them to have it completely arranged and then strangers were the strangers were there strangers were they strangers to them.

They employed them and they considered them they considered them as they had them, had them from the rest who gave them, had them and the rest heard them and the rest heard them and the rest saw them and the rest saw them and the rest had them had them here and had them had them and counted them and counted them. Who makes all who eat eating and all who are eating eating. Who makes all who are eating eating and who all who are eating eating. Who makes all who eat who are eating who are eating eating, who makes all who are eating eating.

No one knows how many vegetables are vegetables and how many are early and how many are late.

A settling. Half of a hill makes it a place to have them say say so. Half of a hill makes a place for them makes a place for them.

Half of a hill and makes a place for them. Half of a hill and makes a place for them and say so.

Who has heard of heat. Who was heard of heat too. Who has heard of heat to please themselves at once so that a horse is not nervous at all. Nervous at all is the reason for this distance.

Sitting on a horse at all.

At all at all.

Sitting on a horse at all.

It is not perhaps difficult to face that way. A face in face to face a face that way.

Not a bit tiresome.

She says that skylarks should not be here. But says he cuckoos are there too. Not as pleasantly she said. She said not so pleasantly. Afterwards there was the arrangement that while some repeat all repeat two and two two and two four. Four and four four and four. Two.

CHAPTER LVIII

Fifty-eight fifty-eight ate ate honey honey and butter bread and butter butter and honey too and she moves paper. How much paper makes a morning let us think carefully, news paper and that paper and soap paper and smoked paper and red paper and all paper and a house. A house if built will be surrounded naturally surrounded. And this is the plan. Everyone to be asked and as everyone is asked they will be told and as they will be told they will join and express pleasure surprise and regret. As to being properly fed we are properly fed at the expense of a great deal of effort expended by Mr. and Mrs. Pernollet. If one wanted to say so one would say that the letter l saves it. If one wanted to say so one would say so that the letter l saves it.

CHAPTER LIX

And as he has a week.

It is not as interesting to listen as that.

It is not as interesting to listen to as that.

It is not as interesting as that. It is not as interesting as that. It is not as interesting to listen to as that.

And there is this too.

This is opposite.

Can one be deceived in Hope. Yes. Can one be deceived by Hope. No. Can one be deceived when one has refused to recognise her again. Yes. Will one be deceived after one has refused to recognise her again. No.

She and Eleanor think so.

Can one be deceived by Eleanor and by Hope if one refuses to be so if one refuses to recognise that it is so if one persists in refusing to do so if one has to have them as they are to be there and to do so. Can one be deceived by Hope and Eleanor if one has refused to recognise them again and continues to do so. Can one be deceived by Eleanor and Hope when one has refused again and again to do so. Can one be deceived by Eleanor and Hope when one has not been deceived and when one has refused to be so. Can one be deceived by Hope and Eleanor when one has not been and one has refused to be so.

Can one be deceived by Eleanor and Hope can one be deceived by Hope and Eleanor can one be deceived by Hope and Eleanor and has one been so. Has one been deceived by Eleanor and Hope and has one refused to be so. Has one been deceived by Hope and Eleanor and has one can one does one refuse to be so. Does one refuse to be deceived by Eleanor and Hope and has one done so.

Eleanor and Hope and has one done so.

Hope and Eleanor and is one deceived by Hope and Eleanor and is one to refuse to be so. Is one to refuse to be deceived by Eleanor and Hope and has one done so.

Eleanor and Hope and has one done so.

After this they do photograph.

After this and they do photograph. And after this and they do photograph they photograph near to and at a distance.

All of it which is longer and they were frightened all of it which is longer and as they were frightened, all of it and this is longer and they were frightened.

They were frightened.

As this is longer.

As this is longer they were frightened.

They were frightened as they were frightened as this is longer.

CHAPTER LX

A mistake.

It is and nearly is a half and it. It is and it nearly is a half and it. So changeful.

Having had to have it here and is well for them and most. How easily and all. All well.

It comes to that that it is here. It comes to that that is is here.

It comes to that that it is here.

Hear how it had to it had to.

This makes it as much more to be evenly allowed.

A novel makes a man.

Do so makes a man.

A novel makes a man do so. A novel makes it made. A novel made a man do so makes it and made it do so. And a novel makes a man do so and a novel made a man do so and a novel. How can it be becoming to be and he and he and we and becoming to be.

Why does it take so long, why does it take so long to take it as long. And now a change.

He has it he has had it he has it and he has had it and he has and hiding is no town. If there are five then there are six by this they mean that a city is silly. If that is silly then very well and tell her. If that is very well and if it is that that they tell then very well then very well and tell then tell and then tell very well then tell it very well tell it very well that if there are five there are six and if there are five there are six then a city is silly. Tell this just as well. To tell. To tell this to tell this and to sell, sell it for this just as well. This can be a part of a Lindo. Lindo who. Who is Lindo. And who is Lindo. Not you. And not you. And not you. And also and very nearly also and also and not you. Who is Lindo. Very well who is Lindo.

CHAPTER LXI

He has heated war. And as a result the rest of it all the rest of it has to be enjoyed and enjoyed.

Having lost all interest in Ida.

Weak young men. Good enough for weak young men. And they are weak young men. Fifty and forty makes ninety. Forty and fifty makes ninety. Fifty and forty makes ninety and forty and fifty makes ninety. Not ninety weak young men not fifty weak young men not fifty weak young men. Weak young men.

Can a novel be of any more appropriateness than it is and not be expected. Can a novel not be expected and not be of any more appropriateness than it is. Can a novel not be of any more appropriateness than it is and not be expected.

Considerably more than that.

He finds it easy to say it all and as it is easy it is very easy and all. He finds it easy to say it all and as it is easy it is very easy very easy to say it all. He finds it easy to say it all. She finds it just as easy she finds it just as easy, she finds it just as easy.

Who finds it just as easy.

He finds it just as easy.

Next.

CHAPTER LXII

Is it more to be addressed as is it more and is it better is it better and more to be addressed as she is to be addressed or to be addressed as she is addressed. Is it more a pleasure or is it more an agreement or is it more and more.

How can a father a mother a son and a daughter all live together.

CHAPTER LXIII

Minnie is what I remember Minnie Singer. And Minnie is what I remember Minnie Singer.

If Minnie is what I remember Minnie Singer. If Minnie Singer is what I remember Minnie Singer if Minnie Singer is what I remember if Minnie is what I remember Minnie Singer.

There is no agreement about which about which and about what there is no agreement about what about what is to be said there is no agreement about which about what it is that is to be said. And so remembering and dividing and rehearing and disturbing, she makes it as adroit as possible. Adroitly.

When they take when they took when they have taken it away and they have heard that all of it and ounces, ounces are as easily heard and seen as if hundreds were thousands. Makes a model say so. It is a careful little lake that has to have a lily. And a lily too.

Action and reaction are equal and opposite.

CHAPTER LXIII

Does she want to and she does, a wife. Does she want and he does and his wife. Does he want to and he does and does he want to and a wife.

And a wife.

Does he want to and a wife. Does she want to and a wife.

There are a great many duties to be divided between a mother and a daughter and a son and another, the same father. The father and the son and the mother and the daughter the same son. There are a great many duties to be divided between a son and a daughter and a father and a mother and the mother and the same daughter. The son and the father and the daughter and the mother and the son and the daughter.

CHAPTER LXIV

Would it be the same if it passed if it passed and they see seated. Would it be the same if when they had handed it to them and they were religious would it be the same if it followed that. Would it be the same one at a time and would it be the same in use. Would it be the same if they thought so would be the same as they heard and had it. Would it be the same if we were mistaken.

The principal difference is that hours and hours and hours and hours. Who said ours and ours and who said ours and ours. The principal difference is that they said hours and hours and the principal difference is that they said hours and hours. And the principal difference is that they said hours and hours.

Field and felt not at once and delighted and pleased to see Sunday Saturday Friday and to believe it to be Thursday.

If by carefully looking and deciding if by carefully deciding and repeating if by carefully repeating we follow them. How can two be carefully explained.

As many questions. How many Josettes are there. How many are there. How many are there and how many are there.

After that hundreds made just as many.

Change numbers so that no one will know that five follows six and ten follows three.

Anyone who says that the younger ones did not go out with the older ones is entirely mistaken.

CHAPTER LXV

Makes a mountain makes it than than if it was to buy another business. Makes a mountain makes it than than if there was a question of ownership. Should a woman be taller. Should animals be fed and should a woman be fearful as much afraid as that and should a man if everybody asks about him should he be reliable. Having heard of her and having heard of him and she and that was entirely another family in that family twice had they been unable to please her most and best and alike. They have been unable to recover themselves and establish it as a certainty that there is no difference between a beginning and their beginning and their ending and an ending and likewise.

Each one is a share.

If each one and their, there is if each one and there is or and if each one and as there is or as there was and they had had five more who were useless, useless and useful, there is no more need of times than at times.

Easily made please easily made please easily made please.

Please easily made please easily made please easily made please.

I hope that there will never be any more comfort from it. And there is.

Suppose it is arranged so that presently and instantly they had come to come down quickly and when they were down they saw that all the others had not been awakened and after that and at that time all of it was older. Older than that if there is to be an arrangement of places where they had to be and were, and were.

How can everyone who can hear and say so how can they walk afterwards and see it all around. All around and makes it easily necessary to wish him well.

Could four fathers be four fathers.

Could four fathers be four fathers be four fathers be four fathers. After that everything and everyone and everyone and they wished to be as well as it could be placed where it was necessary that coming farther all had it in order. As night and day. This can be shown to be his. Yes and yes.

CHAPTER LXVI

She makes it as easily as old and rolls and let it be. She makes it as easily as rolls and old and let it be. She makes it as easily. She makes it as easily as rolls and old and let it be. Here and see. Who makes houses which are surrounded by trees. He makes houses which are surrounded by trees.

He makes houses which are surrounded by trees they make houses surrounded by trees she makes houses which are surrounded by trees. She makes houses which are surrounded by trees.

When four and three. Of course it of course it of course it and it. Of course it. This makes how do you do necessary.

In which direction do they go to see so and so and accept it as necessary that birds repeat themselves.

In which direction do they go to get fathers and mothers and brothers and say so. It is easy to believe when one hears someone under the window say she was all alone and they would ask someone to go and stay with her. It is easy to believe when one hears them say that opposite in the evening when they do not close the door that means that someone is there they only close the door when no one is there. It is easy to believe when one hears one saying and say it wait a minute because if you start now you will have to start again it is easy to believe this every minute. It is easy to believe that a great many are understood when some who are littler than others are able to be pleased by having known of them that they are to be as well addressed as if it were in the morning. Very lately it was in the morning.

How do you do is still necessary.

Exciting. What is exciting. It is exciting and having had to have and hear and having had to have it and having had to hear it, she says strawberries grow and they have been seen to grow. Strawberries have been seen to grow.

A new place for places. In this way they are named. Allow me allow me to participate.

A renewal means that as rapidly as that as rapidly that, it means as rapidly that. As it means as rapidly as that as it means as rapidly as that.

Let a little less last. Yes.

Let a little less last. Yes.

CHAPTER LXVII

A novel makes more than a third, it makes less than is heard it makes more than is inferred. Inferred is as well as even in summer and in winter. Heard is as well as ever and in summer and in winter. A third is as well as ever and in summer and in winter.

It makes more than a third.

It makes more than is heard.

It makes more than is inferred and it makes more than a third and it makes more than that than that is heard. And never noticed.

As you will and as you shall and as you shall and shall and will and will you.

How are all of it how is all of it to be worn. How is all of it to be worn how are how are and very well.

This is the way they do.

This is the way they say they do.

Two, two went and stopped and around it was meant to be if on their return they had had no intention. And they had arranged not planned it is louder to arrange than plan louder if by a lake and a lake is several days older every year. To be best and most.

What is it that when it is worn is enjoyed. What is it that when it is worn is enjoyed. What is it that is enjoyed when it is worn. What is it that is worn when it is enjoyed. What is it that when it is enjoyed that when it is worn, that is when it is worn that is when it is enjoyed that is when it is enjoyed when it is worn. What is it.

Further and he saw that idem is the same and means twenty, sometimes it means thirty sometimes it means twenty, sometimes it means more than twenty and very rarely does it mean less than twenty. Idem the same, very rarely it means less than twenty, idem means twenty, idem the same means thirty, idem the same means more than twenty, idem the same very rarely means more than thirty, idem the same very rarely means less than twenty.

CHAPTER LXVIII

Having had a piece of bread and butter. Having had a piece of meat and bread and butter, having had a piece of cake and meat and bread and butter having had a piece of cheese and cake and meat and bread and butter what follows. Strawberries.

Having had a choice what follows. Rivers. Having had a half what follows. What does follow when do they follow. Where can they follow. Why will they follow. Having had a half and looked and as well as that. Will they lend us money. Will they lend us will they lend us will they send us will they send us honey. He knows that it is easier to stand and lean and she did it than to find it gone away and they know it. As well as that.

It takes nearly all of it to be seen and it takes nearly all of it in between in between one can always come back to the afternoon and the morning. By always coming back to the afternoon and the morning and by always finding it so well placed that it would be more advantageous if there were more of them by always coming back to the afternoon and the morning and by really really red at night is the sailor's delight and red in the morning is the sailor's warning if by always coming back to the afternoon and the morning, if by always coming back if by always coming back to the afternoon and the morning there are as many after all who call who call out and say good-morning and it is in this way that they decide that not having had need of her and not having been able to arrange for him Mr. and Mrs. Pernollet are not admiring everything.

This makes plenty of plans if they were planning. This makes as many fans if they were fanning this makes as many names if they were naming it at all. They do very wisely and very well every day possibly.

How are Hilda and Helen to-day. How are Hilda and Helen every day. Helen and Ellen they say they say Hilda and Ellen and Helen and they say they say good-night to-day. This is the use of it. Not liking it to be called. And yet it is very remarkable that everything has been looked at everything then something is overlooked. Something is overlooked. Why do they not say that the wind blows it away. It is very remarkable that there is no appearance of having answered when called. How deftly and definitely and when it is in all of its various ways easily added to added to insistence. Sometimes it is longer. Forget well.

Here they prefer to give and to make. There they prefer to make and to give and to relax. There they prefer to understate and to reply and here they prefer to emerge and allow.

There have been arrangements made for every bit of it.

There is no obligation to eat cherries with tea indeed we have decided not to make any further use of tea. It has been brought with us and this introduces us to an entirely different subject.

To have never been as content before.

How very rarely is it remarked that a man and woman habited in that way have a habit of walking. Finally it is concluded that they are about to be there as soon as that.

And then in pursuit of continuation may they may one intervene and intervention and beside.

If as they please if beside on their knees and after kneeling further can they jump and jumping over one another. What is the meaning of principally. He is principally used to it. It would be of great interest to be able to know whether those having had more experience have decided or have not decided or have decided. To have rarely seen what is more and more on account of it. Everybody can change a name they can change the name Helen to Harry they can change the name Edith to Edward they can change the name Harriet to Howard and they can change the name Ivy to Adela. This makes it impossible for all of them to say what they mean. Ivy can be shortened it is rapidly followed by five bells. Bells are not used any more, sometimes there are chimes and sometimes there are and sometimes there are no more than that.

It would be quite wise to have followers.

NEW CHAPTER

A new chapter is one that has placed in front of it more and more cousins. More and more cousins. Supposing everybody married how many marriages would there be in it. Supposing everybody had Howards how many Howards would there be for it. Supposing everybody had Hildas how many Hildas would there be added to it. Supposing everybody had hurried how many more Kates would there be in it.

CHAPTER LXIX

A scene introduced into a novel not a scene introduced into a novel.

A scene introduced into a novel. For at once it is remarkable that when they have been one two and three to continue to have adjoined and as adjoined is so so after that they can be saturated with green. Saturated with green and to be seen. To be seen and saturated in green. As before when they are not as all they were to have and rest believed that when they are to have to follow once and left and met so there are in this case to be an added when they see and for this they have had it all and for this resting when they had it darker than before. Then there are always added to and blue. Blue cloth never makes a monster. And afterwards when they originate and derive and thrive and as a placard for it there to have it see that up and down and too much as it can be helped. Help yourself. After that at each time no one is any more related. As a matter of fact no disappearance. No disturbance as a matter of fact no disturbance. As a matter of fact no delight no delight as a matter of fact. As a matter of fact no incline, no incline as a matter of fact and as a matter of fact and as a matter of fact no condition as a matter of fact and as a matter of fact no partition as a matter of fact. As a matter of fact no deduction, no deduction as a matter of fact. As a matter of fact at any time as a matter of fact this time as a matter of fact their time as a matter of fact all that time as a matter of fact as a matter of fact all that time as a matter of fact.

Now easily so and startled startled comes too and to this for it is not half as well when they are afterwards and actually displayed displayed and acting in this way to stay. Can and it is not to be as usually and unusually and recognise softly, softly makes an addition to soften and so gradually and so in as much as they can hear sounds and sounded. That is to be anxious and interested and louder and for this as a reason a reason can be a standard of exceptional comparison and in this and on this account reasons can be compared, comparison and so candy exchanged exchanged in little pieces to them for this and as wishes and would she stand if she were really ready to stand and in the meantime to act as if it were stopped as it was not when there were as many as they were when they were just as ready. Can there be a second when there is a third and a third too. They knew that they had had had to have it and so and so to consider what it was and then always always as they had to give and receive both when they had seen and been seen and then start and once more startle as startling and startling and then as if rested and the rest and for it and for the rest and then as well.

Could eight make six and after that five and then three.

CHAPTER LXX

And leaving it out. Leaving it and to last and leaving it out. No doubt. Frequently they have attachments and they frequently select as much as they had to have when they sent it in this way and they sent it in this way. Practically inviting them to stay in that way in a way whose pleasure is it was it or could it have commenced to arrange when there were different additions in their final hesitation. No use in changing it this time at once.

A novelty to them.

Nicely heard.

As nicely heard when they are five at least and afterwards explained and refused and impossible to leave out and to leave what is at least this time as well as commenced as well as finished. No occasion to make a union between a signal and all around, between a signal and repetition between a signal and a choice between a signal and equally surrounded between a signal and then at least between a signal and rapidly mounted and between a signal and as well as connected and a signal and the rest, when there is time and very lately.

She very nicely knew four years when she heard a change in the desire of one who when she was a mother and for that and so then another mother so that she as adapted to it for when a little more is added then easily and almost sweetly can be sent again and again and as ease and please. Etienne can easily tell the story to his grandfather and she can easily know that the least that could be said would be said more often and as widely as that for there is always a father and a mother a grandfather and a grandmother and then a man a man can have as a mother screened so that to that and farther when there is a seaman a seaman can be an officer and indeed if it had been changed who would have been joined.

Not as nervously.

There they commence to come again to come to come to come again and not repeated if they can come and come again and repeated then as it is difficult to follow when there is more and more region and religion more religion and more region more and more region more and more region and more and more and more regional balancing and region and regional and balancing and region. This time unexpectedly and quite as well as that to them and for them and in time and not to-morrow and so as well as regrets and regretted and not at all as related related meaning told and having heard that not again and not again and not again and the third time and not for this use and not for this use at all and not for that use not at all not for the use not at all, if it is not better to do it at all and refuse to consider what is very considerable certainly.

CHAPTER LXX

It is not very agreeable and that is what we have always thought that they are something else. Yes it is not the proportion and unless you know of something of that kind then she has forgotten. This is tighter and as attractive as markets, markets are as attractive as that and all that there has been seen and decided and remarked and remarked and fairly definitely by the way it is put together and are of it probably and a pretty good idea of it from that and from others that was probably done to produce the finish that it has. And now it has it had it can it means it folds and finds and has and has and heard and hear and sell and well and call and see and find and left and caught and leaves. Leaves is what a door is needed for. Leaves is what a door is needed for. A stone that resembles another stone. It is right.

In a very short time, they had a decided reference to a very

short time and as it was better to have added and anyone differs
from there and anywhere. Differs from have added and anywhere and anyone and differs from there and anyone and everywhere and differs from everywhere and anyone and there and
differs from that and there, their part. If we must part let us go
together.

To introduce into a novel to introduce in a novel. To introduce. We introduce.

We introduce.

If at the same time and not often oftener they and was it as
well that she went back she went back.

If at the same time and they did it at a distance use it again
faster. Fasten and faster is not the same. If at the same time and
by it, by it afterwards, afterwards and at the same time and the
same is the same. If and the sum fourteen is a sum. She knew
blue as well as every other every other one. So silent so silently
and by rocking. When they and this and enterprise and three
times peace. This makes it soon. Next.

She had wished windows and she had wished. She had wished
she had windows as she had wished. She had wished windows
as she had wished had wished wished windows. Not once or
twice. Have happens once or twice. Have happens once or twice.

Introduced and introducing have happens introduced once
or twice. Believing what water there is.

A novel too.

Where is it what is it. What is it. Letting them return the
rest and so forth. She was not a printed necessity to print for.
Printing.

It is here and out it is there and about and in between there
should have been an interruption and mean. No one draws
conclusions. Having put her in and put her in having put her in
and out as well as out. All out about all about all about. It does
does it. A novelty too. And so are you. Not as well as at an
address. Addressing coming back to using introduce and introducing.

Who leads Bonaparte and Pyramids, at once. Who leads
Bonaparte and Pyramids at once in hats in hats houses. Who
leads Bonaparte and Pyramids in hats houses hold and held. In

hats houses hold and held one after the other as who leads Bonaparte and Pyramids and hats houses hold and held.

CHAPTER LXXII

He signed it himself.

A little later he signed it himself.

It can be good and what is the difference. The difference is this paper ordinary wood white wood ordinary wood brown wood, ordinary wood red wood ordinary wood all wood ordinary wood or wood ordinary wood in wood.

In wood. In wood in wooden in wooden in waiting in waiting in that case how many how much wood is there in it. In which case how is there wood when they know as well as we do that he can run quicker than the one that comes to be nearly all always twice and very nearly as careful. He is very careful never to join.

Cut with it to-day and then to-morrow and after that it is very different flowers are different from them in that they differ in men flowers are different from them. Flowers are different from them in that they differ from them in the difference between flowers and flags. Flowers and flags make and made and made and make and make and made. Down here they were not easily induced to have them with them have them with them not easily and complained. If they have a pigeon pigeons are known to be shared very nicely by them as they agree.

She said she knew that there are ten days in between.

Everybody is named Etienne.

Everybody is named Charles.

Everybody is named Alice.

Everybody is named how are they named and having.

Everybody is named naturally and daily and everybody is named everybody everybody is entertained with attention entertaining.

CHAPTER LXXIII

Before the flowers of friendship faded friendship faded.

Sunday makes Monday and Monday Sunday.

One week or eight days and he was nervous.

It is to be asked does he do it because he prefers country to country or does he do it because he prefers morning to afternoon. Does he do it because he prefers pieces to pieces or does he do it because he prefers one to one. Does he do it because he prefers smaller to larger or does he do it for the purpose of not yet. Does he do it because it is at least as well or does he do it because he is delighted. Does he do it because five is satisfactory when it is when it has been added or does he do it because he is remembered as well. Does he do it because he is able to do it or does he do it because he hears it as well. Does he do it because he is placed beside it or does he do it because it is arranged so well. Does he do it because it is as well divided or does he do it because it is followed as well. Does he do it because if it is done now or if it is done now does he do it as what has meant to reach to the day when afterwards when time as it shall have to arrange that in the meantime fortunately by this and that of course.

Nearly is not the same as a conversation and imitation.

Three cases.

First case, Charles married and Charles a printer. Not the same indeed living in entirely different places although in both there is no difficulty whatsoever in continuing prosperity.

Charles married, taller not older, wealthier not wilder, stronger not quicker, and as if arranged. He knew some one who knew him. He knew some one. He knew some one who knew him. He knew some one. She having a father and a mother living had parents with whom she was living. They were to be obliged and they were to be obliged. Obliged is reasonable and obliged is reasonable. They were to be obliged and pleased they were pleased and obliged. He knew all about October. The beginning of October and the ending of October. When is October. October is the tenth month in any year.

Charles the printer will sign his name just the same. He will sign his name and then came remonstrances which were listened to.

The third case is that of Etienne and repetition. Etienne.

CHAPTER LXXIV

No one uses Emily.
No one uses Emily.
There are three times three and Emily.

CHAPTER LXXV

Would they wish it.
It is nearly at once.
Would they wish it.
Making a condition of the four of them and if they were
here.
Two of them are here.
Would they wish to make a condition of it that three of them
are here. Three of them were here. Would they make a con-
dition of it that one of them is here. None of them are here
just now.

CHAPTER XXXVI

It is easy to change novels to two.
One and two.
Through and through.
You and you.
One and two.
Too many bow to two.
Too many.
And it is easily understood that they have permission.
When red white and blue all out but you when all out but
you red white and blue when red white and blue all out but you.
It is a very extraordinary mishap that in there and many rocks
which have been seen at a distance if they have the same name
they have to have it heard and said separately. There is no
prettier house than that and no one lives more prettily in their
house than that. They had their name they heard the same they
had the same name.

He knew he had his and this occasion and he was determined to understand lists. He knew he had his occasion and he was prepared to arrange lengths. He knew he had his occasion and very often it was the same one. The same one has the same sound at once and more than undoubted. How can he have both. There was a way after all of going there.

It is very necessary to have it open and then to remain not as far back as that but very likely anticipated. They change their minds.

What is not as good as it was. It was not as good as it was.

Excited well excited well well excited. Excited well as well. Excited as well.

Not as well and not as well and not excited and not excited and not excited as well. In this way hours and hours and hours and hours and if it was not unusual. We did not know why they asked. Our cloud. How may really able counts and counting are whole or in part in question and in question means red on black. I very much doubted if it could be.

If he says now he says and now and if he says and now and if he says and now we are content. It is in this way that a great many really had had and did return then when it is arranged or pre-arranged.

An announcement. Did it and didn't it. We know very well why and what is said and said and he wishes assistance to be given him. Readily and at once as it is very necessary that it should not be nearly as much later to-day. To-day makes days and days. Entirely. And easily. And following. And amounting. And reassembling. Fortunately counts. Can I be of any assistance and as well as that and as attentively. He intended to be older, the difference between that and older at once and older.

No one knew the sight of startling at sight and startling and he says it was made by these and it was by others. They were the ones that did not continue to give me confidence. What can we mean.

As much troubled as by it.

Rapidly returned and so much as he did and as much as he did.

Never as the rest to be when they and having so placed it that is was not found and found. Everything is as as well.

Not using Emily at all. They felt a really anxious moment coming and anxiously.

Not using Emily at all.

And anxiously.

Anxious is allowed.

CHAPTER XXXVII

To be worried about whether to be worried about whether whether to be worried whether to be worried whether and they went to go. Whether they went to go. They went to go whether they went to go and repeat easily whether they went to go.

Around a mound and mind and kind. To like that kind and remind remind and reminded, have it and ashamed and nicely to be placed where they can be. Be can be changed to see.

Finally fed fairly well.

To-day to lay and to obey exchanged for Sunday.

To let and to let them and to imagine to let them and to manage to arrange to manage to exchange and to let them. Should cousins marry.

They had said one another they had said their mother they had said their brother they had said their cousins and their mother. They had said one another they had said more than that and then one and two make it easily arranged that they were not easily believed to be as soon as they were named.

Name and names names and named, named and names and name and named. Named.

Names who names who named who name, who name and name who named and named who names and names and names and named. Starting from the left and naming them and starting from the right and naming them and starting from the right and naming them and starting from the left and names and named them. To be mistaken literally mistaken to be literally mistaken, literally and listening, to be mistaken listening literally and listening and literally to be mistaken and listening.

It is always so.

Happens and happens to them and when happens to them happens when happens and happens and happens when, when and happens and happens to them. Literally and listen makes her very not restless not quiet not remained not burned and so when will John Byrne entertain Dempsey.

CHAPTER XXXVIII

Easily here and easily hear who will have Emily easily hear.

Who will what they will there to and there as a kind of intention to them. Conversations cease.

What.

Conversations cease.

Or!

Conversations cease.

Or.

Conversations cease.

He and it was as said of him, of him and it was as he said he he and of him of should of him.

A newly separated light and lighter. Lighter as used for light.

CHAPTER XXXIX

When she does not live where she used to she has moved repeated from the third.

Afterwards from a direction and nicely.

Do they need to go and go and it was as nicely as in a minute.

For the fish.

It can be arranged that when there is air there there is air there as well. It can be arranged that when there is a house and fire tnere there is a house and a fire anywhere and it is arranged that when they have said that they admire the butterflies and dragonflies they admire all the dragonflies and butterflies. A night makes more noise than if no one is certain that they are taught it themselves.

Hanging fire.

And so does geography.

Rather more and rather most rather they and rather then and it changes quickly.

Where does it change quickly where there are chairs and shares and astounding astounding and surrounding and light and alight and so to remain when they asked the name of that.

He married her. She married him how very often is it true that her father married his mother or the other her mother married his father.

How many times is it true that if they had intended it they had it to do.

Surely no one need be worried before.

And so a novel seems to be a novel seems to be a novel. Novel and novelty and sooner and he did not go there. And if he had we had already eaten his share. Where. Here.

Announcements.

Marriage is an announcement.

Returns is an announcement.

Silver is an announcement.

Have had it is an announcement.

Able to-day and anyway is an even number when there are more numbers than even and odd. Ivy can always be attached and detached and changed from six thirty to six five.

Always happy to see you.

CHAPTER XL

It was and if there was a doubt a doubt based on it here, there was and if there was a doubt a doubt of this and here. He would not have it rolling up and down and now and then and why and so and if they had it when they chose and if they cut it as they went and if the last when it is told and all and pink and black and will, and hills and there and why and should and when and mountain and out and been, been when, been where and if they had when this is like the time and fall and fall and led and by this way and way way back and sit down.

Not at all surprising that it takes so long to come.

What.

The sound.

The sound of what.

The sound of the stone and stone when it is stone is nearly assured.

It is easier not to start.

And easier not to start.

It is easier not to start.

And easier not to start.

It is easier not to start.

And easier not to start.

It is easier not to start.

We often regret veal we often regret. We often regret occasionally we often regret occasionally that he was not better informed.

Having never known either it is not at all difficult to come to a decision concerning which is to be the more admired and admire and not foolishly and not beside. Beside if he prepared the stairs stairs can be in houses when houses have this use. Use and useful. Useful and of use. They have decided that for the future for the future and in the future there will be constructed as a house and as an industry and as an allowance what is easily copied and copied and neither she nor I can remember what it was that was pretty and prettily prettily and perfectly perfectly and allowance. Allowance can always remain a favorite in color and so there will not be any interference whatever and going on. Ending with on and only, only and in order in order and in order to in order to do it as it has been done. Done and done. This means a bet yet.

CHAPTER NEXT AND ONCE.

Once is always inclined inclined and meaning separated. He knows copying that. A chapter should never be mentioned altogether as if they were absorbed.

We had them last year but not so pretty.

CHAPTER XLI

Did anybody say it went around, did they did anybody say it went further. Did anybody say that no one was expected did they and did anybody say that we went away. To remember very well.

Dedicate it to a place to have had a little more occasion to have festivals when months and months and months as different as to months and months.

Every one can easily tell the difference between the two.

It was afterwards that there was at least an hour.

Why does it.

He can they can and they have to have it as much more and no judgment. And in then and by it as it can be all of it in quickly quickly is as well as heard. Entirely as much.

It was very well and very much and very much at last and there and very much and very well and very much at last and there. Renewal. There is no use in accustoming oneself to it. To understand why why he wondered why that and not that. Commence commences.

After every little while after every little while and after every little while. After makes anxious and anxious makes diverting and diverting makes August and August makes it now. It is never necessary to answer at once.

Hear me out.

Why.

Hear me out.

Hear me out.

Why

Hear me out.

Hear her out.

Why.

Hear her out.

Hear her out

Why.

Hear her out.

Hear her out.

Why

Hear her out

Hear her out

Why.

Hear her out.

Why

Fortunately there is almost all of it there.

How can it be as well as that when there is an announcement that no one goes or comes here without permission.

It is not easy to have it enough enough to say so and so and so and so. Having admired it all. She has admired it all. He has admired it all and now.

To wish that it had been all right. All right.

Right and left makes no difference when there is a reason for it.

It is very remarkable that following what is placed so that it can be seen all eyes are attracted. When a little later it is left over and she did not ask for two when one sufficed she had given two she offered one she refused four and she added enough enough to ask if would there be a mistake and arrange. How many surprises make one two three and if four are four then would there be as it were inside out. No one understands this but I do and if I do then why do they need to agree to arrange it as if every time before there was as much and many many meaning white and four. Four makes four and four if there had been four then three would have sat together four would have sat together one would have sat together and really and really as much. As usual.

Sitting still.

CHAPTER XLII

If she knows this.

He would have had it to say anyway. Threes. Having heard about doors and pours and stores, stores of grass and glass and this as plainly. To be five and three to be four and three to be three. Theodosia, Susan and their friend, she was a friend to them truly and they affectionately and surely returned and re-membered that they wished to leave twice once. Afterwards they forget their mother they had not remembered their father and later all five together returned together to visit their grand-mother and after that they left and went to Portugal. No one would could or should suspect that they had come at once. And then as if to please themselves having been distressed at a possible

animal it was singular that the evening after there should come
the nearest and in a way as dear to her as ever. So happily not
the same. More than that it was soon discovered that far from
being respected as rich and useful the mother of a very well
cared for child and the wife and protection of an interested
and admired husband should surely arrange everything and she
did. More and more three houses had been bought as one and
in a way it made no difference. Could one have gone to a school
where afterwards if there was a difference of opinion about the
stature of a friend a friend would just as easily be fairly well
endowed and remarked. Many hope that remarkable has no
merit and no fear of completed criticism. To criticise is to pain
and this must be remembered in connection with bread and
bread and bread. Four if all are added. This has been what has
had and made a rose a blue and a lilac colored paper and every
time a lilac colored paper is blue it is gratifying and so charming so very very charming and surprising.

CHAPTER TWO

Chapter two and chapter twenty-two and then to remember
chapter twenty-two.

CHAPTER XLIII

Three times it makes a difference to them.
It is useful to have it and everything else. It is useful to have
everything else, it is useful to have everything else and to expect
that a father not caring to sit at table with his daughter or with
his daughters and not preferring to sit at table with his son
and not preferring to sit at table with his wife does prefer to
sit at table with his mother and his son and his wife.
It is not at once to be preferred that Stephen unknown and
Susan unknown and unknown to Stephen and unknown it is
to be at least to be neither the one nor the other and pronounced.
Can she be right and if she is amusing can she really learn
french and portuguese and can she really if she is amusing and
can learn french and portuguese and can have a younger sister

and having had a considerable time elapse between her birth
and that of her older brother they were as well to do as if they
had been as well known as that and ever. It is not nearly as convenient that they come and they go as if they come and they
go. He comes. He comes who comes who comes who comes
she comes. After they went to stay there. It is remarkable that
in the North the North being North and in the South that the
ones in the North resemble the ones in the south. It is remarkable that they are that kind and also when it is understood that
it is also true. They had plenty of time to do it. How very often
are they known for three things. Religion and she has her doubts,
violence and she has her regrets and industry and contentment
and she has her intentions.

To begin to allow. To allow it.

We sent a message about ham and cheese and afterwards we
were just as obliging and obliged. Who knows how difficultly
everyone asks her to do it again and so not to be at all deranged.

Sometimes everything says so. And so.

At last everyone has have had and had to hurry and to be
as peaceful as that.

Four names mentioned. Ivy Louise, Jemima Lucy and Therese
after that Charles and the others one does not know. Supposing
everyone addressed each one and said good-bye good-bye we
are going now and were answered very well be very careful
you are very careful you have left and are ready you are ready
and you are going you are not going at once as just at present it
is difficult but if you will stay absolutely still I will and he will
and success attends all his efforts. After that everyone who has
come has been as adaptable as ever and in a way it is very pleasant
that after careful observation she has concluded that after all
it is very easy to arrive at having what has been a difficulty for
a certain length of time.

It is an additional advantage and then after all would they
if they were told to would they would they need to be told
that just as long as it is necessary just so long is it necessary.
This is what makes it more or or finally she looked and what
was it that she saw. She saw it later very much later and indeed

she saw it earlier very much earlier and indeed this is all very well but not as well as ever. Come again Saturday to-day to-morrow and Tuesday and more often if you feel so inclined. All will make every effort to welcome you entertain you and please you.

CHAPTER XLIV

Ida and Myrtle, Ivy Ida and Myrtle, Ivy Myrtle and Ida each one of them and all could they be told that they were that their home was that their town was and it is nestled at the foot of a fairly high hill and in that way they are certain to leave it either to marry well or to go to another place and there keep on living.

Following as well. Following as well as that. And following as well as that.

When they had that as well and they were and found it to be nearly as soon as if they had not liked at all. And kindness kindness is shown by fifteen having the use of it at all. So many make the most of it. Obliging. They are obliged to be careful. And originally originally they undertook it in order that they might be as welcome as they were. And they were there and afterwards it can be stimulated and easily encouraged and with-drawn and so they allow this which is neither earlier or later. After that they have left as much of it to do as before. Who taught them. They were taught in the way that is understood. Higher and higher and then they succeeded. All of them.

CHAPTER XLV

Who can be shorter than that. With whom. She said that as far as she knew no reliance could be placed upon their judgement. And replaced.

To begin at once for that and come up and sup. It is regretable that we were spoiled because in that case perhaps it is better better to think in threes.

Perhaps coffee perhaps sugar perhaps fish and perhaps hurry. To think in threes makes fours and she told them. She said she

did know the difference between five four forty it never comes
to forty thirty and eighteen. All these have it to be that they are
equally intrusive and she finds it unequal and satisfying.

If they say after this it is easy to say and this after this. In
this way there is a reply and now twenty-two too. She knew that
if she knew who would always compare it comparatively afterwards. After and now. Has Louise been Louise. Any one can
easily.

When you are very sleepy you sleep.

Increasing a novel. How to increase a novel and stay further
apart and nearer together and further in and fairly around and
really about. Having heard that they were having heard who
were having heard how and why intelligence is refused and they
amount and it amounts to it.

Could a sister be a sister and a brother be a brother and Louise
has no brother in finding the leather suitable. No one can or
should connect Louise with her brother or her half brother.
Gradually everyone comes to be about and gladly would it be
practically a vacation.

She thought of their possession and they thought of it at once.
It is very easy to be allowed to have a distance and come to stay.
They found it in every way enjoyable.

Gradually who knows how.

Very small means smaller very much smaller and very much
smaller not as to size but as to intervals. Intervals can be used
to describe space also can be used to describe annoyance and
also be used to describe directions. All in all.

Who knows and how do you do.

Alternately.

It had been asked by them and for them and additionally of
them it had been asked additionally and with these as additions
and added to conveniently and as replacements after that can
always does always is always exchanged by replacing.

Having expected that she to know two of them.

Helen Needle and Helen Holt.

Helen Holt was an Englishwoman. She had a mixed ancestry.
Her mother was Scotch and her father was both Scotch and
European and more than that was and was not unexpected and

she knew that she intended and attended to all that made it possible for her to be called here and there. This made resemble and furthermore there was no reason for it someone who was of an entirely different arrangement. This one was one who was to be named and as she was married and as she then inherited her fortune and indeed they did live as they had been accustomed to live there was no change in their circumstance.

He had been and she had been called away.

No one entering abruptly or leaving abruptly does desire that if she were fond of solitude she would notice that in different parts of any country generosity depends upon what is and what is not held out and held up and held in that way. After that it happened that a year and a half having passed she and as they were prepared to go they were prepared to continue as if she were her mother her father and herself and any other and he too if no one said that they had seen thousands thousands make thousands. Everybody who can count can count to one hundred.

Does any one know from this that both of them were both of them. And not in preference.

CHAPTER XLVI

When she was and help me when she was what was she to me.

A description of avarice and reason to know.

Suddenly soon clean soon as it was and mounting. There has been one two and three mounting.

Bit of it and see it fit and when it and alike.

What is the difference between thank you and what.

It is of little use it is of and because of this that they find that they are more comfortable here than there. Easy to say and every day daily and every night nightly and easy to say and every day who arranges what. What is it.

Why does it look like that and to read again. Reading is never mentioned. Reading and eating and sawing and seeing. Four more surrounded. If they go away from here and go there and there they see it made as it is to be filled with either. A question did he marry a woman, or how has he had it when he saw the very great difference there is between names as long as that. What was his name.

To come back. When they were there they used to have her see him see her and afterwards it being Friday Friday is the day if Thursday is the day before. And to rise. There is a difference. There there is there can be a great many. Here there are and less often very few. To choose them and to have to be obliged to remember that Zenobie is Mary and Jenny is Louise and Helen Cavour is Helen Strong. Always Helen always strong and if she were as often right as wrong. They will be cooler.

Not useless. Not a bird. Not a cherry. Not a third. Not useless. Not at all. Not either. Not small. Not in particular and not as best, and not in their place and not as if they had spoken about it. Is she usually right.

Why does she not inquire about how each one did not stir.

Each one.

One, one.

One completely one.

One one and then after afterwards was pleased.

One and every day.

And one.

Why did she not inquire.

Back of it in front. Back of it two two and two, this makes two with two hows how-do-you-do's and eyes and arms and really. And in front to budge and believe, believe that black is high and white is low in this sense that pine-trees trees and trees and hay and trees and trees and hay and trees. If this could be to mix which is nothing.

CHAPTER XLVII

This nearly see.

When it in their and aloud and by the time they had land and sea. Sea can always be used see see can always be used as a very little river.

Introduces, she says she walks quicker, more quickly than a little child and following following those which not she but certainly someone someone has cleaned and they are, what, they are cows, and bulls and oxen, they do not use oxen in the United States of America and for this reason they are introduced here.

How many things can happen.

First they went away.

Second very little boys are never brothers.

Third. It arranges.

Fourth. They lay there.

Fifth when we did it.

Sixth. Having had louder than louder this makes it a decision that we prefer to have them come coming and come here. All older older than those than they than how than in which and then rarely and then as much and then in them.

Can one be darker and one be lighter and afterwards they are as different if they left it and left them there. And in use. When they had had yet had.

Believing and relieving.

Can all can all have it as it were out of sight really.

This makes it as it was as if gloves gloves were made.

The history of gloves.

Gloves were made the history of gloves.

And how.

Gloves were made and the history of gloves and how and the history of gloves and how and gloves were made there.

Higher easily and the chair as chairs and not the pair as pairs.

There are many days many days two days two days four days four days three days.

A novel makes rudeness.

To begin now.

Once upon a time and usually they fastened it in that way that every now and then and awkwardly they saw that they had better and at most two marriages. Marriages too.

Younger.

Choose names.

Have hair.

Hold hands.

Hear her
Have them
How and how often.
Heated and really aloud.

He he was as soon as that remained, remained as soon as that,
leaving as soon as that seen as soon as that and as soon as that or
as soon as that here as soon as that so frightened as soon as that.
A mistake. Mistaken too. Having wondered if after all he would
after all be after all well after all and there after all and after
all, two marriages after all marriages after all marriages.

To return to names.
And return to names.
Preoccupied is different from occupied.
Everybody smiles.

CHAPTER XLVIII

Teases and pleases has often been said, wed head instead.
Always returning to that.
Did it say that.
To be pleased to be displeased to be as to be has to be.
Once, wait and await.
Twice State and understate.
Three times, ask to be injured in that way.
Four times, Having had it had and stranded and then to be
too merited and to leave, two leave two.
And all for you.

In this way flattering flattering engages and nearness and
engages and let us engages and please engages and stems engages
and branches engages and they and why and do they engages.

We need transference of letters and parcels and doubts and
dates and easier. In this way they and we are pacified.

A novel is useful for more reasons than one.
Joseph in boats.
Josephine in addition.
Josette in carefully reasoned hours.
Bertha when they have wishes.
Albert in the meantime.

Frank as necessary.

Herbert as arousing.

And Hilda inasmuch.

And Honor when they have heard of tapestry and Robert when they announce it, and Emil when they marry and Frederick when at most and Jenny when they find it and Louise when they had it and Hope when it was and Arthur all at once. Is there any difference between William and Edwin between Clara and Martha between Helen and Anna between Henry and Raoul and also Paul and also August and also Hazel and also Phoebe and also and also Lucy and also Edith and Nancy and all who remembered Kate. All who remembered Kate are here.

When if they had a vase made of what is was then it looked pretty, it was satisfactory and all who mean to be all right do mean to know that they are as it can be when they have their gloves and windows and their trees. Who are so many that they have to seat and sit and once again come to be there as if they were to be as well as they had sat when they are found to be so bitter yet and well around it as they had to hold it when it was as nearly for them in the way where they had had and now for them it is beside and very, very nice.

A very little anyway is better anyway.

Not nicely not easily not Hope.

Three weddings.

The first wedding is the wedding there.

The second wedding is the weeding when they have had everything that way.

The third wedding the third wedding is the one at which Louise was present.

Friends and familiar.

Now as two and astonishing.

Harvest are harvests and so are harvests when they are heavy and here.

Imagine a thousand.

Imagine three thousand.

Imagine two thousand.

Imagine forty.

Imagine more in between.
Imagine right and left.
Imagine at once.
Who knows who.
Wedding.
Who knows when.
A wedding.
Who knows which.
A wedding.
Who knows that.
Wedding.
I thought of it.

CHAPTER XLIX

Next time.
Little and a little.
They said five and it was four.
She was glad to hear it.

CHAPTER L

Not looking.
Looking.
Looking.
Not looking.
Mistaken.
Not mistaken.
Not mistaken.
Mistaken.
When it was as soon as seen what can have been as a fan. It is lost.
Arrived.
Not arrived.
Not arrived.
Arrived.
When it has been as it was as it was and will it now. She is very well and a sister of Camille.

Using it.

He she and they they she and he she he and they they he and she.

And after that a line.

We have not asked it for it.

She just goes on and on.

You can always tell.

She goes on and on and setting the table.

You can always tell.

Very well.

She is very well.

You can always tell.

We know three Emilys Emily Dawson Emily Chadbourne Emily Harden Emily Chadbourne Emily Dawson Emily Harden Emily Dawson Emily Chadbourne Emily Harden we know three Emilys Emily Chadbourne Emily Dawson Emily Harden we know three Emilys Emily Dawson Emily Harden Emily Chadbourne, we know three Emilys Emily Harden Emily Dawson Emily Chadbourne we know three Emilys Emily Harden Emily Chadbourne Emily Dawson Emily Harden Emily Chadbourne Emily Dawson Emily Chadbourne Emily Harden Emily Dawson Emily Harden Emily Dawson Emily Chadbourne Emily Harden Emily Chadbourne Emily Dawson, we know three Emilys Emily Chadbourne Emily Harden Emily Dawson we know three Emilys Emily Chadbourne Emily Harden and Emily Dawson, we know three Emilys we know three Emilys Emily Harden Emily Dawson Emily Chadbourne we know three Emilys Emily Dawson Emily Chadbourne we know three Emilys Emily Harden Emily Dawson Emily Chadbourne we know three Emilys Emily Harden we know three Emilys Emily Dawson we know three Emilys Emily Chadbourne we know three Emilys Emily Chadbourne we know three Emilys Emily Dawson we know three Emilys Emily Dawson Emily Chadbourne we know three Emilys Emily Harden Emily Dawson we know three Emilys Emily Chadbourne. We know three Emilys Emily Chadbourne Emily Harden we know three Emilys Emily Chadbourne Emily Dawson Emily Harden we know three Emilys Emily Harden Emily Dawson Emily Chadbourne.

We did not know.

How many are there who are what, no answer.

How many are there.

She needs me.

She needs me and she needs me and she needs me.

All this out loud.

And now new and opposite.

They who are they they are there and when it is easier then it is as they need to have it often exchanged rose for roses and pink for pinks. If it had not been led, led this in this as this to this may this why this should this would any one prefer a stream to a stream or nearer to nearer.

Reply there.

Eighty forty twenty-two twenty forty thirty-two thirty fifty seventy-two seventy twenty twenty-two or two.

They need to have fifty for fifty sixty-six for sixty-six or seventy-eight for seventy-eight and walking.

Who knows that they are angry.

They do.

Who knows that they have wishes.

They do.

Who knows that they have thanks.

They do.

Who knows that it is earlier.

They do.

Who knows that it has been picked up.

They do.

Who knows that

They do

Who knows this

They do.

Who knows that in the pleasure of being lost as found.

They do.

And who do

They do.

Twenty-eight eighty makes ninety-four.

Before.

CHAPTER LI

Naturally was found was found around.

How can they change from white and red to grey and blue. How can they too.

How can they when they who they by them by them as it can be that doves and she that called and he that they and she that he that he and as to astonished and flatly flatly denied not arranged as beside.

This makes it at once that she did do that without it without that and after every day after every other day after every other day after all after that after their after in their way. Whose is it.

Three chairs and place three chairs and place and left and left three chairs.

To leave three chairs.

To leave three chairs there and to give three chairs and to seriously decide to leave three chairs. This is and is not an arrangement easily intended when they have very many deci-sions to make. Let us not promise. If he is not as pleasant as he was nevertheless he will be not their choice but their decision. If he in speaking of conversation says that he is approaching she need not have meant to be different as they say. If she decides has decided can decide to be a bride it is very well all very well. And so no and no how to have meant it.

Parts and apart and start are all used to use and use it. Not as for their pleasure and profit and so to make it seem the same as one. Theresa or Tessie, Josephine or Jenny, Louise or Louisa to make them all the same as one. Charles or Charlie to make them all the same as one.

And that we will do.

Who are Mr. and Mrs. Mont Blanc and who are Mrs. and Mr. Mont Blanc. It is so easy to be mysterious so they say.

Now not again now not again and now not again they need to sit to stand around. Supposing a man in Morocco had a mother a wife and a daughter and he left Morocco and came to live where he had plenty of water would he be as happy not happy would he be as busy as he had been in Morocco.

Suppose a man in Portugal had a wife a son and a daughter and another daughter and he came to live in a place where there had been plenty of water would he want to would he be ready to place his wife in another place which he had bought for her where he would not sit with her or with either daughter or with the son he would not mind the son he might not have another daughter would he mind leaving altogether leaving his wife or one daughter or the other daughter would he mind altogether altogether leaving his wife altogether leaving his wife not with this daughter or with that daughter would he mind leaving his wife altogether in the place which he had bought her with or without either daughter. As the daughters were both young they would naturally stay with their Portuguese nurse which they did. In this way there would never be any reason for one who was older to be as it were older every reason and the one who was a little younger to be as much as a little younger.

One can always feel that three who were there were asked but that later they would not be at all as much and more than that. How often can he.

CHAPTER LII

All seen all seen as to novel.

A woman and can be surrounded by three, there are no others who have extras.

Any wedding will do to say too.

It is very remarkable but in some countries there are more weddings than in others.

There are more weddings in some places than in other places. Who is about.

If Albert is Edwards if Albert and two if Albert is Edwards how many are through through with it.

If Albert is Edwards how many are through with it.

Each day each day.

He needs him. If they are needed.

If they need him. If they are needed.

Plenty of had to do coming coming plenty of it had to do coming.

He needs a happen to have he needs a happen to have he needs a happen to have had he needs a happen to have had he needs a happen to have had had happened to have had and not like that like it. And begin and happen to have like it and begin and happen had happen and begin.

There is a difference between the lives of Ida Amy and their brother and Theodosia Hilda and their brother. Ida was twenty-five their brother was twenty and the sister was ten years old or a little older. And there was a father and a mother. The father was gentle but did not want his daughter to marry an Italian, the mother was a little younger and was getting very much older and she did not want her daughter to marry less better than she was to marry later. All this happened to be satisfactory to them.

Theodosia was ten and Hilda seven and their brother seventeen or older and their father and their mother and the Portuguese nurse another and if the brother had another brother and if the father had a mother the father did have a mother and if the mother did not have it either and she meant them to stay and they did for a little while.

How was the life of Ida and Amy and their brother different from the life of Theodosia and Hilda and their brother.

Not altogether.

Not different altogether.

They both were to be older and younger they both were to be added to not in number but altogether. They were never altogether. They never saw one another or had seen one another all together. This did not make the difference between one place and another one city and another one country and another one fountain and another one and one another and having lost a father and a mother they had one son and a daughter the son was older and another father and they had one daughter the daughter looked older and one mother the mother was as old as ever and one mother she was another mother and so much. Every time a family is another, three sons and a daughter and they were as richer and richer than their father and their mother and the father and the mother were as richer and richer than their father and their mother and they used everything over and over. To separate them now.

A NEW CHAPTER

Actually a mistake.

Would five miles be more than eight if it were a matter either of more or oftener or if at once they asked.

At sight.

At sight of it.

At sight of it, counting two there were seven.

They had originated it by means of an accumulation and as to arrangement who held horses held horses. Not in use.

Simply. Simply makes a seam. Seem. To and two and too and two and to two and to and to two and two and too and two and to and to and too and to and two and two and too and to and to and two and two and too. To whom.

Needless to say who would have gone.

He knew her and at a time.

Needless to say who would have gone and for the first time again.

Arising by as much as occupied. And so in a place. Remember the place. And counting and recounting.

Once in the middle once in a way once in the center once to play entirely. Announce now.

Remembering that they chose the name all the same. And likely.

Let us see and sit. So they say and said.

Advise now.

Three.

Not as acceptable as two.

Four.

Not as acceptable as as repeats itself.

He made her attractive.

She made him as attractive.

They made them as attractive. They saw and just as soon just as soon. That is the way to understand misspent.

No one is knowing more than knowing it in the morning in the evening at noon. Supposing they had to stay anyway. Supposing they were aroused. Supposing they had astonished and astonishing dependents and supposing supposing all are examples of remaining and in consideration.

They spoke of that.

If pleasant at present.

It was a satisfaction to see her seal. She knew what it meant.

That is the way they say that fifty is more than seventy and seventy more than forty and seventy-five seventy-five is as much as that.

To return to their having been there for hours.

CHAPTER LIII

If he knew a single white and yellow. If he knew a single a single so be it.

They make Annas Anna.

If it was a desire to have had accidents as accidents, accidents as accidents if it was a desire to have accidents if it was a desire to have accidents as accidents, accidents not chosen, accidents not accidents not as chosen if at and as and as to accidents and chosen and reminded, industriously, can at a glance be at their price and at their joining and as around as in a piece. A piece to a stand fairly and very entails a relief. This is the first telegram.

Will not do and to do.

Second telegram if not at once and so selected.

Third telegram an answer.

Fourth telegram so much in London. Fifth telegram return to two. And a telegram. A telegram meets me. Y.D.

CHAPTER FIFTY-THREE.

CHAPTER LIV

And no more.

Would it make a difference to them.

CHAPTER LV

Now and then.

To reason with Bertha and Josephine and Sarah and Susan and Adela and never Anna. What is the difference between chocolate and brown and sugar and blue and cream and yellow and eggs and white. What is the difference between addition and edges and adding and baskets and needing and pleasure. It was not a mistake.

There is a difference between fifteen hundred and three thousand. Who knows that.

Next.

There is a difference between twenty-nine and thirty. Who knows that.

There is a difference between it and themselves.

Now to hear to see now to see to see to me.

After that no doubt.

Afternoon.

After.

Afternoon.

After and afternoon.

She knew what I meant.

Has she found it. She knew what they meant. Has she had it. She knew what she meant. Has she held it. Has she held it as has she had it. Has she had it as has she held it.

Or a nephew.

If he had a cousin

Or a nephew.

And three.

Three means thirty.

Thirty means three thousand. If he had a cousin a nephew and three.

Always an investigation.

If two drop two drop. Drop two.

Drop two too. Not to have added to it.

A nephew at most.

Not most and best.

Not best and most.

A nephew at most.

This whole novel is about a nephew and his wife, an uncle and aunt a cousin a mother another and a father.

This is the way they begin and win.

In a little while when reaches and riches when each and each one when either and every little more is allowed for in a very little time he said and they said that they would take it away take it back.

Announcing.

Did any one annoy a mother. Did they.

So and did they so and did they.

Little by little.

And little by little by little and did they little by little and did they. They did.

Plenty of time in plenty of time.

This is all about the way a nephew and his wife and his friends and their friends and all of them are older.

Thank you so much.

A little use in it and of it and a new time to arrange a place to arrange a place. And allow it allow for it and really not really not although although they are they are there now now they are there now and how do they feel about it if it is no annoyance to them. To them and there is. There is that there. There and here. Here and not not now. And not now. Not now now.

Actively.

Happier.

Who has heard a little more than that now and here there and then at once as allowed and separated and for it and by and by and now and when when and how in the way. In the way as it is all as all right and for them. For them for it in an untried it untried it. How fairly fairly always well as at once. Did she need more than she had when she had mentioned it and not liking pansies. And how not liking pansies.

Any once in a while and so much and as much and it it was it was earlier. Not repeatedly thanked. And not not and not. Did she see that they were as she knew them too. Two and two. Thirty and two. Thirty and thirty-two. Forgetting numbers.

Who is forgetting numbers and not who is not forgetting numbers and not and not and who is forgetting numbers and who is
not forgetting and forgetting numbers and not forgetting any
numbers.

Take them along.

It did not take them long.

In a way two in a way.

It did not take them long take them along. Two in a way in a
way two in a way.

As it did not take them long take them along two in a way in
a way two in a way as it did not take them long take them along.
Two in a way.

CHAPTER LVI

The central theme of the novel is that they were glad to see
each other. He because he had and she because she had and he
because he had and had again and had again come again. The
central theme of the novel is that if they were as equally told
told to tell it. Supposing they had been there as it was often
afterwards helped. She was no longer having it given to her.

He had held himself to be at least as often as ever in the midst
as in the middle of it all of it next to the beginning or authority.

Having either one as often as they as the end and as their
equal to it as their as there had been. As large.

As a novel next.

He was very much inclined to be feeling that he was and he
was one and one and one. This if there were numbers were
numbered and if a thousand made fifty fifty could always be
repeated. This was their mistake.

Next.

If in a parcel parcel can remind any one of parcels if in a
parcel they had prepared they had prepared not only to keep it
in that way then there would have been a decision and if not
avarice then avarice and platter platter as used to platters. This
made minutes every day and to-day to-day makes me mention
disappointment.

He knew very well and not he did not he did not know very

well he did not he did not know this and that very well that very well he did not know that very well.

If after all they would know if after all they would know if after all they would know if after all they would know if they would know if after all they would know he would know if after all he would know who would know, if after all if after all if after all if after all if he would know if after all if he would know. Remain here. Remain here remained here. If after all he would know if after all he would know he would know. Standing and sitting is no more than worried and worrying. Change sighs. If sighs are changed change sighs.

A story of a young man a man who was very nearly perfectly certain that perfectly certain. The next time in winning.

A story of an older man who was perfectly certainly perfectly certainly perfectly certainly certainly quickly certainly perfectly quickly perfectly certainly perfectly quickly, not as not as not as not as it.

Use it for me.

A novel nicely.

She says not to be always ready to do it. Not to be always ready to do it she says not to be always ready to do it. She says not to be always ready to do it always ready to do it she says not to be always ready to do it. To do it she says not to be always ready to do it. Now and most most and best best and most most and now. And now and then when it would be just as well was just as well.

Would he by and by would he by and by would he would he by and by would he like it by and by would he like it by and by by and by would he like it would he like it by and by by and by would he like it as well as she would like it and would she like it as well as he would like it and would he like it as well as he would like it.

Following two by one and three by two makes counting as counting. Out loud as out loud and what happened as what happened. What happened.

He Henry Althimus and wife read it correctly.

Next.

She was as well as that.

Very well.
He knew a name.
Very well.
And then later.
He knew it at once and later.
She would not find it as loving as charming as it may be added.
At once. It is going to be added. At once.

Not so much as an end. Or ending. Not so much. Not so much
is as different as as much. As as much and is as different. Is as
different as as much is as different is as different is so much. Is
as different as so much. Is as different as as much. Not impossible
at all impossible and not at all and not at all as at all as at all and
not as at all as impossible and not as at all.

CHAPTER LVII

If he felt that he was all they had and dedicated too who was
surely who was too surely reasonable. Imagine feeling imagine
hills and imagine it. And then quiet and quietly. Three have it.
He has it. Three have it. They have it. Three have it. And have it.

When a great many were admitted they came from the same
direction and in time and timing. All land is precious. All who
had exchanged for exchanges chickens for vines and Mildred for
Ernest and borrowed for older all of it as all of it as preceding
and predicted. Around me.

All of it as they do how do they do.

All of it and fully.

All of it who has who has who has who has who has who has
to. He has to.

Who can replace crowds.

That was how they were a care.

Lovely and loved a devotion is to be easily held for twelve.
Twelve can be a dozen. And did they change for them. For
them and how and how for them.

Every little while to-day.

And so how. How do you do how do you do said easily.

In this and that and that to spare and spare should shed and
sheds are fair and fair supposing nobody wins do the police in-

terfere. Yes they say they do. And when they do who needs them. They need them as they say if afterwards they attract if afterwards it attracts if afterwards and afterwards. Many people retire definitely.

This makes a while a while ago.

Canning and follow.

Next to and next to a door.

Poles and follow. Next to bountifully next to.

After all who is there after all.

After all they are not to be counted there were so many there that they are not to be counted.

Having begun with it.

All right.

All right very likely.

Influenced by them all right very likely.

To return to Margaret.

Margaret was convinced that once they were suited they would as well as ever that they were remembering. And after all would they. Would they accountably and would they. After all three times. The first a cousin, the second an interloper and the third an enemy.

CHAPTER LVIII

Begin now.

She said that he said one half hour.

Why do they have a different way to make squares every time. Because in one and just the same and because in that one as well as all the same.

Season.

To season means that she would have had a signature.

Having happened to-day to-day.

When they came and holding she said had never and they went away as at once.

A single central cream and creamy. Dream and dreamy.

Let us wish willing.

Everybody who is told is told.

Everybody who is told is told.

Everybody is told.

To do not and having. Supposing Ethel Mars has done it very well. She has. And Emil Henry. He is not there. And Miss Anna Hunt, there is a difference the one of one and the other of the other and Henry Mann, he is just as able to be repeated and after all when they were best. They were best when they had sailors. Could a sailor be a man.

Every little once in a while they made them look like that look like that. And so forth.

It is easy to be a nice brother sister mother father aunt and uncle and altogether will they answer will they prefer to follow will they prefer to arrange will they choose and will the choice and will the rest of the middle of the half and the arrangement be as much as there has been of increase.

She would be so disappointed.

Now then near.

It was that she could by and by and have it as they could as well and for it in the case of their having been in the rest and rest and rested and finally as if they had to answer in a minute. Can consider. Having occurrences not in the way of dent and venison venison can be increased by hearing and by hearsay and yet if it is easily followed why can larger cities astonish and do delight and held in here and was a mistake to speak phenomenally. No one should remember what was put in there. No one. Repeat no one. Say no one. Say no one. Ask ask them ask them have them are they are they who are they talking to when they are careful to arrange which and where. She is so easily easily what she is so easily. If everything that was said was repeated everything that was said was repeated if everything that was said was repeated if everything that was said and repeated if everything that was said was repeated if everything that was said and repeated.

Little little a little never mentioned. Three things at a time. Have they and they and when. This makes it seem that they are as a color. Let them see older. Let them see them. Let them.

A little anyway. He said that if they never went and looked not in all would they be as well.

She said to them that if she cried beside what would they talk about.

He said if it were at all likely would the one be known.

He said she said she had said she would return and return she did. She did return. Return and returned and always as if thinking about it it was meant.

Very well meant.

As if they had and had it.

She is nearly as expected.

When all this time after all in the course of conversation after all and all this time after all in all and as all had he learned that in the course of conversation as in the fall as if as all in all by now and nearly enough come to the next and greeting greeting by this time and application and fortunately and by this by their with their and their all their for their use. Use it as in the course of conversation in its entirety.

That makes a meal. He said somebody who had said and had sat and was seated had been seated had been had been seated and seated as if in eating eating had enjoyed moroseness. This has never been accustomed accustomed is different from custom. After all not after it was in the week. Nearly in nine. At the same time they came to say yes yes yes yes yes. All five are as yes. Yes. All five are as yes. Yes. All four are as yes. Yes. All three are as yes. Yes. All four are as yes. Yes. All two are as yes. Yes. All two all two all two all one all three all two all four are as yes. Yes.

The next was that no one and as no one nobody and as no one nobody nobody as no one name and came makes houses and how how and houses and nobody and name and came and how and it does not occupy occupied or either. She and either was a chance to act and activity and actively do. Do pearls do does Goldiva do does Rosina do do they do do and do one does yes. Yes.

Julia Ford Helen Maud Maud E. Lathrop. Just like everyone else pale with a mote. Very much very much encouragement astonishment accomplishment and intact. Please plant plums and after this at all.

She was finally attentive to having little things returned and for this she had had lingering at once. And then who announces buttons of three or four happen to have three or four, literally happen to have three or four. Three or four happen to have three or four. The right kind but not enough happily to-morrow to-morrow should have been said first happily to-morrow after she had been here and regularly regularly is an item. Everything else. Say Elsie.

Elsie Allan Edith Sidney Minnie Maxwell and she dreamed of Charles.

Charles had leave to come and go and in this way he was not careful of why he was divided between love and affection. Love and affection perchance and disuse hours and powers and powerfully.

What was it.

If she could go on saying so and she could why not, if not. That is the difference between they never appreciated and they always called it jeweler.

Now then.

A victory.

Victory victorious as well and entitled.

Dear dear Gabrielle.

Dear dear Therese.

Dear dear Myrtle.

Dear dear Olive.

Dear dear Clara.

Dear dear Claribell.

Dear dear Elsie Edith and Dora. Every time.

Change quickly to men.

Ernest Robert Thomas and Edward also Michael Arthur Bernard and George Buchanan.

Very quickly.

After that.

Very quickly.

CHAPTER LIX

Now and nearly.

Nearly and now.

Nervous.

Nervous and now.

Nearly and nervous.

Nearly and nervous nearly and now.

Now and nervous.

Nearly and now.

He shall be placed where he can be called here and there. That makes one way. He can be accounted for as having very nearly always been meant by them. Now and then. Never having finished their best way always in there by that time hard and backward and arriving. Arriving means musical.

This is told by then by them.

He never wishes to see either Dora or Minnie Meininger.

Neither does he wish to see Henry or Dorothy Dane. Neither does he wish to see any more or Louise Hilda Paul Sherman or even Maxwell Grant and indeed if he had his choice he would prefer all the rest. And no one knows why. Why does he. Settling down simply to pleasure.

It is a great pleasure to give it to me.

CHAPTER LX

Nobody can.

Suppose everyone thinks.

They did that.

Returns.

They did that.

Have it.

They did that.

Allow it.

They allowed that.

Heard it.

They heard it.

There is no likelihood of following allowed.

And now and then.

In their rolling it rolling is to state.

Dear and dear here and here. Really hair, hair is as well as ever and also seriously.

Now a whole help it to them themselves.

To let us pray.

If after all they did not pay for a name let us, and if after all when he said he had more than complained would she come to them as if it were to us.

All these things makes gold golden and behold and beheld and gold golden.

And now regularly beginning with not seeing if as if they said they had they had had they heard they held they hold they are to please them with singing and after all not with plenty of room.

So then.

He was satisfied to say that they had nothing to give away.

They had nothing to say.

He had nothing to say except that they had held and were holding meat as meat and paper as paper and heavy as heavy.

They had nothing to say except to say that they believed it to be day by day.

He had nothing to say except that they had turned away.

They had nothing to say that was easier in that nearly as if it was as if all told. Look out. Look out and not in and corals.

She meant not to be able.

That sounds just like that she meant not to be able to. That sounds just like that as if she meant not to be able to and not any more.

Always having it about. And always having it about.

Having meant to be married and marry. This is the way it is. They they were older and they they had adopted and adopted having been married and able to and having married. After that sixteen sixteen after that they were after that they were there together after that and after that they were adopting after that adopting able to and older.

After that sixteen after they were after that they were adopting after that they were adopting being able to and older after that they were adopting marrying after that they were able to and older and after that they were adopting after that they were adopting being married to after that.

Remember all forty, sixteen after that and sixteen after that.

Remember all forty before that remember after that remember all forty and sixteen after that and sixteen after that.

Now what.

She could be had after it was later as it could louder and out loud. She asked about whereabouts.

Consider a novel as news.

Helen came and stayed.

Helen came and stayed.

Janet came and Janet came.

Jane and James and James and Jane came.

Consider a novel as news.

First.

After that.

By it a little.

And she knew it at once.

So then out loud.

Everyone.

And so forth.

All and one and so forth.

By and one and so forth.

CHAPTER LXI

She looks up to him up to him and after all who did it who did it who did it.

After all she looks up to him and who did it who did it who did it after all she looks up to him and who did it who did it who did it after all she looks up to him who did it.

It was very nearly useless and so they had extra and maybe they did.

Now and ninety ninety and five George and Georges and once they did have to have every day farther and farther to them.

Begin it begin to do all of it so that this. Did she know them then. She did. Let no one witness witnesses witness.

Come in.

Come in Helen.

Helen.

Helen.

Come in.

When she is in she can have many more handkerchiefs hand-kerchiefs and days days and lights lights and all all all too. Next to having forgotten all right. She has easily told that two are all and right. When she said after a while and not now not now not here not here now.

She never minded it and every little while they closed it and every little while they closed it and she never minded it and she never minded it and every little while she closed it and every little while they closed it and she never minded and every little while she closed it and she never minded.

That is one way of eating Tuesday.

When they had had a long time in the country and they said do you look like it and they approached it and they have had had it at least two years she said to have had it at least two years.

Not at once and three not look alike and foolishly the sky and foolishly green and foolishly why when white.

She thanked for them.

Another knew next.

We will always expect to go and come.

He had had it ahead. Who had. Do not be foolish who had.

She went in and out sometimes she went in and out sometimes she went in and out and sometimes it was for salad and some-times it was for something.

Something else had something else who is questioned. Do you how do you and do you do you need to do you need to do you need to and do you need to every afternoon what is every after-noon what is done every afternoon. Every afternoon what is done every afternoon. One afternoon and another afternoon and one afternoon she asked what is done every afternoon.

Nearly novel.

It is nearly nearly not in the meantime in a minute.

All favorably.

When they will seem and do have this and can share where and may this yet and by it. Disturb me. Plenty of at it so that and now and by by it.

Higher is one.

Dear is one.
Stopping is one.
And stopping.
When they stopped they came out. When they came out they came there. When she came there they were there. When they were there a share was there and if it is a share did they succeed did he succeed and if it came to them to be ready to exchange he relieved. Relieved is always best.

Can he have been so nearly as it was when she called away was called away that there was an example of every little while by this time. An instance of the wish who was it and who was it by their and by the time so not so as to delight, refuse to do so. She did not refuse to do so and easily after every little while at once. Follow for them. You do like it.

Introducing pleasures and pigs. Also introducing slights and sounds also introducing what is followed by them when they and as they wish. All at once.

It is more than they intended much more than they intended.

Every day if they had met either met or either met they could really startle is not the same as stare and yet how can harshly be harshly and harshly.

She was so kindly kindly to and never afterwards relate and to relate. Astonished and surprised. A long miserable story. She knew that they ought to have it little by little and so they did and so they knew that they knew and they do dare and lovely as it can be they have it as an instance. Every one refuses for instance every one refuses. And for instance. Imagine meetings. This and they say wishes and washes and feathers and best. And next. Having seen years. And next not only for them. And next. They had not resembled as well as listened to enjoy and never deny adjoining and praise and then. Next and then they have nearly married mentioning and then in outline and then then as to that, follow them follow their follow as if fellow and follow made it that she rejoined. Could she really never have it had it have it hear it there have it had it there had it have it at all. At all. Succeeding at and all. At all announcement for them. Find it now.

CHAPTER LXII

Mary and Jane it was a disappointment all the same it was a disappointment. Martha and Bertha it was a disappointment all the same it was a disappointment. Mary and Jane came and Martha and Bertha came and Mary and Jane and Martha and Bertha came and Mary and Jane and Martha and Bertha it was a disappointment all the same it was a disappointment. Lucy came there is that name Lucy came it was a disappointment all the same it was a disappointment. Helen came it was a disappointment all the same it was a disappointment. Suddenly they change Paul Edith and their mother what is the same as having a son.

Future when they might have had it. At first when they might have had it. When they might have had it.

In and in a minute.

He met her. She met them. They met easily. They meet when they have heard of it.

Supposing they had always had their father. Supposing they had always meant to and supposing he said supposing he said I have not seen that one but others like it. Supposing he had said that they were as many as very many as many as there were in mixing the three. The three make it come to be that after all he did remember. Everything in their being and always anyway the history any way of any nine families a family not having gone away. Nine families a family not having gone away.

One two three four five six seven eight nine. One two three four five six seven eight. One two three four. One two three four five six.

This is the way to show him that he is a queen.

This is the way to show them that they have often been betrayed.

This is the way to show her that she reasons very well.

This is the way to have it partly theirs and partly hers. This is the way to have it partly hers and partly his. This is the way to have it partly his and partly theirs.

After who can be seated and eating who can be.

Next and net. Leaving out to do so.

Then it is so easy to have more of it as well as that who says they can ever see what they have heard as well as that and now and this and for and how they make it do as much as all of that by then who have had formerly in the meantime and so soon changed later.

Remembered for them.

So in this and on this account.

Could there be lists of persons seen. If the lists are made could they be as much as much as as much as ever. They delighted in this admirably.

She met and talked with him about how very easily they would have it cleaned and she said yes and she said yes and she said yes longer and he said yes as long and in the meantime it was very unusual.

That is so.

Then having had indifference to it they made permanent arrangements and very likely they would in the meantime accordingly having had their attention attracted in having that they intended to deny it at once. And only then they could be very nearly too likely to be undertaken. This always remains in mind.

Would she please yes would she please. Would he settle it altogether yes would he settle it altogether. Would they learn that forty and forty made forty-four. Would they be pleased with rings and would they trouble themselves. Would they please wear a hat and who would after all be their assistant and finally leaving finally how many more how very many more plenty in evidently afterwards having reunions. Nearly and this. For instance.

She had had it easily arranged that just as accidentally. No one repeats it. Repeats it makes its effect. She need not prepare letting it have it as often as there was and we never would be pleased to be never to be never to be to be to be as well as to be. This is easily what they said. Let us repeat the whole of it. The whole of it.

He they them and theirs that is not as well as ever. Next.

They and then and themselves and they had they had never to this and never to this and to their happiness and pleasing.

Would she go with him to the country.

Every little while imagine it.

After all in this and whether whether do they. It does make a difference whether it comes after or before and easily when they need it to be darker it is as easily lighter. So now and every once in a while.

Imagine a door a room and plenty of ice and snow also as often as they came in they went out. Also imagine that if from then to every evening she would not be able to have it ready would she be joined. This makes her different from the one who had as frequently had her head and her hand equally prepared and was not in any way obliged obliged to and as obligation. Can no one see why prizes are asked for and offered. Why certainly they do aid in the arrangement of schedules. She was surprised. That made that not as important not as important.

A new noon. Why do they catch fish or fishes and by this kind of day day in and day out.

Can any one follow me. Certainly they can. Certainly they do.

Supposing Paul is Paul does Paul or do Paul and Paul and do Paul do they after all have it easily remembered. Can he have chosen in the time in which he had been away can he have chosen to have been there. That is the way that she explains it. All of it again.

It was as a fault in him never to mention Negro dances.

CHAPTER LXII

In a habit and never he had had it here.

Lead it right.

Follow the house.

And save it.

In to use as in a habit and never to decide it after all.

Settled and unsettled.

A part of all who can be halted just at once and they should always be renounced. Letting and letting and every time letting it alone.

One all day.

Twice all day too.

She needed to to do to and to having a preference.

Did I make a mistake.

There then.

A little later when there is when there is a place for it places make all sorts of all sorts of places make all sorts of thunder. Always change to thunder. By and by always change to thunder.

He not a he she not a she she not a she he not a he relief and relieve make dishes and dishes and sets and ceiling. He never knew because if it was at all at all all of it. And now there is an instance to always prefer instance to an instance.

Actively two beds.

Actively too.

Actively two and two.

Actively to arrive at a considerably usual and usually returned. So much for it. Everybody does do it as well as that.

Now an arrangement.

To-day.

First yesterday Mrs. Craven and he knew it was she and I was not certain.

Second Mrs. Marly and of course she did not hesitate when I told her that I had heard it and she did not hesitate. Third Mrs. Paul Paul William and after all it was to be expected that he would be as soon as that and taken. That was all.

Next day before that.

She would know last night and to-morrow more than three days later and would he nearly be so well so so and so. Then next he could and he was not there he could really reason that more of them were in that and found. Coming to it and after it she said it had been put away.

CHAPTER LXIV

He knew how not to not to he knew how not to. After that he knew how not to.

Relieve and receive and receive and relieve.

Acutely.

Receive and relieve.

Acutely.

Always to prepare.

Just like that in calculation.

Red seen as yellow. Yellow if it were yellow would not be admissible as admissible is only blue and red as rosy. So then neither of the two.

In conversation.

Do you believe in ignorance.

Do you believe in receptions.

Do you believe in rotation.

Do you believe in little less.

The next reply.

Do they believe in separations.

Do they believe in acknowledgments.

Do they believe in respective.

Do they believe in pressure.

Never to ask for an answer.

Did she like it.

If there were to be another one would she like it.

If there was a question of getting it again did she like it.

If they had it as they needed it did she not remember it before.

Did she like it.

And then preferred beside.

Did she like it.

Now using uses and used to it.

And never as well as yesterday was to have it in intelligence and beside that they were industrious. How many were different. Two hundred and fifty.

CHAPTER LXV

It is easy as easy more easy easier it is more easily known.

If a thing is exactly like it who makes it who makes her have it. If she has it who makes her use it. If she uses it who makes her hold it. If she holds it who makes her attach it. If she attaches it who makes her divide it. If she divides it who makes her leave it. **She did not leave it because it was found.**

CHAPTER LXVI

Every little time is longer.
Every time he sat down.
Every time he sat down.
Every little time is longer.
Why is it not at all an easy thing to have more than more than one at a time.
Everybody means four.

CHAPTER LXVII

Forgetting sitting.
Now and then.

CHAPTER LXVIII

She knew how she threw threw it. Never to be confusing.
Glancing makes it seem as if it was by that time by this time at this time and in this way.
How could they receive attention. Liberally.
An and and a Negro an and in order and an refusing to resist and a parasol and after and before resemblance a resemblance.
Part of a parlor. To be really used to it.
He gave me.
In a little convince and in victory. Men so and mend meant too meant to they convincing really relied on Helen or Hannah.
Hannah which is short for Hannibal.
Having once more read about Russia England and Russia and never mentioned it. He needs hours.
Are two women together different from two women together.
Article and articles.
Hand and feet and foolish.
Coming back to day and night.
This makes it always as easy as that. There are two times when they are very nicely nicely at least and making five millions making five million turned around. Finding it funnily enough.

Was she interested in little in a little less. Was she as she and she can carefully she can carefully say that they might be as well as if they had asked did he know him. Always and yes.

To change the length of wood. They did.

CHAPTER LXIX

How could one hundred and sixty-nine be mistaken for sixty-nine. Sixty-nine has been has not been mistaken for one hundred and sixty-nine one hundred and sixty-nine has been mistaken for sixty-nine.

Plentiful.

Religion.

Furnished

Preceding

Remarkable

Relieved

Attributable

Reality and landscape.

Exercising in all of it they need to be authentic and how how do they need to be authentic and how do they define registration and believing and reorganisation. Supposing Janet Scudder asks Paul Chafin how he likes Russia. Supposing he answers. Supposing she continues to repeat have I had it and he says yes have I had it does this make that difference or differently. If she engages to do nothing at all and afterwards remembers how it was understood would she be perfectly and perfectly meaning in and because of it and would she by this time have had it as it was to be when they had heard. In this way. She can say. That they do deliver and deserve deserve is the same as observe and rely rely upon it. Mrs. James Franklin how does Mrs. James Franklin like having the rest of it from time to time. Very well and having said very well and all very well it is all very well now and then and again. Mr. Henry France might easily be pleased altogether pleased and he might very readily very readily indeed come to be prepared to have it very likely to have it be ready when there is occasion to have it ready. I wish to know what you would say if you had seen it.

CHAPTER LXX

To be returned at once Negroes, dear me and having heard it at once. She asked did she hear me now. What is the influence of Robert Robert William upon Robert Robert Paul. What is the influence of Emily upon not to repeat upon Katherine what is the influence of Emily Evelyn upon Emily Emily Ida. What is the influence of Emily Ida upon Emily Evelyn. And after this at once. The next and the next after the next. What is the influence of Walter as if there had been as many as if there had been any. Think of it. Pleasing themselves. If you do not like it do not do it. Pleasing themselves. Think of it. She sent it they sent it. They sent it back. They sent it. They sent it. She sent it. She did send it. And after now and then and places he more frequently than she remembered places.

There has been and there will not be any mention of her name.

I can feel the beauty this is what has been said I can feel the beauty this is what she has said. I can feel the beauty this is what he has said.

Very nearly what they have said. He asked me why did I not say what I knew to be the case that they were nearly as often right as wrong I said that there was every reason why I should say it and why I did say it and why I do say it. He said he really allowed for it.

Reynolds is not Reynolds.

CHAPTER LXXI

Having heard may having heard may it having heard may it be having heard may it be having heard it.

Please unite plans.

To feel that it would not be satisfying if she was not satisfied. To feel that it would not be satisfying if she were not satisfied that it would be satisfying.

Three four five, referring to having had heard and hearing. Referring to they knew she knew. Referring to entertainment and entertaining. Referring to would and would there be would there have been in the morning. She could have inherited it in the morning.

Once just at once he he could be the usual extra and having added it in time. And she was not as might be and might be supposed to be supposed it of them. Not in comfort. Once more just the same as they had afternoon and wishes.

Now come back to heavily come back to heavily.

Cannot mean in that room and why in that room. Cannot mean in the room.

She knew the name of her father and her mother and she said that she preferred her father to her mother.

Would he not the father and not the mother would he tell her that he would rather return he would rather hear further he would if he might return again.

That makes it as much as if they had in their being two and not at once neither of them came.

Could she be listening not if she did not hear it and heard it and they have twice two. Leave this to conversation.

Leaving out altogether that they were to they were to be they were to be there. Just like what just like it at all.

She need not be careful at all.

CHAPTER LXXII

When they came to see me say came to see me when they came to see me.

Forty-nine make forty and nine and climbing and Clive and as it were alive who is useful.

Usefully, and shorter used and fully and shorter.

To be prepared to have it an action.

It is very easy to put the dining-room fire in the parlor.

That was one day.

It was very easy to put this arrangement into practice.

That was every day.

He knew nights.

He knew days.

He knew day in and day in.

He knew what he had left out.

This makes it four times three.

She was ready.

Needed a novel too.

When this and mainly mainly to be there and not in there and not in there and mainly to be there and mainly. Who has asked whom. Can they need they and need they and can they and unimproved. In little places who has weights weights can be corrected by fertility and fertility and public and public and do too. They need need it and they have and have has been heard of. Ending heard of.

Letting out names in novels. And letting out names in novels and letting out names and letting out names, letting out names. Letting out names in novels.

A novel is usual.

As usual and a novel is afterwards when they have been there in plenty of time have been there.

Is it earlier or later that they say they prefer eating to drinking or eating to praying or eating to managing or eating to relief.

Back to back and back to back and back to back. Six times and so and as so and as it was because it was for butter cheese cake fish and fish and tea and tea tea too. Who knows noise and who knows noise. Action and in action and it will be successful they say.

Planning and plenty of time.

In an hour and a quarter and as they had noon to-day she was wishing she was wishing she was wishing for it all day. Having always come back to more rivers than women.

Always having been obliged and obliged to lend not to lend not to give a difference between green corn and bread wheat and rice plants and all. All at once and please buy and please deny.

It can easily be remembered that a novel is everything. And they had.

CHAPTER CII

They knew their number they knew that their number was this and she changed it.

A little piece of day by day.

Introducing women and then to have it as in their way. Let
us need that.

One two and two and two. Nieces. One two and two. Pieces.
One two and two and two and two. Three pieces. One two and
two and two. To separate new ones from novels.

I believe that everyone intends to come.

I believe that everyone intends to use them.

I believe that everyone has by this time arranged for it.

I believe that everyone is at least prepared.

I believe that everyone has very likely to have been attracted.

In these three ways there are injustices and decisions and
hearing.

To believe in surrounding hearing surrounding in surrounding.

To believe in plenty of time.

To believe their chances.

To believe ineradicably.

To believe funnily enough and they might have thought of
it.

When they cannot stop it altogether when they cannot stop
it altogether.

CHAPTER CIII

She included me.

They make many many make them in the meantime.

This is thinking.

She had seen me.

This is nearly

She had nearly seen me.

In the meantime.

In the meantime she had nearly seen me.

When Paul is said to be as usual and when he is said to be to
have it arranged to be used why then why then is so easily in
the middle middle of it and oh how nicely.

Birds may and they may and wider to change larger to change
larger altogether. My and my own.

When they can and cannot cannot care and carefully enough and carefully enough and carefully enough and as their meeting and as their meeting when they can.

By all the time and by at length and by nearly all of it and by it as it is never to be as it is never to be nearly as it is and nearly as it is.

She needed it and changing to wait she needed it she needed it as changing to be more to be careful.

Imagine two sending two at a time to them.

I wish to remember that they were different as different.

Was she to wear was she to wear and wear what was next to it and just as if they had gone and gone there. I knew that they meant that always and that always and that meant positively.

To wish to make it perfectly resembling and resemble.

He Conrad Clarence Charles Changer and Conroy everyone of them just at first. That is nearly.

After that they who were nearly willing that he made them made them more than met them for they met them meant to have it here. They need always have been heard to say once and once a day once to-day. This makes after this to be sure after this. Nobody knew he knew.

Catherine Caroline Charlotte and Celestine.

In the place of no one not yet.

They need changes that is twice.

Once if they have been women.

Twice if they have been in between.

Twice if they have sanctity in disclosure.

Once if they have meant to be related.

Once if they have exchanged purses.

Twice if they mean to truly.

Once if they have especially depended upon them and upon their having been in their way. In their way makes it more than ever an instance.

And so they suppose.

It was a chance to disturb their even their even their own and even their own at once or once or twice.

To know how and that as ground and that as around.

Supposing choosing four each four two times four is eight and opposite to four. Returning to and before. This makes their having it in that and their state.

And as splashes.

Now then sudden

Now then return

Now then and now and now then. And now then. And now then. Now then now then. It is easy to say continuously.

It went very easily when thrown.

Nicely and taking it nicely.

They effect stretches.

Do be do be do be due to be.

They need to arrive around. It is not at all after all when they went away.

That is their that is they are that is their and meet that is they are there to meet.

Meeting and met. Continue to make Conrad and Charles and Clarence and they they have to be as well known as in the afternoon.

To change forward and back from time to time. They need to reassure themselves so that this as that is after that. In their motion motion and made it.

After all.

CHAPTER CIV

Making altogether forget beginning three.

Herbert Harry Hardy Hill and Howard.

This makes their houses at once after that in the meantime. Changing lace for base and cups for changes changes after all. They knew their way.

They meant all of it. They made it their mistake.

Flocks of following are sensible. And they excite roses. It would be very much to be pleased with if they had made no part of it.

Opposite. Hilda and Ida as much hide her as much and had it had it something to do with it and Hannah and really Hattie. All at once really.

He knew she knew she knew he knew.

Arrange a novel briefly.

Never to return to all.

All or nothing.

Until the land had been paid for in full.

That makes them when when they had had it. That makes them then then there and there as if there had been rain. Rains all the time.

Never but it had been here for this.

Needs and noses knows know is know is in as much and they have had to be. When it is when it had they had eyes then they had. To be sure.

Ought to be as they had.

They had it there.

Forward and back.

Back to back.

Back to back. Who knows. Plenty of time. Who knows. Had the same name. Who knows. When as in the meantime. Where is where is where is where where it went when when and when is always always is in a while by that by that returns to and in conclusion.

CHAPTER CV

It is useless.

She needs Pritchard.

They need Richard.

Richard so much.

Never to go never to remember that never to remember that there is as part of it.

If Abel Arthur and Edwin went to a place and asked for something that would be effectual if it were used not as intended but as they intended would any one feel more than delighted. That would depend very largely upon whether it was the habit to inquire in what way had it a use and if so when would there be need of more of it. After every little while there was disappointment. He knew twenty of them.

Now and then makes more of it more of it and she went away

and said it is not more easily when it is as easily as ever. She
knew that in hoping for her father and her mother she was hoping for her father and her mother.

CHAPTER CVI

He thought he would please him by getting friendly.

As likely very likely very likely they will wish it. Every
now and then they arrange to do it and it is not needed here
and there and they avoid that when they are nearly there.

It is meant to be changed.

At length.

He knew that if he listened to two to change. He knew they
had their ease and their easily and their as easy and their as
easily as they were as if they were used to it.

Now plainly to be seen.

She might say Oh Josephine. He might say oh Alice. She
might say oh Josephine he might say oh Caroline. She might
say oh Josephine. He might say oh Katherine. She might say oh
Josephine. He might [say] oh Nelly. He might say oh Isabel and
she might say oh Josephine and he might say oh Elizabeth and
she might say oh Josephine.

The next time that they have happened to come here they
will be as pleased as if they had intended everything.

They knew their name.

He said it was perfectly certain.

They knew that at the same time.

They knew that they had it as well prepared as anything. And
pleasing. And more than all the time. Who was able to have them
come as often. Come again makes it just as well.

Not as easily as ever not.

Always.

Not always.

Repel and repelled repelled and recalled recalled it.

They joined just as much as before.

Before and more. And now a chance.

Supposing there is an arrangement like this supposing five
and they are not a part of it but in front of it. Supposing they

disarrange it and supposing they came to be behind one and before they came who has whose return. It is never as safe in return as it was as it was as it was as it was. As it was as it was. They had meant to have them in their way in their way right in their way just in their way as they are in their way. A great many see each other one another. This makes three at one time four at one time nine at one time ten in no time and thirty-five exactly. They came at once too.

Commencing again in singing. Nobody sings. Always as they had it for themselves for themselves once or twice always as they had it for themselves all aloud by and by always as they had to themselves as they heard from them there. To know is different that he knew. He could come to be left and right.

She made it very detailed.

CHAPTER CVII

This was a part of it. He arranged it for them.

And as it was when she was near when she was here when they were there and anyway who makes it all who makes it all nearly. Once when they had it all at once. When they made that and he said thanking was thanking is and never said it any more. Put it there my dear friend.

In the middle of it all there was this said. He said it that they had it and after all remember the best of it at first and at once. Who makes houses who makes elephants who makes bananas and who makes tube-roses. It is very well to say who makes elephants who makes tube-roses who makes bananas and who is charmed. It is very well to say who is charmed it is very well to say who makes tube-roses who makes bananas who makes elephants and who is charmed. Who now and then is charmed. Who makes tube-roses who now and then is charmed.

Finish famous for it.

And can it be aided as at once and very likely by this time so that it is settled and pleasantly and pleasantly at that for instance and as allowed for and in their estimation when they have had it for them and by them and with use and relief and as kindness and formidably and just as much as when they had indeed carefully and nevertheless by joining. She knew more than that.

How do you do necessarily.

CHAPTER CVIII

Kindly and kindness. More than might it.

What is there to tell about millions. Thirty-five millions when mentioned.

She met me.

Thirty-five millions when mentioned and when mentioned thirty-five millions when mentioned.

He is very well able to come again. Again and again after all Wednesday. They need not be delightful to them and for them and nearly as they had and if it is not older it is not as if it is. Thank you for them.

It is very agreeable to have it here.

Why.

Because naturally it is very agreeable to have it here. He meant it all. She meant it all. He meant it at all. She meant it at all and they had that and there and by and all and when they meant this they meant everywhere.

Who has houses.

Who has.

Who has said who is to be after all there.

Who has said it.

Who has announced that they are as much as ever prepared to be irresistible.

They make honey into maple sugar. So they do.

Need any one wonder why they are to be given what is she what is he to be given, he is to be given all of it.

Well well it is very astonishing that some things are not observed.

They make roses easily not so easily.

After all it was a mistake.

Allowed a chapter.

They allowed a chapter, they allowed a chapter to appear.

Come and come and come to them and do.

CHAPTER CIX

It is certainly very affecting to know that whatever is said about it is said so as to prepare them to be older and younger and to be after all after all and to be there and there and to be when they can wish.

I wish.

I wish I was.

And after I wish you wish. You wish you were and after you wish you were you wish. You wish you were.

Were you while you were you were you as pleased as that it is very easy and easily to say please. Please can be attached to please and some refuse chocolate. After that they change.

To often wonder if Edith is at all well.

And to often wonder if Edith is at all well.

Next to neglecting is protecting and like to be explaining to everybody that all is everything.

CHAPTER CX

It has happened that they have seen she knew their doors.

It can be traced to this that when they have felt themselves to be claimed they can be often as much as was meant.

He can learn it with them and their having said when they and their having said.

Announce me.

Pronouncing them to be left partly to themselves.

And do they drag.

They do like it when there is nearly all of it next to it.

And by this time.

Coming closer and the best way the best way by this time they have meant to be individually in unison and so Paul can be a name.

They mean the rest which is it.

Now and hours.

Please pay the man please pay the girl please pay the same please pay it so that it can be sent away.

Please leave it here.

Please send it now.

Please have it changed.

Please see it as it is to be left there for quite a little while yet.

There is a difference between to need and they need there is more than an allowance to allow for it.

Changing names the name is Paul and it is called Paul the name is Helen and it is called Helen the name is Edward and it is called Edward the name is Anna and it is called Anna the name is Arthur and it is called Arthur the name is Bertha and it is called Bertha the name is Oscar and it is called Oscar the name is Ida and it is called Ida. And so they have to have it every little once in a while.

CHAPTER CXI

Not as nice as they can come to be that they can see.

Preparation is not different from in preparation and when could they have made them all there and inclosed.

By nearly now

Come too.

They have had and she knew how to whistle.

Not as in their voice and all to leave it. Who comes to have it fortunately. Buy it a little. Do buy it a little. When addressed.

Happening to have farther farther do they prepare. By this next to their own day.

Come to the home.

Come to the home two buds and two roses and she said she so much preferred them to leave and now as actively.

They had one more.

Good.

They had one more.

And you

They had one more.

You.

They had one more.

They had one more.

He prefers it because he was as nearly as ever in a grotto.

And this is the place to have it as it was to be intended. Come to them again.

A next wish.

Not to fail.

A next wish.

That they should repeat.

A next wish.

That they wish to be after as much as ever to be sure to be sure Tuesday.

Not any extra wishing Tuesday.

And so now yes.

Once and twice a color. Once and twice can be called shoes whose and they came whose whose and they came and saw we see so.

Not to be so much like them just now.

Everybody who has assisted in finding out all about what they had to do and were a little careless about arranging for it for instance in closing a door they might not have turned that way and in having had plenty of time they might perhaps have been easily misled. Supposing they had wanted to arrange about it would it be easier to explain or would it be easier to return. She might so very nearly have come to be as usual and they might do as much for them.

Would they be afraid.

One two three. Would they be afraid.

Not so much by their persistently and choosing and by and very likely to be unable to change change and challenge make how do you do natural. They have every reason in making this and allowance allowance for it and be in time. Once when they had indeed by no means had fairly and submissive submissive can exchange, they need to have been when they wished for this winter. Now that they have allowed for it they need and do have more than all and alteration they can surround and be be doubtful are there fifty or seventy lions to their name. Who can breathe as easily. When they have been in no way easily courted courting makes all who have known what it is to love have known what it is to love and love them. How do they arrange what they like when they are undisturbed. Do you an-

nounce me no one can be so shown and shown can be pronounced usually usually for this reason. They can select. They
can select them. They can select and remind themselves that
they are by this time always more and more often in between
saving and saving. They saved them. And more as it was in
particular that they had shared partially shared that for this
reason. A reason. By not at all. And fortitude. Fortitude makes
why was she as late and why was she as late and why was she
as late. Read forty-one. In reading forty-one they have a great
deal of pleasure in and at this time and they have no manner
of knowing why they consider that it is so. Not to repeat. No
not to repeat. Who goes away to-night. They all do. And so
they do. And so they do.

CHAPTER CXII

They need to be as well as that and they have that as well
as this and so they sit and they are all as much as when they had
the same for them also. Not as nice as pleasurable and weather.

They could and will and they might there and they might
there as they might by and by as much as it is true when they
are ordered to very extremely remember it. Thanks for the
name.

They might have and will it be always as they have said
why they could and undersize arranged and more than as if by
and by when not at all and always by request and formerly
welcomed. In season and out.

He needed a novel.

CHAPTER CXIII

There can be two kinds of ladies and cakes two kinds of
children and bread two kinds of men and rice. There can be
two kinds of birds and weights two kinds of dolls and Simons
two kinds of losses and cups. There can be two kinds of change
and changes two kinds of miles and mingling two kinds of
settling and their. There they are.

They came to bow.

When they came to bow they came to be here. And when they came to be here they were received and remained as long as that. Supposing he had to have and had to have been having and had it. He certainly had more than they had had when they could do it all all of it. Not as much as when there were more wishes more wishes more while more while more when more when more while more wishes. It is always foolish to rely on minutes minutes and after a while and could they hear me and why could they not be just as pleased by it all. There there and there and they had no reason for remaining by the way who has a nobody can so often and obediently see.

Imagine lacking it at all. Just imagine lacking it at all and just imagine lacking it at all. They needed it as they why did they breathe either.

Miss and missing who knows how.

Next.

Make and making who knows how.

Next.

Next.

Next.

If you like to dearest.

I should not be at all surprised if he were to be there.

If you would like to.

Not to be at all surprised if he were to be there.

If you would like to dearest. Then.

Dear

Dearest.

Come and eat.

Very well come and eat.

Who could come.

They could come.

And when could they come.

He had often been threatened and he always was able to nearly not hear. He had an illegitimate daughter who was a very pretty girl and Nelly would know who her mother was Nelly always had that kind of information. Nelly and Frank did look as if they had and Ada and Harry not at all that is to say melancholy is natural and not at all. Mike and Jane are often

pretty nearly ready to forget about who was able to come and
John and Josephine may easily have left and James and Bertha
are prepared to feel very content if only they are not disappointed. How do you like all that.

They do realise that.

Come and kiss me when you want to because if you do you
have more than done that which it is a satisfaction to have been
most awfully obliged to have as a delight and more than that.

So much can one change be an advantage to them.

Supposing they arrange for Thursday if it is at last Thursday
Thursday if it is the last Thursday, Thursday when they came
Thursday came Thursday seventy when they went to seventy
certainly of course not by permission and not by and in countenance they can as usual be inclined to realise religiously religiously makes an announcement. They can but try. Now and
then they mean to be there is a difference between in between
and have to be and come to say and shall they have hours and
hours and he he does have what they can to all be this and that
by chance. Now and describe the party. Four can establish with
them that they that they shall be shall be all all to be lost and
left left left right left they had a good place and they left and
by and by they might have come to be originally very welcome.
Welcome is as welcome does and they mind mind it because
when he says that as young as he was he was stilll and until a
father and he was a father and a father was a father of a son.
So can a mother a mother be the mother of a daughter either.
That is why inevitably they can there can be these can be and
now as and come, as and come makes as traditions. Let them consider either. They knew that they might have heard third word
or to be preferred.

Pitifully not annoyed.

CHAPTER CXIV

Now that it is best to be and say and do and leave and how
and now. Now that it is their time to have it in their arrangement by the way and do they do they do.

Lit and left and by this now shall they be felt to be at once and can makes no and far too well and noise noise can be attached attached makes no difference to attracted. And bowing.

When Harry and Frank and Paul and James and John and Robert and Ernest and Edward and this and that and because this and for that and nobody knows their name all the same all the same to be sure they have left it all here and by this care who shall be as much mistaken for them.

Supposing he was French and became English and supposing he was Swiss and became Danish supposing they were supposing they were hospitable.

All who have have given.

When it is and all of it have it to be that they can having placed it in their care.

He did it very well.

CHAPTER CXV

By this time they do not use other pink any other pink.

Nobody loves to come and go.

They are darker than their fate.

She makes it very easy for them to be well and happy and also nearly often by and by and there.

Exchanging there for there makes it that first they came first they came first they came first they came. Exchanging there for there makes it first they came. First they came. Exchanging there for there makes it first they came. Making exchanging exchanging making there for there makes it exchanging there for there makes it exchanging there for there. Exchanging there for there first they came.

Not as they came.

They knew nicely.

They knew that nicely that they knew that. That is one.

They knew that they knew their there they were there there there there their there or in there. There they were.

They knew that in that all there is of have it had it how and how do they pardon publicly. Who pardons publicly by then.

Not as well as ever and not at first. So then arousing and she knew by its name who came.

And made it.

He made it.

When he made it it could be just as well as bitterly and how can it be one and one. As might it all do more. Do more do and to do more and to-morrow. Who can reply to exchanges.

One to one

CHAPTER CXVI

Able to be apart.

What happened

They were good to them

What happened.

When a little all of it was as they meant to share for the piece that was partly left they made it all of it as different as when it had not been completed they were the first admitted. They were near it and so when they had and they had for themselves and by an arrangement they did not interfere not between and not before before can always be in plenty of time so that they have it as safely as ever as safely as ever to-day.

Having to have and buy it. Who bought it. Many people had told that it was a delightful place a very pretty place a nice place a very nice place and he said it was nicer than he had thought it. That makes them wish for them. Not a day not a family either. She needed all she did for them.

Connected with pass it pass it for them and connected with thank them thank them for that. There is no more use in mentioning all of them than there ever has been and no more after all when they had held it as they held it at all.

Now and nearly.

Two hundred and twenty-two and they stopped counting.

It is all as well can be so much for them as can be felt and they make it that farther than at all he when he did and remembered that he had given her to us he would not come having of necessity occupation in full. Who meant that. Mother and daughter who meant this godmother and goddaughter who meant who meant and after all she was not born and all the rest. Can two things be returned and given. So that they can be be one only one tortoise shell two red violets three one at a time. Just as easily as not.

What happens is this. Very much very much and as much and as much and then markets, markets are open in the morning and except on Monday. This has been held to be then. Then they come to go they do and finally shall pronouncing make it as much as when they respected. They respected tact and generosity.

CHAPTER CXVII

She might be white and she might be white. They need to have had it helped and they consider hers to be best. The whole of it which in the meantime is pleased. Pleases and as she knew that they had when there was and finely. Finely means longer at most. Most and best.

Did she give it.

Always to ask did she give it.

Did she give it. And to always ask did she give it. To always ask did she give it and did she give it.

They made their mind up that she did give it.

They measure it from end to end. Do they. They arrange for it and they wait for it. And they do. They believe that they have not had that they are not about to have any further trouble concerning it and they do not have any further trouble concerning it. That is to say just now and a very little later they begin to countenance what has been in no respect idealised. Then every little once in a while they arrange for it they begin they allow they rearrange they continue they become they become once in a while they become ready to collect it altogether and to very likely and probably to have it matter just as much. How can those who have been after all pained by oversight and more than that by intentional shoving how can they be more than easily courageous and yet they are. They are. They are that.

He was distressed by it. He knew that they could show themselves more often if they were considerably and considerably and considered considered as in a way not to be followed. Imagine

them at once all at once and they knew that they could at once
and at first be reasonable be followed and be beside that, beside
that by and by and by and by. By and by to by and by and beside to by and by. To hear them coming. They come. Come
along.

Leaning and once in a while.

Supposing they had usually they usually had more than yet.
They aroused, aroused and louder and arouse and arouse and
just as regularly regularly means once a day. Who can compare
regularity with noise. Everybody. That makes it more of a to-do.

Nearly by and by.

Everybody knows about it in time.

CHAPTER CXVIII

Politely.

They can be easily heard at a distance and they can be easily
heard close too and they can be easily heard when she was as
if when she would be as having been younger she would then
not have heard and known that to inspiration and to inspire
and to inspired and not to be told at all and certainly not as well
told. Not as well told.

She knew that of another. Not as well told and she knew that
of another and not as well told. Not as well told and she knew
that of another. She knew that of another and not as well told.

I knew that she had heard of them of them of him of him of
her of her of her who and when were they looking alike all
alike and we we knew why we were wanted and we were so
nearly for that reason and because of it did she know that she
had had a hat.

No one likes to know that.

And by this to-day to-day can there be years for every day
and year for every day if if there is no difference between may
they stay.

They pronounce then.

In the immediately continued having placed where it could
not be placed they might have been surely had been could and
would have been their own. Supposing one considers four out

of five or to be more correct three out of five or perhaps with greater exactness exactness as to it supposing four possible out of six impossible and that again always is incorrect four possible out of seven possible and impossible and two very good indeed indeed perfectly satisfactory and so forth. So in this way having arranged for their not being particularly anxious as soon as they had been finally entreated as between then nothing is ever afterwards an annoyance indeed not by this time and their time. By their time and by the time that they have meant it for this because after all should they be as rich and richer. To be sure to be sure wonderfully and to be sure that they could arbitrarily entice them from their own decision and because of it could it be as well for them all. Indeed very difficult to think together.

CHAPTER CXIX

She did number it.

There can be choices.

They can be used to it.

They can decide.

They can be relied on.

They can be as much as much so as ever.

They can be nearly always anticipated.

They can be addressed.

They can be easily they easily can be disguised.

They can be prepared.

They can be utilised.

They can be delicately undeniably recalled.

They can be as much as they can of that.

They can be sent.

They can leave or be sent.

They can have their attention and they can be as much delayed.

They can be all of it can be returned to them.

They can be as much as ever in their way attended to by those who when they have meant all of it have by and by not at all as well as ever and as much behind.

They are as much behind as that.

They are ascertained to be reasonably kind.

They are indicated as having been nearly more often prepared to go than to come. To go than to come and to go than to come. To go than to come. Than to go than to come. Than to go than to come. To go than to come. To go than to come.

To change them to having hired porters to carry it up and down. To carry it up and down and around and to defend themselves as best they can.

Can a novel be changed into a story of adventure and when.

A novel can be changed into a story of adventure when it is found out that there are nearly as many times when there is a use in remaining there than there was. They knew that they meant it so. They had had it as well and they had not been blinded by it to the exclusion of having gone there too. Can anybody think what will happen. By nearly all of the time she meant two months and so did she. And she meant that they had been collected and so did she. And she meant that they had their reserve and so did she. So did she. She knew that they could not be at all as they were when they came. She also knew that they had more than enough not more than enough unless they asked for more and not asking asking is always when they were to be not only added but rested. They are rested. Supposing four sisters are older. Two sisters might be between twenty-five and thirty-five. Four sisters might be between twenty-five and thirty-five. Four sisters. Four sisters need not be here. No they need not be here. They were to be nearly divided into one and three. When they see this. There can be no return to them and it was only in connection with that that they were here. Here and here.

CHAPTER CXX

Was there a mistake.

Rest awhile.

If they say and it is an established fact if they say that he has gone away is there anybody to ask about it. It is so very easy to change a novel a novel can be a novel and it can be a story of the departure of Dr. Johnston it can be the story of the discovery of how after they went away nobody was as much rested as they had hoped to be. It can also be an account of the discovery and the return of various parts of the country which have been gradually losing their identity and then after all when there is more than there has been of daylight they can after all be anxious. A novel may also be partly that they have not at all wondered why they had not had all of it and partly it may be that they have stood and are standing as much in this way as they did when they were underlined. By and by a novel may be dated by their having been very often eager about swimming it may also be arranged in such a fashion that they had better hear themselves return to it and very often and very often and how often and how often can they be radically after all by themselves and to their delight and to be happily when they were rejoined. Who can think about a novel. I can.

<h2 style="text-align:center">CHAPTER CXXI</h2>

He knew her address. He knew his address. And he knew his address. And he knew his address too. That makes three times. He knew his address. That made it come to be sure that he would really have to return what in the manner of more than ten thousand he had made thirty-three. Thirty-three thirty-three thirty-four. Anyone has all of that to be to-day to be sure.

It is an excellent idea to take away a distance to take away to a distance to make it a distance to make it in the distance to make it to make the next room the distance to make it the distance that it has been taken away. It is a very good thing indeed to make it to have it taken to make it to have made it to have taken it into the next room. And after it has been taken into the next room naturally there is no way to wait as long as it is necessary to wait particularly as any one can go away if it is necessary to go in there. Go in there. Where. Having carefully arranged that they will never be frightened they have carefully arranged that they will never be frightened and having carefully arranged that they will never be frightened and having carefully arranged that they will never be frightened. Having carefully arranged that they will never be frightened and having care-

fully arranged that they will never be frightened. Having carefully arranged that they will never be frightened and having
carefully arranged that they will never be frightened. It is a
serious question this question of enrolling them. Supposing they
come, then they certainly do come and supposing after all that
they wish to come, from now on everything that is said will
have some connection. Everything that will be said in connection with porters will also have the same meaning in connection
with carriers and subjects and animals and advancing and re-
tiring and going and coming and returning and collecting. Everything that will be said will have a connection with paper and
amethysts with writing and silver with buttons and books. In
this way she knows what I mean and he knows what I mean and
I know what I mean. Very well then. Once upon a time and
quite often they meant perfectly well everything that they had
carried away with them they meant it perfectly well and I said
that I would like it and never having had any pleasure in that
it will not be like that. Again it has been a pleasure to say that
sometimes they looked different sometimes they looked different and at these times they might when and if they were younger
they might come to be at least very old and so this was in their
way and they might be perfectly generous and they might easily
be careful of what they had when they came in and out and it
was always just as much pleasure as ever to them or to whom
to whom or when. This makes what will never happen to be all
of it. So that. She was not at all different differently more than
it could have been expected. This is in a way cloudlessly.

Supposing he had a wish. What wish did he have. Did he
have a wish when he looked at a star and if he had a wish when
he looked at a star would he care to have them believe him and
would he equally well hope that it would be all for the best. If
he had a wish and he wished that he had been able to have anticipated them in their actions would he then like to have them repeat what they had done or would he only care to have them
have it as their next intention. If he had had some success in
wishing would he afterwards allow everyone to have it commence quickly and would he by and by would he like to have
it happen that they would change it all when they saw him

come away again and if he liked this as much as that would he
be very careful that he would not need to have them remember
that they were there. He had met all of them and in that way
they were nearly all there. This follows that and after that this
follows and after that this follows that after that. He could be
almost always very nearly there when there was a difference
between center and central as also when there was and when
there is some difference between behind and mind and between
carefully and carefully. He knew that he was always anxious.
He knew that they had plenty of time. He knew that they made
the most of it. He knew that they always liked to be up and
about. He knew that it was all for the best. He knew that he
was as obliging as ever. He knew that they had begun just as
often he knew that they meant to have half of it he knew all
about it and he knew how it happened and he knew that they
could collect all of it. All of it makes it so much all of one piece
and does it when they can be heard. Can they be heard in here.
They can. And so when this is begun every time they have been
attracted they are attracted. And so easily. Come to arranging.
An arrangement is never an annoyance. One and two one and
two never does make more than remembering all their names
Louise and Eugenia and remembering all their names Arthur
and Paul and also remembering all their names Rosy and Henrietta and remembering all their names Maximilian and James
and remembering all their names Ellen and Maddelena and remembering all their names Ernest and Herbert and remembering all their names Harriet Janet Emily and Agatha and remembering all their names Edwin and Charley and Godwin
and Louis and Frederick and then then who is near by.

They come to be here by this time. And any other kind.

Very much of that belongs here. Very much of that belongs
here very much of that belongs here and very much of that belongs here. Next to the next time there is belonging to it that
he was very much mistaken. To be neary placed in the way of
asking them when they are coming again is what is fairly nearly
half of that when they have been very well pleased and have been
encouraged and allowed to arrange it and pass it along so that
when he reaches they mean to have it almost always plentifully

changed plentifully changed makes practice makes perfect. Who
said who went.

CHAPTER CXXII

Who made it all. They made it all.

Supposing a novel is historical.

They made it at all if they made it at all. Suppose it is nearly
best to go away. Supplied by themselves and always left there
and showing that they had every reason to laugh aloud.

A visit to America. In visiting America they found themselves
there and they said who is perhaps the most important and they
answered you are perhaps the most important and asked to make
it afterwards afterwards they meant to be there they said they
would look for it and if by that time they had not decided then
very likely they would never fancy anything about it anything
about it they would be in their attitude advocating that they
should try always and often and have it fastened fastened can
be through and through and through it. So much better than
if they wished. There is this the wept of the wished on wish
and after that they might look about and see it just as well.
Just as well and pensive and answered and obliged and missing
missing it who made flowers into bouquets who did. Who did
make flowers into bouquets. And who did make flowers make
flowers into bouquets of flowers who did make flowers into
bouquets of flowers. And who did make flowers into bouquets.

CHAPTER CXXIII

One two and three, four five and six, seven eight and nine,
ten and eleven, and eleven and twelve, and twelve and eleven,
and eleven and ten, and ten and nine, and nine and eight, and
eight and seven, and seven, and seven and six and seven, and
six and five and four and three and six, and five and four and
three and two and one.

One and one. One and one. One and one and one and one.
One and one two three four five six seven.

Now to go on. It is very nearly plentiful it is very nearly very nicely it is nearly very nicely arranged for. It is very nearly very nicely very nicely very nearly very nicely arranged for. To run and balance and orangutan. Now then they never went away.

He knew better just then and he had some help. He went to the door and he asked them would they prefer to repeat it after him. If they would would they be just as willing as if they meant to ask themselves how had they known about it and might they need it might they have to be very nearly seen and might they not think better of it. They do not if they have it around about them they do not often allow it to come to some result, there can be a result and a conclusion and after that she came in and out. Why when they went would they have been careful of themselves.

There is no difference between at that time and at that time there is no difference between how do you do and how do you do there is no difference between every little while and every little while there is no difference between singling them out and singling them out there is no difference between charming and charming there is no difference between relating it to it and relating it to it there is no difference between they made it more nearly the same and they made it more nearly the same there is no difference between not more than there is and not more than there is there is no difference between what is more used and what is more used, there is no difference between nearly as many and nearly as many there is no difference between as many as that in all and as many as that in all there is no difference between when there can be no thought of why they had no further need of that and when there can be no thought of why they had no further need of that there is no difference between as they went there very often it made no difference to them as they might just as well be praised and as they went there very often it made no difference to them as they might just as well be praised and there is no difference between they had leaned forward not to see but to be comfortable and they had leaned forward not to see but to be comfortable. It might just as well have been in a minute.

After that they might.

Not to do as they would have been afterwards make an arrangement that they might do more than have it here do more than have it here and letting them hear that that this is why they happened to have left it. They never have said they never have said happened to have left it with all that can be put in and this and more and wishing and advantage. And not entirely used up and not used up entirely and why, because when they they as nearly he mentioned someone.

CHAPTER CXXIV

How perfectly astonishing, and a way of being as well off as ever.

There are a great many kinds of their having used up all they needed and they were willing to give themselves just as much as they had before. They made no mistake when they left it all where they could neither easily nor very easily be in plenty of time for it because consider consider that they had after all nearly as much beside that as they had had before. Before what before what and before which and astonishing. They might just as well and very often and having had it to hear and be made there and therefore can they be more mildly if they have attached themselves to hundreds of thousands. They might be equally and adjoining and they might in that way no eagerness is established because and this is why they change, they often and believing it when it is all at once they have no sense at all about it they do know that if they have understood before they can be just as nearly by the way as they were before. They do not get used to it. They do not like to have more arrangements made. They do not do they not they do not declare themselves fully and each one by this time more than fortunate and they have it as well as uneasily, they make it fairly obviously and just as plentifully as and never mentioning grass and grasses this changes it this makes it that they prefer to leave it so. They might be all of them they might be now they might be in that as an arrangement in that arrangement in their arrangement for themselves and it is never formed into two. Each one is it one or is it as many as divided into all of their time and yet the rest of them do not do it they leave it to them because when it comes to their having no doubts about it they have not had any one one at a time. It is very easy to come to them here.

Here and there is here and there is here and there refusing to be repeated here and there, well what do you make of it.

They know that it looked very differently to them they did not even love it all the time they did not even benefit by it by themselves they did not even expect it to be fortunately for them fortunately for them they did not expect it to be fortunately for them as they had sent it away by themselves just at once and by their help would they. She knew it about the middle of it. What is the great difficulty that they have. The great difficulty that they have is in replanting in supplanting in contending in rejoining in recognising in recollecting in distributing in devoting in connecting in representing and in attending attending to it for them and for themselves and with one another and hand in hand and nearly and all in all and for it. Can they be calmer so. To return to the regular question do they do they as they are neither obliged to nor pretty nearly ready do they and does it amount to that. This makes me nearly ready. Nearly ready to say so. If they go do they go away together at all. Do they need more than they have already do they have to be kind and nice and sweet and tender and happy and lively and having changed it from snow to snow and snow they know that there and there are pretty nearly having refused numbers just to-day. Consider whether they would be at all interested. It is not mine this time.

CHAPTER CXXV

They were perfectly able to take care of themselves. And their ears.

Once again and they had not been very well ferried ferried across. Imagine all of it in time.

One two three one two three one two three one two three.

In a carriage and out of a carriage and they never mentioned a carriage again.

One two three one two three one two three one two three. One two three one two three.

They had amounted to it it had amounted to it and they amounted to it, it amounted to this. Just exactly as if they were there. There is no one more so and as it happens. As it happens. Blue birds on a black hat. And as it happens. Black birds on a blue hat. And as it happens. Blue birds on a blue hat. And not next to as it happens. Black birds and a black hat.

There that is what they mean. Now and then then and there there that is what they mean. If she likes it cold if she likes it cold if she likes it as cold if she likes it as cold if she likes it as cold if she likes it cold, if she likes it cold. They have half of it. If she likes it cold.

If she likes it cold if she likes it cold if she likes it cold if she likes it as cold. If they have half of it. If she likes it as cold. If she likes it cold. They have half of it.

Not nearly as dark as it was.

Now everything about hat about Hattie. Hattie has gravely misunderstood she thought that head meant head and hand meant hand and half meant half and here meant here. She thought that this meant this and they meant they and there meant there. She also had purchased for herself once more all that they could use and she had made this mistake they did not dislike it they did not come away they did not disobey and when she meant to be all in all she was all in all and so forth. That is what she meant by what she said.

Now and then is easily after all.

Once more going to come.

They had happened after all and after all who knows who can know who can know after all it happens that after all they had precisely and precisely is always precedence and precedence is one after another after all why can they have it once and a while. She is partly to blame for this. Do you know why they both prefer it do you also know why they both want to come. They both want to come because later on later on they can and they cannot be left behind always to speak of it all alone. She is to be when they come back.

CHAPTER CXXVI

Having finished with that.

Perhaps they meant to believe them perhaps they did and so might they know the difference between Smith and Shielded and if they did would they comply with it as nicely she might have been nearly as often there as before and she might not and she might not have had it too early for all these days and she might be nearly often fortunately she is fortunate and she had had it better just as much better and when she said she had all of them everybody believed her and it did matter it did matter just how much just how much was effaced. They all had it principally they might find it and too they might come to be all at once just as good as for it and when they did come to say had it gone they never knew how many had come to speak to them about it. They knew that any one could be there altogether.

After that every once in a while an incident.

Never always ready to refuse and least of all when they meant that urgently urgently by then and safely by then and not missing it never at all missing it because they could never come to be alright. They might have been nearly as safe and as often as not they would just as soon come to be here. And it does not make any difference.

CHAPTER CXXVII

Everything that happens has it has it once in a while has it for them has it has it happened to them has it happened to them all the time.

Not nearly not nearly to be sure to be sure when is it that it makes no difference. She knew this for a change.

How did you feel about it altogether. How did they feel about it altogether. How did she feel about it altogether. How did it happen to have nearly been just the same. Because they had already gone. Which was a comfort.

Tell them just how you like it to be.

Also tell them that it does not displease you that they should try by asking everyone just what it was and what was the value of it. Also tell them that they need not be at all indifferent to it and that as she came in and out it changed it but could one be sure that they meant it just as much. Meant it just as much is just as easily said and partly partly is always as nearly so as once before. Once before and as they held it.

Returning after a while.

It was very well said that they might be old.

Would it be better for them to please themselves.

After all who makes it be as nearly as that.

She never could be certain certain to certain to be almost as once.

He being René Crevel is not partly to blame.

He said that they had meant to be there and they were not there and they had believed that they had been asked to be very careful about it. Every once in a while they might be there and just as soon as they instinctively withdrew they were very much more careful than they ever had been. That makes him every once in a while obliged to be as well. They knew that they cared about it every two months. Nearly every two months. Would it be just as well to have had it happen and altogether to send it to him for them and so they might easily arrange for it altogether. Should he be so much so one at a time.

CHAPTER CXXVIII

Always thinking of it.

CHAPTER CXXIX

If they had made up their mind.

Supposing that he knew that there was snow falling.

Coming to change it for everything. And they made mischief and they had come to say when they could that they preferred it anyway. They needed it and now as nearly as that not having made it acquired.

Not and do they do that.

Having exchanged russian for russian and spanish for spanish and American for American and then for then and there for there.

Who makes it do.

Everything alike.

Everything just like and everything like and everything alike. It was she who disturbed me. Not when they were always there as much so and believing it to be lost and there was as much as they could possibly have as their own and they needed to have especially to have they need to especially have it by and by. Not when not there and now.

Not here and there and now.

This is to be very well known.

Would they begin again, would they be very often as pleased as if they had heard it about themselves and would they be dreaming if they were smiling, would they know the difference between saying it and saying it. Reminding them that they are saying their same thing. Begin now.

When they met and saw them all and they were there and had it very nearly all the time for this use. They might have been just now they were and as it came they had to fasten it and so they can see by the same half that they heard me. Now then. Now and then.

It happened that the one who was the heroine had been asked to go if it were not troubling her unduly was asked to come and if at that time there had been no use if at that time it had been of no use asking would it perhaps not be at all and more when there could be no difficulty might she not present herself. And if she might what would she say and what would she say when she was attentive. When she was attentive she would not only not be alone but nearly for that reason and when they were almost as well heard they might she often thought that it had lost its value.

CHAPTER CXXX

Everyone reminding one.

For that leaving it alone.

Howard did resemble Lansing.

CHAPTER CXXXI

Invited to address.

CHAPTER CXXXII

Continued as a way to have without doing any injury to the hand or the rest continued to succeed in arranging it all.

Invited to address them.

They made them ask them ask him ask him would he be able to address them.

He made them ask them would they be willing to have him address them.

He made them ask them would they ask him would he be willing to address them.

He made them they asked him would he be willing if they asked him would he be willing to address them.

CHAPTER CXXXIII

It is if it is at all needful to have it come after or before it came when they were after all in plenty of time every once in a while.

This makes them finally have it be nearly as after all when they could come to claim it as if they had never after a while been inclined to prepare themselves. Every once in a while and in answer and in answer every once in a while.

CHAPTER CXXXIV

No one writes a letter in that way.

Please do not wish us to have it as a disappointment.

CHAPTER CXXXV

A novel is nearly finished in this time. After a novel is nearly finished in this time she will tell you about everything.

I am taking it I [am] certain that you will be very pleased to have me tell you why I did thus and so. As you may easily know it is not at all difficult to remain here all the time. They come to stay. At the same time it becomes increasingly unnecessary to know that if they had not been pleasing to them they would after all not have been obliged to have ended this here for them and they did not they made it obligatory. To see and to see here. See here. You know as well as I do that it does not make it different. It does not make it different and it worries me and they have little afternoons and more than that they can be more than that that they can be and that can be read out loud. More than that they can be in that in their way. Suppose they had been in a moment in their meaning meaning in their midst and allowing that allowing them they had managed to have finally just as well and as it is in every nearly as much meant as that. She knew that she knew where.

They made it come to be at least as before when they had arranged it by piles.

Every once in a while two in twenty-five sometimes three in twenty-five and sometimes none in twenty-five. This has been to-day an example of it. One in twenty-five.

Could a country have been singing in a minute.

They knew.

Could and would they be perfectly frantic.

They could.

Could they be by the time that they had it hand in hand could they listen to me.

They did.

When they had been nearly as if when two and they had never said not at all could they know the difference between fifty and fifty and a hundred.

They could be as used to it as if they were never neglectful.

Be nearly as happy to-day.

As soon as he heard me he said how are you going to leave it when you have been nearly as much as all the way by this time for it itself and she might by and by remember that if they had made their definite attention they would say have I. She might even be obliged to need me. And she might also not have been nearly as often disposed to remain more than cautioned or exercised. Did she not be very carefully at once by their arrangement satisfied. Was she invited. Did she did they observe it when they were almost ready to have windows changed. She knew they made the most of it.

Having always returned to their same residence.

Once more.

CHAPTER CXXXVI

An announcement of how nearly it was plainly attempted.

As plainly as that.

And for this purpose.

And just as much.

And nearly there.

Nearly there makes an enemy know.

Know too.

For them.

Who has heard that we are going when we are asked.

CHAPTER CXXXVII

A rather funny thing has happened. Beatrice Jones sent a copy of what she found and at the same time Matthew Jones had been at great pains to make it possible that everyone would do me honor.

CHAPTER CXXXVIII

She needs it now.

Does anybody know why they love me so.

And in this way they are obliged to have it more than in preparation.

She and he might have heard that they went there after all.

And beside that.

He and she were everlastingly arousing themselves for it and so when she had not had any preparation for it now and here now and here comes nearly to the same as by and by and yet they do, do they have it all the same. All the same makes it very much as much as much as ever and every once in a while and once in a while to be sure. To be surely pleased to stay.

Supposing that there had been no difference between the first and the eleventh, supposing also that there had been no difference between the eleventh and seventh and supposing also that there had been no difference between the seventh and second and supposing there had been no difference between the second and fifteen and five. I said that it was either then or not nearly as often and he said I will be there.

CHAPTER CXL

To continue to go along.
He knew he knew he knew me.
We knew we knew we knew them.
They knew they knew they knew her.
She knew she knew she knew him.
It is easily fed.
What is easily fed.
This is easily said.
That is easily said.
Then it is easily said.
By then it is easily said.
Come and stay with me.
She made it as much to their advantage as to mine.
Put in this way it is very remarkable that there are not any changes and that they know each one of them why they came when they went away what they had to do what they wished to give and why they went away and also before and afterwards they neglected nothing they did not disturb themselves they did not disturb this and they had been almost always kept together. We asked them for how long and they knew that they can be as anxious and as reassured as they are every once in a while. Beside all this they made it very difficult for me. When they had prevented and pretended and when they had fortunately to always fortunately come together then when there is no longer

any reason for preferring a tinkling she knew that she would always say that she too had had it and knew it was not as if it was not as verified. Verified is very well.

That was a surprise to me.
She was never angry that they needed me all the time.

Wood and wood and how much of it is dangerous. This is what they want to know.

If they want to go will he say so.

Will he say so to me.

If he will say so to me whose is it when he leaves it here and he has not said very much about it.

Let us think of it altogether.

Altogether as much.

Now and then reflectively.

Those whom one does not like to have around it is only necessary to discourage.

And when if they are discouraged they remain away one can but congratulate oneself upon the fact that for the moment they will not return.

Nearly at once they then when they are nearly ready to go somewhere they can be in the nature of things asked about it. A very little begins to be somewhat effusive and as the chance has come a very little nearly all the time by this afternoon they can be awfully well pleased and they can say was it arranged and as it was arranged they have added shall it be that they have added something or shall it be that they have added nothing shall it be that they have added nothing or shall it be that they have added something.

It can easily be seen that a novel of elegance leaves something to be desired.

In the main they have been just as reasonable as ever and it is very well to remember that really all of it not that all of it is very much too much but as up to this time not formerly but recently as up to this time there has been a steadily increasing tendency to in no way have as much more why should one then make that as a mistake. A mistake and mistaken have not exactly exactly and exact and as if they had as much as to be as in avoiding that never to be very likely because of it. Why did I think not of a garden but of the very great difficulty of passing unperceived. But I did think of it and not in connection with two but only in connection with one one who had hoped to have already accomplished what should have been achieved once in a while. She might be just as careful and yet never have in any way any reason to be asked might I be some assistance to you. She meant to overstate nothing. She was nearly always early and they were very anxious to leave it all to them.

Would she leave it all to her. She might if she had sufficient confidence that if she did so that it would be well done and in that case there would be no occasion for arranging it in this way. To be sure.

She would be very foolish if she preferred coming to coming and she would be very nicely pleasant to all of it when they had heard it every once in a while. She could be anxious to hear him be seated.

CHAPTER CXLIII

It was a very pleasant day yesterday.

CHAPTER CXLIV

It is pleasant that to-day is as warm as yesterday.
Alice-blue and an Alice-blue wrapper.
Who did say what he had to say.
Then why do they occasionally have to have little amounts of it every little while.
This is theirs.
He said he had been named Arthur but he did not care to have it as well pleased as he was. He was obliged to be very well every day.

What can they make successfully. They can make lilacs and hyacinths and she knew very well that some flowers look like oranges.

Supposing that there is a difference between action and succession and between they had decided not to come and lighted cakes. Everybody knows their name.

If she left on the third of January which is on Sunday will she come here before that. If she does will she come alone and will she say I have never been prevented and in that way it has never made any difference to me. Not to feel very much as if they could continue to have cakes lighted not to feel very much as if they could have to have cakes relighted. Cakes relighted candles relighted candles relighted cakes relighted.

CHAPTER CXLIII

Not to have felt that it was at least as nearly perfect as it would have been if she had been charmed.

Supposing she knew that a war would popularise differences and she did know that a war would popularise pretty well pretty nearly pretty much as much as mills. No one knows what millers do.

Do they.

Do they know what they will save.

Do they.

Do they know how do they know what they have arranged for.

Please ask them to arrange mills so that mills will be at once understood.

Please ask them to arrange folds so that folding is at once understood. Please ask them have it at once understood.

Supposing victory is in the balance who makes it difficult to buy them. Elmer Harden does because he having been brought up in Medford hesitates to give information which will lead to the purchase.

In this way it is just as different as it can possibly be from Allen Tanner who has known intimately Paul Winship and

Matthew Standard. This has influenced him so that he can long-
ingly write that he knows it.

Do you hear him.

Yes you do.

When they see you they do see you. And so forth.

CHAPTER CXLIV

It is easy to arrange that they should go away.

CHAPTER CXLV

Let me say it here here let me say it.

Once more to be told that I called Miriam Miriam.

Let me say it here.

Once more not to be told that I called Miriam Miriam.

Here let me say it.

I remember all about it.

There is no difference at all.

She meant to be foremost at all.

Now and then they need to lend it at all.

If anybody came and they wanted it and they were given it it
would be just as well that they had been very much the same
thing that it had been very much the same thing to them.

She gave an address.

Tenderness.

It is very likely that nearly everyone has been very nearly
certain that something that is interesting is interesting them. Can
they and do they. It is very interesting that nothing inside in
them that is when you consider the very long history of how
everyone ever has acted or has felt that nothing inside in them
in all of them makes it connectedly different. By this I mean this.
The only thing that is different from one time to another is what
is seen and what is seen depends upon how everybody is doing
everything. This makes the things we are looking at very different and this makes what those who describe it make of it it makes
a composition it confuses it shows it is it looks it likes it as it is

and this makes what is seen as it is seen. So then to make it easy let us say that nothing changes from generation to generation except the thing seen and that makes a composition. Lord Grey remarked that when the generals before the war talked about the war they talked about it as a nineteenth century war although to be fought with twentieth century weapons. That is because war is a thing that decides how it is to be when it is to be done. It is prepared and to that degree it is like all academies it is not a thing made by being made it is a thing prepared. Writing and painting and all that is like that for those who occupy themselves with it and don't make it as it is made. Now the few who make it as it is made and it is to be remarked that the most decided of them usually are prepared just as the world around them is preparing do it in this way and so I if you do not mind I will tell you how it happens. Naturally one does not know how it happened until it is well over beginning happening.

To come back to the fact that the only thing that is different is what is seen and when it seems to be being seen in other words, composition and time-sense.

CHAPTER CXLVI

She may be coming in any moment darling.

The next through and see believing that they change it on the way to have it met. There is a great difference between when she said and when she had it. Now seeing it all supposing that when she was as young as she was it was nearly dislike and then when they had it for themselves and once and all the time and bequeathing and they made it theirs they knew that they had been here all this time.

How do they like theirs and themselves in it.

She knew why she was in their way. And she said do they mean to be as careful as that.

It is not at all difficult to remind it of itself as having been by this time and needed.

And remembering who said when they had been as in a wing a wing is a part of a house.

CHAPTER CXLVII

Let me have it at once. When I went to them about it they were just at that time quite free and for this reason they could be completely obliging.

He thought that if he had left it and gone away he would have enjoyed roses bird-songs and what ever he would do more or less at once and in a very little time it came about that mostly because they were ill at ease he felt that not only because of this reason but by this means human means and in furthering furthering it too.

She would never enjoy having it known as Dorothy. Supposing Dorothy and Daniel could be as they had been when they returned from all of it. They were so nicely behind what was naturally very alike and by this time.

Paul did not believe that only one child was unadopted.

CHAPTER CXLVIII

Do not hear me if they have undertaken it when and where they can.

Having had and hearing them tell it to themselves like that.

Not being interested in Geneva or Arthur or Edward or even in Susan and Hilda and having always arranged it so that they would very likely be there. It is very interesting and in a way naturally peculiar that in so many ways they would never consider this. Quietly never consider this.

It is very well it is very well it is very well for them to do it.

CHAPTER CXLIX

I do like to be nicely here as well as she does.

Does she want to go or stay.

As well as she does.

And she does should she open the door with her left hand when the right is not at all occupied.

There has been a decision arrived at and as yet it has not been as much so as before.

Before and before.

Please please before.

Having resisted this temptation.

In every little while

At once.

In every little while Charlemagne who was an old king as well as as old said when there are two they should not be helpful they should not help they should not help each other.

And they knew how they heard it they heard it and they heard if there were mountains.

So twenty-five makes between thirty-four and thirty-five.

Easily.

Genevieve remember.

Remember.

When on the twenty-eighth of January and largely when they had reselected it.

Having had not feeling that in this one it having been continued around who are around when they have their share.

It is not as remarkable as wondering and not as remarkable as their supplying supplying it in every way.

Would she know their name.

CHAPTER CL

It comes it comes it comes out. Not only fancifully but really. It comes it comes it comes out. It comes out not only fancifully but really. What can a novel do a novel can tell everything that is true it can tell everything truly it can tell that it comes it comes it comes out not fancifully but really. And then another subject is calm, how calm. Another subject is calm to calm. Another subject is calm their calm. Another subject is calm his calm. Another subject is calm just calm. It comes it comes it comes not fancifully but really. It really comes. At this time at this time is different from no time, at this time it comes at this time When she had been satisfied when she had been satisfied. When she had

been satisfied that they could see to it at once. And they do. It
means that she will have every reason to be satisfied.

CHAPTER CLI

Begin again
Fanny irresistible
Jenny recalled.
Henrietta as much as that.
Claribel by and by
Rose as plainly seen
Hilda for that time
Ida as not famous.
Katherine as it should have it in preference
Caroline and by this time
Maria by this arrangement
Esther who can be thought of
Charlotte and finally.
They can be so prepared that they have this one at a time.
She knew commonly that all of it might be one and once and
one more and one and one.
She also knew them alone to be sure and when they they
could be easily and at once told might they as they had it in
plenty could they be in authority.
Florence can be a name.
Romaine can be a name
Finally can be a name
Constance can be a name.
More than that if they had seen it as much as when they had
merely been more or less thoughtfully considered as much as
the difference between when they had had it as they might by
this time or would they be equal to it altogether.
No one can arrange glass to be rosy and blue and all the time
too and very much more and really from door to door. She was
nearly as easily heard when during the time when very many
without doubt meant to be ready to say yes and if you like it.
Not much more than at present.
It is very surprising one may say astonishing that once in a

while they have been nearly seated and expectant and at this
time windows might be open or closed depending entirely not
alone upon the weather but upon the quantity of noise there
would be if the windows were open or the windows were closed.
One might open one window but even then there might be some
objection not because of its being colder or warmer or even
because of more or less noise but because there might be an interruption as the result of there having been some notice taken
of the fact. In this way there is really no necessity for this and
for that. Merely by this time.

It does not take as long.

She is afraid she would.

On and on Eugenia is here

On and on and on.

On and on and on and on Eugenia is here.

Never stopping just as much as she did.

To think very well of that.

Supposing a thing was this. Supposing it happened to them.
Supposing they were not really pacified when after all they had
it as carefully as they had begun for themselves and to be right
after all.

Right after all.

Coming to have only more.

As a pleasure.

As a pleasure they had certainly half of it and half of it when
they said stop they said stop to them.

It would be nearly all the time as if they had it.

As if they had it did they hear them say. Did they hear them
say as if they had.

Change each one two.

Supposing that after they left they were called back.

Supposing that then he said but you did return it to me and
they they did they did it they did it too they did it too and they
did it then.

They could be very carefully allowed to be here and there as
much as ever.

Is it very pleasant to have a portrait painted and just what does
that mean.

To be followed by once in a while and particularly when they had often and once in a while and to be followed and to be once in a while and to be often and to be once in a while to be sure of it too.

CHAPTER CLII

Following.
Following makes two.
Following makes two and they changed their minds.
Following makes two and they changed their minds.
After all it was not only that they had never been there but that they had never been there before.

CHAPTER CLIII

Imagining that a very little one is shorter.
It cannot be helped that when they are after all finally persuaded that each one individually answers and says when we are there we are very nearly as careful as ever.
Be finally on time.
It is very likely that when they have each one individually and as easily seen that they were often called to come that each one should have and should be noiseless. After more of it was nearly as possible alike how many kinds of days are there here and there. To be very well endowed and after all to be so very much sooner than was to be expected. All this can excite someone.
Who knows where they go.
They go there very often and they seem to enjoy it.
Once to leave and once to leave and to leave at once.
When they had been and in a way it is easily understood that there is no conversation. Begin again. It is very easily understood that there is no conversation.
Nobody knows when they have seen and they have heard and they have called called to them.
Everyone can remember that General Grant had a brother.
A brother and a brother-in-law.

It is very kind and it is very kindly it is very kindly. It is very kindly it is very kindly. And it is very kindly.

He can if you please.

CHAPTER CLIV

She knew they knew they knew this they knew this too.

It can happen that everyone is seen at one time.

Slowly and certainly and when it is spoken as it is when they drew away to whom might they say that they were addressing it.

And nearly as much as if they had by this and when they were equally released by and because that if as a last resort they might be as much as beside when they wish to leave that there.

In this as they having sent it before they came to beg them to believe them and they might differently disturb themselves as much it might even be as very likely as ever that they had had all of it to be left here and there. To be left here and there. Behind what is always chosen who can choose places who can choose this and three and who can choose two in a day and who can choose when they have believed it and when they have believed that and every once in a while they can be always and as careful and around it. To continue means that they please.

How easily can one think.

Think yes of it.

When shall it be.

How much have they left.

Who is nearly satisfied and very likely if they do and when they come and changed.

It happened in this way. As they were there satisfying themselves in a way not entirely but just as well as if they had meant that if it were asked it would never be answered angrily, when all this was meant to be very clearly explained it would easily follow that one after another.

And now not exactly.

In there when in there when in there when how.

In there when in there when in there when how.

She makes it have to be as well as that and they have it to say for that day only.

Now and then it is exceedingly determined when they shall have the rest to be.

Telling that she went away and to stay. Telling that she went away so that they might say that she had not gone away right away. Telling that she had to-day to go away as she had to say anyway who may be more often here and there. And after this not at all.

There is never any altogether the easiest way is to leave out anything.

And this makes this for this and very happy to have to have to.

A novel out loud.

CHAPTER

Imagine three or four.

Imagine three or four or three or four.

When she said to be sure did she say surely as much too.

It happens in a minute as much so.

Once makes once or twice twice more.

When if they had and could they sit when this you see remember me when they are there as well as when by this and now for them.

By leaving it alone.

She was neglected when they did not want her here.

CHAPTER

Hours and ours.

Hours of having had it for us and as it was to be given to us it was ours.

Leaving it at least always.

There is a question that can be asked do they care to go out when there is every likelihood that the weather will be stormy. There is also a question to be asked. Have they any objection to going out when it is cold as cold as it ever is here.

There is often this question to be asked and there is also this question to be answered. Is there any reason which can be considered as a reason which prevents him from doing what he has

undertaken. The answer is that in all likelihood there is no reason there is no real reason that is to say that there is nothing that
is in the nature of a prohibition that could prevent him from
doing what he has undertaken. Everybody who is very likely to
be allowed to come and go never dislikes what has been asked
of them. They need and they have it firmly impressed upon
them that from time to time there is a great deal that makes it
most uncomfortable for each one to leave it here and to leave it
alone. We are very sorry that we are not seeing Katherine again.

CHAPTER CLVIII

When they are three they are these three and they often and
one wonders as to which one desires it there are often four.

Papers which have been given to them are very often of so
much importance that they are the reason of their not only
needing but even adding to their own comfort.

She never knew why she thought of it as that.

CHAPTER

This is a long history of them. They did not and this is all
as they said each one of them knew two some of them when they
were accompanied were accompanied as much as before more
and before. To consider each case separately to come to consider
each case separately this and to come and to consider and to consider each case and in this way they have not had it only for
themselves alone but also for another especially there. These are
their names. Ernest Ernest Ernest Walsh and that surprised her
because she had expected me to say Olga Walter. The second
the second was Robert all the Roberts end in s Robert which is
Roberts and he said might he come and to say the words the
poor man's overcoat and here and there he knows his name. His
name is Robert Coates at this time everybody expected me to say
Charlotte Perkins. Another name which means more is Francis,
Francis can be early and late and so a Francis when they had in
mind might be Francis Lake so he might he might be Francis
and he might be Francis Lake, Francis Lake is never opposed to

a son and he is also once more not as much as that too then.
Having not admitted that mistake. What is a mistake a mistake
is relying upon what is nicely near and at most sincerely.

Every time that they do I do.

CHAPTER CLX

Every little while they smile.

And afterwards.

Now that is all.

It is very foolish and easy of them to have it said that they
have to think of that.

Following what she wrote

CHAPTER CLXI

To easily understand why they prefer that a fire is made of
wood. To as easily understand why they prefer what they hear
to what they heard. To easily understand that they need that as
much as this. To easily understand that they allow it themselves.
To easily understand that they have all of it as much as they
wanted it. It is easily understood that they remembered it all. It
is easily understood that they had arranged everything. It is easily
understood that they had very many more than they had had. It
is easily understood that they might be there all the time and it is
easily understood just what they had to do is just as easily understood as that. It is easily understood that they made it there. It
is easily understood by this time.

CHAPTER CLXII

It was just as well he did before.

It was just as well that he did before.

It was just as well that he did what he did before.

It was just as well that he did decide to do it before.

It was just as well that he did decide to do it before he had his
mind relieved about it.

It was just as well that he did it before he had his mind relieved about it.

It was just as well that he had had to do it before he had his mind relieved about it.

It was just as well that he had to have his mind relieved about it.

It was just as well that he had done it before he had had his mind relieved about it.

That makes number one and two.

They were better altogether nearly as much or more likely to be recalled to have it recalled to them that they had never preferred it altogether.

They had not had it nor had they had it held before them as an arrangement to which they would or they would not agree accordingly as they would be more or more likely to be willing to have it prepared.

This is number two.

If she was nevertheless as much or nearly perfectly satisfied that they would be very pleasantly situated if they were more or less able to have it be when and where they were altogether reasonably felt to be and they felt it to be an advantage.

This is number three.

It was by no means not only half and half for it and by themselves but when they had often had it and defended it as they might altogether and they had not only because of wishes but also as they had the habit of seeing it as a thing to be known very well. When they had this as an outline they could and might they be just as well satisfied to return it they could not knowing it as a disturbance they could be partially forced to have them know of it. By and by.

This is number four.

Number five and then number four.

When they had more of this and having been made to really know that it would give him this satisfaction the satisfaction of liking it and liking it as well. They need not be obliged to go.

This is number five.

Might they have known that they would be very very welcome. Might they have known that they would be very very welcome.

CHAPTER CLXII

When is it to be all of that for them.
And how about it when they have to get it.
And when they had to have it left to them for that.
Behind it.
For this and with this that they made them here.
When they had this
For them

CHAPTER CLXIII

To state return to state.
They stated it as this.
When they were leaving they had explained. When they had
explained they had explained that when they were leaving they
had explained. Not having undertaken to be arranged by leaving.
She knew that that was not what they were for.
Having been explaining as to leaving and having been leaving
having been leaving having been explaining having been leaving.
He knew that that was not what they were for. Having been explaining about leaving and having been explaining having been
explaining about leaving and knowing that that was not what
that was for. They might have been reconciled to it. And in
agreeing agreeing that this was that that that was that that that
was for. Stupidly stupidly if you like. Agreeing, agreeing if you
like. Stupidly agreeing stupidly agreeing if you like, if you like
it that that was that that that was for. Stupidly agreeing if you
like it that that was that that that was for. This makes it that that
was that that that was for. And very pleased with the answer.
Another was to stay is this that that is that that that is for. Another way of staying is this, that this is this that that is for. Another way of staying that that is not that that is for. Another
way of staying is also this. This is also another way of staying.
Another way of staying is this. This is this that that is for. That
had been nearly all as well. All as well as that that this is for.
Another way of agreeing is this that that is that that that is for.

Another way of agreeing and another way of staying is that that is this that this is for.

CHAPTER CLXIV

By this time.
Asking him not to let me in.
By this time always
And he was as influential as that.
More than by this time.
Supposing women were needed not only to tell what happened but also to have it said.
Formerly for them.
When they had had a half of it here for this and by this and by this time.
Imagining two or three times.
For themselves and they knew that it was placed there to be there to be there to have there to have it there to have it placed there as they needed it almost always.
She knew how to be bold too.
So bold too.
Having decided that among them there are some in the first rank and they must be carefully avoided as they have nearly all of them very much to do with it.

CHAPTER CLXV

Having come to this point in the novel it has come to seem quite as easily done as before and what is as easily done as before and why is it as easily done as before.
It is as easily done as before.

CHAPTER CLXVI

As every one.
As population.
As advantage
As in this way.

As they had.

As they are this is it.

Supposing forty-five is a reunion. To reunite in a city. Supposing forty-nine is a reunion. To reunite in their place in their place they were reunited in case in case in this case. They made a change in treasure treasure to be when they had seen forty-one come to be left when they had deprived themselves of that. In their and on their account to be in there in between. This makes it come to be fortunate very fortunate.

Supposing he knew how to how to be supposing he knew how to hold out out loud. Supposing he knew how to hold it out loud. Supposing he knew how to hold it how to hold it out out loud. Supposing he knew how to hold it out out loud and walked away.

Every time there is a white and black and grey to-day. To-day is most of the time. This can easily make it that much different and they divide it. For them by that time.

CHAPTER CLXVII

A little longer to the minute.

CHAPTER CLXVIII

Would they be likely to be heard.

Would they be likely to be heard.

Would they be likely to be heard.

When they would be heard.

When they would be likely to be heard.

And need to nevertheless.

To return to interruptions. Interruptions cannot be more nearly by and by than if there had not been more needed. And almost most of it. It can be nearly very often near to it when if there is more than they had had they had had it. And not to be at all left out. And how did they do it when they were all in little as little likely to. They needed it for this and by this time. Having the habit of being one of three how many can there be to make two. Two have heard it as they said it to them and not to

be nearly as prepared as that. He knew how they had heard it
and they were all of them very well and they had had by this
time wondering if it could be possible that she was older that
she was there also all about this. All about this is just as well as
ahead.

CHAPTER CLXIX

Letters are often written in the morning.
That makes more of it at one time.
She knew what to do.
Having left it for them.
At this time.
To listen.
She knew what to do and she knew what to do for them at
this time.
Arranging it as they need.
Some do not have it as if it were as if they came.
Some do not need it as if it were when they came.
Some do not need as it were as if it were that they were to be
nearly as much prepared for their coming. In this way they knew
that it would be as welcome to them as if they were preparing to
be more and more nearly when they had that for themselves.
Twice seventy-five is one hundred and fifty.

CHAPTER CLXX

They need to be as they need to be out loud as they need to
be and when there was more arrangement they had as much as
they intended to delight in. This is what they mean and by and
by and by and by as carefully.

CHAPTER CLXXI

Would it be as well that everyone, a historical novel is not a
history of everyone.
Having had and he left it for them.

They made it as they wished it when they did when they did they did have to be sure.

To reply to a historical novel by at once changing it to blame.

Once upon a time there came to be left altogether to himself the one who came to see him too and very likely they did exchange saying who could have been made to look as well and as often as they had occasionally wished it to be by themselves. They very nearly were then to be held as well as they could to do so. When nearly all of it was as certain to be left where they had to have it now. Now do they say. They made it as very likely. When they had heard and left it to be more or less after all spent alike nearly as much as they had undertaken it as they say. By nearly all of it.

It was as commonly by all of them left to them as they could be very well after all nearly by and by for them.

Who left them.

They did.

And come again.

There need by very many capable of having what was fortunately as to be like it. Like it is in exchange and with it is in exchange and there is in exchange. For this you see as who can be nearly once in a while.

Historically undertaken.

He had more nearly wondered why. And did he believe in really having it as much as reprehensible and never to be perfectly at once.

Now and once or twice.

A historical novel and noon.

He said that in and at noon there was more care taken of it.

After that they had never had more than they were to be shared. Share and share alike.

A historical novel beginning as soon as when they had added it to their remaining pleasure.

Pleasure and as pleasure.

It is in no way necessary to accustom the rest of it to it.

Pleasure for them then

A historical novel is one that has to do with her having been remaining.

It is not at all necessary to end with the commencement.

They do know what is and where it is by this time.

Once they were to be after all back again after a while.

Need they have said that they liked it as and never either wanting or alike.

Do as they do.

CHAPTER CLXXII

A historical novel and begun it is continued every time that this has been and begun and to be happening in their best way if all of them wished to be there.

CHAPTER

It was to be had to-day.

They promised it for this morning and all this morning they had it. One at a time and save it for nine. Nine is as well as it is when they have it as much as they have it splendidly.

A long sentence to say so.

If he used it as it said it would be as useful to him to him to them then. When they had this to do for them they did for them they did it then. When they had been as much there as anywhere they were very well after all following he had had a son. He had had a son and one, one two three four all who have meant it to be there before. Arthur had a son naturally. James had a son and naturally. Manuel had a son had had a son had a son. And after this it did not matter.

CHAPTER CLXXIV

After this it did not matter.

This is now to be a very long history of their son and they were after a while their father. James and Manuel and Arthur and another and each one and not anyone had had a brother. Think of it each one not anyone not anyone had had a brother. George had a bother he said he had a brother but that was not as important as one another. He had said it was not as important

as one other. And one other it was not as important as one other.
Paul had had a brother he had had that when his father having
had a sister he would be another. And this would be then what
would be when they had to have one and the other. This often
happens in revolutions.

CHAPTER CLXXV

They made it for them and he had it as well as having it and
he was to have it have it here. Having it here is never more than
having it here as they could as they could having it here as they
could. It is never the same as having it here when they could
having it here when they could.

Coming to not at all.

Coming to not at all and coming differently coming to not
at all.

Coming differently coming differently to not at all.

Coming differently to not at all and it was to be hoped that
they as well as they were paid and repaid and repaid and paid.
No one can think as differently.

CHAPTER CLXXVI

Never stop to gather them together. Never stop to gather
them together at all.

Never stop to gather them together at all and speaking of it
to them.

Never stop to gather them together at all and speak of it all
to them. Never stop to gather them together at all and speaking
of it all together to them altogether to them and speaking of it
at all to them.

What can it do it can be all to you.

What can it have it can have and does have it all all the time
so that when and where they please when and where they please.

Altogether at one time and at one time and altogether and
very much more than when they had been reconciled.

What is it that happens when they have decided that they are
very likely to be there.

This that Bernadine will come too.

What will be very likely to happen then.

What will be very likely to happen then I do not know what is very likely to happen then.

Is there any difference between not at all and differently

Is there any difference between what was as nearly by and by as by and by.

Nobody said that I did not know of it.

CHAPTER

In between and more and more history.

Once upon a time they came every day and did we miss them we did. And did they once upon a time did they come every day. Once upon a time they did not come every day they never had they never did they did not come every day any day.

Four coming down and up makes it look the same.

A historical novel at once. And after a historical novel at once and after that the history of a historical novel at once.

He was older at eighteen.

He was older at twenty-six.

He was older at twenty-seven and then that was all that has been said. She was older at eighteen she was older at twenty-six she was older at twenty-nine she was older at forty-three and that is all that has been said.

She was and has left it to him and he has not been very well informed. After a while he often had thought that he would very much like to be able always to reply after every little while.

So much for that.

CHAPTER CLXXVIII

Never needing all of it to-day. To-day is as easily said as when they said it they said it to themselves for them.

This is now the time to describe something.

Something is as easily said as they say it say it when every-one everyone and by this by this as an allowance an allowance of giving it to what was more nearly all alone.

All alone is as easily said as all the time and all the time is as easily said as here and now and here is as easily said as if they came and if they came. They came to say that it was decided.

Nice and quiet I thank you.

Once upon a time when they had not heard anything of having left it there they were very silent and they knew that occasionally they might be as nearly left behind as they had been. They had been as nearly left behind as they had been. Once every time that they knew about it they heard him say it. Who said it aloud. It was said out loud by them.

She knew that she was always very willing to leave it out.

A novel and the future the novel and the rest and the rest is diamonds.

The novel and the future a novel and the rest and to rest to rest so that when they have been very much more nearly as much as they could they might have it left over.

It is extraordinary anyone not there might be there and this makes it always more and more reasonably reasonably sure.

It is very easy to believe a novel.

Believing a novel it is always more and more reasonably certain that they will believe the novel. The novel tells it as it was it was very nice and quiet and to thank you.

A novel to be on this account accounted for.

What is a novel a novel is partly this.

When they had decided to leave it alone and after all think again think that again and again this again and again this is again and again this is in this again and again this is in this in this again and again.

Think again again and again and in and again and again and in this again and again.

Think in this.

Again and again.

Might it be that they would see it.

Might it be for long.

And might it be that this is this as long as this is this for long.

As they might be easily wanting to be known now.

Every once in a while there are more of them everywhere. Once in a while.

Supposing they asked have you ever known that they can come once in a while.

They send an answer it is a great pleasure that very often there is occasionally a cessation and in plenty of time for it.

They ask who is as well known as before.

And they are answered he is as well known as before because by this time they would hope that if he had come to be careless every one would know about it.

They asked are we liable to be very moved when we hear of his suffering.

They hear it said that they can come to hear it when it is allowed.

Allowed can often be misunderstood.

Every day they come to stay and every day they cannot always have it happen that what they said is what is repeated and if it is repeated who has heard it. Very nearly more than at once.

By this time there is every advantage.

To imagine that a novel is once in a while necessary.

Coming to it again.

If a novel is once in a while as necessary as coming to it again whom to whom might it happen that they were softened by it. Softened by it for very much that reason.

They followed them just as well just as well just as well.

Just as well as now.

Need to have the whole of it do they need to have the whole of it.

Whole of it is never time lost.

Time lost is never in arrangement.

In arrangement is not either for them not at all.

Not at all aloud.

CHAPTER CLXXXI

Who can be well pleased by themselves alone.

Who can have it very nearly changing from longer to shorter. Who can very nearly careful by and by and why not repeat by and by. Why not. The reason why not is this if it is then there is every reason to suppose it. Do be yourself.

By that time they have allowed it and they are as careful as they were when they were around and behind it.

Never mind they will wait.

It is as much as it can be can be expected that when after looking and making a mistake not exactly a mistake and certainly not a misunderstanding when she was just as adaptable for whom did she take him, she took him to be just as much the object of their attention as he was. He was very nearly always prepared for it almost as much so and more.

Could they feel it as well as they heard it and could they hear it as well as they called it and could they call it as well as when they came in and out. In and out and a young lady. Thank you so much.

CHAPTER

Supposing she felt that going out to see her sister every evening was something.

How did she happen to happen to go out to see her sister every evening.

When they had brothers and brothers and brothers how many brothers would have it here.

How many have they when they know that this is why they had not asked them to be always ready to have them prepare it for to-morrow. How did she introduce brothers how did she introduce their brothers and how did she introduce his brothers to them.

Feel it to be all of that just now.

Imagining that they were feeling this and just once more they had to have it said.

Have it said is just allowed.

A novel means regularly regularly told so.

He was regularly told so and it was no wonder that he would be just as much as ever would be just as much as ever would be just as much would and just as much and pleasure.

In this case how many could follow.

They said that after all they must be older.

They said they were left as much in the dark as before.

They said was there really any difference between in and on.

They said that they had always hoped just as well.

And now loudly a novel.

A novel meant that they would be as much as this as that. How much needs counting. Anything as much anything more.

Believing that all the ones who had been nearly ready were ready.

One are you ready now two are you ready three are you ready four then go.

They made no difference between explained and having explained.

They might have been ready.

Are you really ready now. As they might be ready now it is not at all necessary necessary and needful it is just as necessary that they should be very much as much as if they were used to it.

Used to it is said by those who have left and right and right and left as if they followed one another.

Listen to me.

I say do you know when they can be spared.

They can be spared and that is my answer they can be spared all reconciliation.

Who does.

Who does what.

Who does and what do they do. They do it so that when they are as well situated as they can possibly be they can be contradicted. After that they might have been often and often, who knows any difference between the fourth of February and the third of February.

CHAPTER CLXXXIII

Why did they like it green in winter and the reason is this, they would be very likely to be able to have it said that they had heard when they were listening that they might be very well known all the time. And this makes it different.

Supposing they had enjoyed January supposing they also had enjoyed February and supposing they also had enjoyed what they would after all would be and follow one another. Supposing all this satisfied them and they were as much attracted as they had been attracted by the way they were always apt to be likened to this and all this at all makes it useful.

When they had been all of them by their opportunities by their opportunities now when they had been all of them more as much as as a place. How can they and nicely nicely never makes them really fairer fairer makes them really safer and as for that and never had it here.

Once in a while and never had it here.

She knew.

Having had the choice of when and why makes it more easily then and there. Who does that.

Once in a while they had it safer once in a while and fairer once in a while and they had it once in a while.

Returned and around.

What is the difference between around and returned. She never minds hearing it again.

Again and again who said farther.

It is very well placed.

CHAPTER CLXXXIV

I know very well that I will tell about another whether another whether another is there.

Whether another is there.

It is very often corrected.

CHAPTER CLXXXV

It is not at all necessary to indulge in the illusions of hope, they can be nearly certain that they will be very well satisfied every once in a while. And who told you so. This is the way they begin principally.

Who might have been expected. He might have been expected. Who might have been expected, she might have been expected.

CHAPTER CLXXXVI

Having promised her mother and his father that she was to be very much later as much replaced as before who can encounter them.

They must be as much in their place as when they had to be in there once in a while and once in a while when they had to be in there once in a while.

Once in a while in there they might and avoiding and by this and alarm for them who have more help than ever before. Ever before and all around all around looking all around for them. If they and in the meantime who has whose attention for it when they were eager they made it do. They made it do every once in a while. Can they happen to have it as much as they needed to have it, to have it and they might be all there were to be by that time in and of that origin, origin can often connect with arrangement and discolor discolor pronounces organisation. Leave it to me. She said they leave it to me he said and they said and they leave it to me. Leave it to me means right along and for themselves alone and she was nearly as much nearly as much is the same and nearly as much when understood nearly as often nearly as often to them aside from their being more than adequate not for this arrival but they need to say who came to see to it and they said as they came to see it would they would they be known as once in a while and very often having been as much as as much happened to have held and heard heard can often be once seized seized make a mistake.

She thought it was very beautiful, whenever she is repeated

there is needless to say this that it must be as well as it is. Also it does prepare itself to be prepared for it.

When this when this when this when this they mean when this when this when this when they when they when this they when this they mean when they mean when they when they mean when they mean they mean when they mean this they mean when they mean when they mean this.

Who does have it to be said to be said to be said who does have it to be said when they mean this, when they mean this, who does have it to be said to be said to be said to be said when they mean this.

By the time they heard it all they had it all. All separates itself from all and so he knew how many were apart and parted. Partly to be sure.

CHAPTER CLXXXVII

A chapter of reasons reasons and reverses reverses or resemblances.

When they came every day.

Let it be too late.

When they had their the rest of their realise it realise it you too.

Letting it be nearly all of it too too they say.

They say that they never used it again.

Knowing the difference between at all or all and knowing the difference between at all. Let us think of their leaving. It may be said that those that are pleased leave and those that are not pleased stay. That is one thing. It may be said that one after another he chose to do that. It may be said that they have it in part and that they do like it all as well as well as they did nobody need know who was there. Commence to.

Leave it alone.

If it is left alone after every little while after every little while after every little while and not like that. After every little while and after every little while and hear it as it was to have been thought to be alike, alike and so may.

Excuse me and not at all and believe and have it said and

show showing showing can be as well as after it after all. Settle
it by that.

CHAPTER CLXXXVIII

It was very early in the spring and a yellow butterfly which
had flown was observed. Also it was to be noted that the trees
which had put forth their buds had mistletoe in them which also
was putting forth buds blossoms and berries. All this made the
morning and the afternoon most delightful.

Having the habit of being accustomed to hearing that they
would like very much to come and go away to come and to go
away to come and to come and to go away having been accustomed to this at that time and having been nearly very
delicately having very nearly delicately warned been warned
and warned about it how many have they given for three. One
may say four. By the time that they were nearly ready they
had been as much pleased and to please them as if they had been
able to make all the arrangements and by the time that after
all they might be there and to come who would be as much able
to place it so that they would think of think and able to establish
it in such a way that they would think of everything. Who would
need half of it. They might by this time not have forgotten to
name them. Suppose you know eight in four and twelve in five,
would that accustom you to separation from and devotion to
this part of it all the time at all. By the way who did send us that.
Once in a while they might be just as much obliged as they were
when they could have been at that time and surprised surprised
that he was no longer visiting them visiting them visiting them,
no longer visiting them.

They might be very occasionally be not really as much persuaded as they had been by they themselves undertaking anything. If she asked did they see that he saw when they had been
altogether fairly nearly as much as they wished to have had as
in this way when they needed it around. And to continue. They
might leave it to them and they might also be very well used
to it one at a time.

CHAPTER CLXXXVIII

Did she and could she and could she and did she. Did she and could she. And as she could and as she could would it be best to ascertain that it was all very well.

Always more and more for a reason, they made it that they could be near enough to it.

Finally they had been after all very pleasant pleasant and pleasantly. Very well I thank you.

It was in this way that they were flattered a history of flattery not naturally as history of a flattery a history of flattery are examples of flattery these are examples of flattery and being adequate to expecting to be told everything.

To think then to begin then.

After all as how to as and how to and as and as and and how to after all and how to after all. In this way it changes from nothing to something it changes in this way it changes in this way and from how to to something and from nothing and in this way and how to and in this way and something and changes.

To begin again and anything and anything and lengthening and how to and as for this as for this is when they miss and how to and in this way and exchanged for by it for the kindness of their women did you say who said they said and and and and believe it. A kind of having it by then. And so they made it much. Who could be as a chance a chance to be nearly as often often interchanged with might it have been at one time their place. After all they know who came too.

It will not need to be changed for that as a beside and when they went coming coming to be here even though they could not have been more than once in it for it when it is not there. Who can think quickly.

They can think quickly. This is the answer they can think quickly.

Who can think quickly.

They can think quickly.

Nearly once in a while is what is said when they are left to be able to be sent away as they had to leave or be sent every once in a while when they need this for that.

This is the history of why they said will you or will you not.

These who were known as they knew it said one day when as they had met often they were arranging to leave together why when they could not have been heard from should they be reasonable. They were reasonable and this is the reason, one one alone when he said no and he said this is what there is to say about it, the second one liking him best the second one because after all he would after all be after all able able to be after all all after all to-day as well as how to be left for themselves all as they could be heard. How often childish. The third is might it be and when it had it as they said and likely, does it show which is which. Which is which may they come which is which.

The three of them come come and when after all it might be one at a time it might be. Not very well arrived at and by and by always having not to be left to know that it would if all the same when is it to be followed by it at all.

And how did he have time he did have time for it.

CHAPTER CLXXXIX

She knew this just as well as she knew that. One at a time. She knew this just as well as she knew that.

If she knew this just as well as she knew that she might be able to do this just as well as to do that. If she knew this just as well as she knew that and if she could do this just as well as she could do that she would be very able to be asked to do this for that. And so when they came here they came without her. Listen to what is said when they came here they did come without her and this was because after it had been understood they made use of it all and they had it all arranged and they needed it at once and they might have been nearly all of it having had it all of it by itself just as nearly by itself. This makes it very nearly likely that they please and them.

When they undertook to be able to ask them to go and come when they undertook not only that but also what was placed

here and there might they might they after all come in and out
and might they might they after all come out and come in and
come in and out and might they after all come in and ask what
are we prepared to do.

This is not question it is an answer what are we prepared to do.

Every time he used he was used to it every time every time
he used he was used to it.

This is because of hearsay.

If she knew that they had been always as badly needed here
would they would they asking them would they. Once as much
as when they had it all. Once as much as when they had it all.

They could be when they did and this and very much and
very much I thank you.

Can three a man a[nd] two women be conversing can they
one woman asking another woman and can they can they when
they are seen when they are seen and this is the difference between having asked them not to.

We can be easily careful.

It is not by their name that they are called.

CHAPTER CXC

Why do they say that when they mean I mean. Why do they
say it when they mean I mean. Even now every little while it
is as different.

One Paul and Allen.

One George and Walter

One Henry and Georgiana

One Albert and Elizabeth.

One Gardener and Neith

One she went to look for them and she found them.

Once in a while she went to look for them and she found them.
Once in a while she went to look for them and she found them.

They might be different if they were indifferent to having
not only changed friends but changed friends. They were indifferent not only to having changed friends but to their having
changed friends. They were indifferent not only they were indifferent not only they were indifferent not only indifferent not

only indifferent to their having changed but indifferent to their
having changed friends. They were indifferent to their having
changed friends they were indifferent they were indifferent not
indifferent to their having changed friends they were indifferent
to their having changed friends.

This time come out.

This time and come in.

To this time and to this time and come in. To this time and
they were this time they were going away as they had been when
they had been when they had been when they had been when
they had been they had been they had been there. They had
been there and they had had had had had been there and they
were there. Supposing they were there usually. They had been
there as they had known how to be as much as when they had
given had been given and was not as if it could be that they
needed for that for that could be nearly as if for and if for that.
They needed it for that this makes it come around. He did not
go more often than that as he was nearly certain that when he
came again folder folder in six. This might be as if when she
she she and she and she he he needed it six years ago and to say
so.

Fifty-five and six makes two. Two and two makes four. Four
and four and four and for that and all for that. Nobody knows
that they changed their minds.

Having forgotten them.

Not as long.

In when they met and meant and in the meanwhile correctly
as well as very carefully she meant to tell it and as she meant to
tell it she could without having been not only not so very nearly
coming to say so.

To be minded of Clara. Clara was a part of that she meant that
she had been alone in not to mention in all of it at one time in there
and as she did not like not only that they had had it as very
nearly very likely to be all of it as they had had it given to them.
So then why should a sister look at a brother why should she
as sister look at him a brother why should a brother be looked
at by a sister why should a brother be looked at by a sister. When
this had been that occasion.

It is very well very well very well altogether very well that

that could happen to be accidentally that always in the same way one after another if they had met them one after another if they had one after another if they had met one after another if they had not met one after another not really is it not really is it not really not really after they had met them after one after another. It is very often disturbing that they could go away.

A novel fifty-five a novel fifty-five a novel fifty-five they say and to go away and to delay to pay and to be settled as to the way why anyway, George can be impenetrable. This makes it nearly follow one another. It happened that after a little while at this time when they did this they were as well pleased as if when they had shown that they would very easily receive it all. They might when they were careful as careful as they did for baskets they might by that time have not had it every once in a while yesterday. You understand very well what I mean every once in a while and yesterday and to-day and to-morrow. Every once in a while and to-morrow and yesterday and yesterday and yesterday and to-day and to-morrow yes and to-morrow yes and yesterday and yes and to-day and yesterday, and yes yesterday and to-day and yes to-morrow and to-day they said that if they needed it so much it would be more than they wanted if they changed from changing and being being being and it being there and it being there not at all and it being there. This makes that be all of them that why that why that is there is to be to be to all to all of it to them to them to be to for it as soon. Now and then be at a time at a time as it it is to be all of it to be to be to to theirs. Obliging obliging is when it is prepared.

Not to be at all when they do they do too. He could easily see that when he had advised it to them. Supposing he was never ready after all and she knew fifteen times thirty immediately this would not be as they say as they say it of them. Who can be showing it by that sound not at all stop it.

It is not explained by an interruption and so forth as very likely.

CHAPTER CXCI

If eggs are white and pale how when they are seen and delicate as well who can be and have a better choice and this makes it

very possible that they have heard that this time before they had
made the opportunity they had explained that they were very
very admirable very very responsible very very careful very
very pleasing and very very welcome, welcome as well. Not only
were they disappointed but as they recognised that after all
there could be all there was of supposing it was as much of a
height as this and theirs to change. She was not tall he was as
tall as he was when he was fairly fairly can always mean both
what they can and why they can be there. Be there as well as
there. They had this and easily when it is to be thought of when
it is to be thought of. They have an occasionally nearly always
having decided as a month and for their wishes. Can anyone
prefer them to be darker or darker just as well just as well as
just as well. One two three just as well. They just as well. And
this time it was and would be to be there a difference to their
reliance reliance makes it be practically be the same always for
this by then coming to have heard very likely as forstalling.
Could they they being their own and betime betime could be
used as having after all in indifferently indifferently to be theirs
as undertaken and then when they had never as much as by and
by and actually very nearly as much as by that leaving it alone.

One two three just to be.

It is not by this time that they are admittedly beneath where
they had for themselves and chosen, for themselves and chosen.
Not once a while for themselves and chosen and how could
she think they joined them. It was by this as they had it when
they needed all of it as their own and only by their when she
can fortunately for me fortunately fortunately is the respect in
which carefully enough by this time. Every time that they had
had it all. All when they were all when they were and leaving
just like very well just then.

Control control the as well as control the contents the might
it control the rest. This makes it not at all as much as it was as
well. This is now to be the story of how she did not come again.
Well are you coming well did you come again well did you come
again well and well did you come again and well and come again
this is a story of how they did not come again of how as they
were as they were she was as they were as she was not to come

again. How many were not to come again and how many how many she was not to come again this is that story that story of how she was not to come again. She was not to come again. She came and she asked and she was answered and she was not to come again not to come she was asked and she was answered and she was answered and she was asked and she was not to come again well she was not to come again. This is the story the first time she came she was not to come again.

CHAPTER CXCII

Daily daily every day what did they say.

CHAPTER CXCIII

There are two kind of liars the kind that lie and the kind that don't lie the kind that lie are no good.

CHAPTER CXCIV

Equally at their best they are equally at their best when out of a window of a small room they are both leaning and they are both they are both leaning out of a window of a small room. They are at their best when they are leaning out of a window of that room they are at their best when they are leaning out of a window of a window that is near the ground out of that window out of the window of that room. That has nothing to do with it.

CHAPTER CXCV

Remembering windows that has nothing to do with it re-membering windows.

Remembering windows has nothing to do with it remember-ing windows. They were both leaning out of the window of that room that has nothing to do with it.

If they were beside all that judges of what would get darker and lighter they would if they had asked not have it not have

it, they added they added to had it they had it to add it. Not
any longer a good description.

Could if a light grey and heart rending be softer could it and
light grey be paler could it and light grey be paler. Not the least
resemblance between that and that.

Price of peas changes with ease.

They need more nearly think of these. Once in a while.

CHAPTER CXCVI

It is never a mistake to state that they are ready.

Could she have a hard life if she were so tall. Could she have
a hard life at all.

It is never by this time always best.

Could she be positive that they were partly the same. When
they had been there when they were called. Could they be by
that time for it for it when they did not need what was it was
it by this time. To change to. Did you need to feel it all at once
he said to me and he said yes they can be as they were where
they were told as alike and told about it here. By then. They
made it have it be by this when do you do it.

It nearly came to all of it.

When she was nearly ready to be asking do they like it do
they like it do they like it do they like it do they do they like it.

Now and then now and then and by it when it is to be their
share.

A whole family a whole family impenetrably to do this at
once and as a while and after it after it to them to do it while they
liked. Could she ask to be found and fond of it at all. If they
had it and to change connect it connected by this time anyway
by this time. Who made two and twenty more by this time.
Listen to it to them now. She meant to be very careful of Sunday
she meant to be very careful of Sunday and Monday and some
day and when they went there and went might it be as they
would choose it for them as they hear seeing she never confuses
their means. In any little while they said so and would it be
very well for them to do it more more than they liked. They
made it be theirs as well as when they did did means divided

by that and for this time and excuse me. Everybody knows that John and James are two names.

CHAPTER CXCVII

Religion

CHAPTER

And for them who do.

For them to be always having it so that they can be as never having heard it when they liked as said it shows it to advantage, they had asked would be very carefully see to it that they would know it when there was all of it and they do say. Knowing it and obliging. They were very well obliged to explain that now there would be as much use for it as there had been. They might be in the way. It was not only an only way to see what they could be afraid of before this and by nearly all of it as the best of it. Do you know how many houses are in it. No one needs to be the one they had to have to have it.

CHAPTER CXCIX

It is always for the best that they should ask it. Once in a while it goes forward and backward and it is that by that time.

Forward and backward and it is just as well that it can be left alone easily. Why do they say that they see you. They see you and it is well enough and all of it alone. When they equal it to them and they can be for this for this makes what makes it different when it is perfectly nearly nearly perfectly all right all around. It is very recognisable that it is not at all all the same. He has just had it. And he was here he was. Nobody can be more exactly once in a while once in a while where they are and not does he say so so that they can be very welcome. Much comes to be much all the same all theirs the same much comes to be much comes to be much comes to be there all the same.

A wedding in arrangement and by their having been almost always let alone. A departure for their going away. This is meant to be an especial and partly their being once in a while some of this time there. May I ask did Mr. Fraser come again. When they had all of them more choice, choice between what they heard and when they heard it especially when they were going to be every once in a while called Tom and Frank and Henry. Every once in a while they were going to be called Tom and Frank and Henry and every once in a while they were going to be called Tom and Frank and Henry.

Every once in a while when the whole time two talking together say they like it and it is perfectly useless to attempt to have no more to do with it why will they wish it for themselves alone. And I ask you why when only they are there need they be very often very lonely. You know that. In the meantime in the meanwhile separated from it by always coming to their relief coming to their relief they do they say they say they do who changes to that when they care to stay. Arrange it. He was so well so soft so much and so be it.

It is at once theirs anyway.

She needed to be brought and for this who made that.

The intermediate introduction to an edge then.

Leaving those who said they came and went alone who had it all. Who had it all where it was left when they had gone away and whether whether they did or whether they did not.

Once again.

Expected him to stop.

Once again.

Once again.

Once again expected him to stop once again.

Having asked him to be Napoleon I very much regret having asked him to be Napoleon. Around and the house. Left and the place shown and the flowers. Seen and the surroundings. Never having been often told that it was very possible who might be there when they say I wish that they had come.

It is as well to be always careful always careful in every way.

CHAPTER CC

They must be lively in order to please.

They had been there when they were told how many times that they were to be followed.

They might have measured to length and breadth in order to arrange everything. And mostly who and mostly all and mostly all.

And all when they went away.

It is not why they come but when they come that is important and important and important. Supposing that he remembered that there had been sometime that it had been there sometime and also supposing that they were not all preferred to leave every little while. Once in a while. Once in a while is so much so much so very much so very much so very very much so very very much so much so much so much repeating so much so.

They need it when they have this time to themselves.

Needing netting and needing and as they knew they could they could do so. It would be very soon when they were mistaken.

It is never necessary to have been left alone to be sure that they will naturally have been here to-day.

It is in this way that nobody ever thinks about another.

When this is fish fish is eaten to be sure it is eaten.

One thing follows another

There is this to say there is this to say there is this to say there is this to say.

Who may you be prepared to come and call away. Who may you be prepared to ask when do you mean to have them say it was a mistake they made a mistake and when it might be that they would have to show not alone what they used when they went away but also what they used when they came. Every once in a while anybody can answer a question and every once in a while every once in a while every once in a while every once in a while they every once in a while and every once in a while every once in a while and too every once in a while.

It might be just as well to be there when they are there it might be. Who might be said to have been here.

A list of addresses and who went to see them.

CHAPTER CCI

If they look if they are close to it and look up will they be sure to say as if they had not.

Once.

At large as large as once.

Finally for a difference.

As novel makes them say they like it here.

If at once they are as folded as they are folded who makes them see places places where they have not been able to be joined by them.

Every day.

Places where they not only have not been joined by them but exceedingly very little as if they were at all practical.

Could one make two hundred.

Why when as they go along do they as they go along mind it do they as they go along.

Positively in this respect.

Fortunately as they had and now not any one and now very often without it.

Positively by this time and centered, to be centered is to be around when they are there.

Mounting do they please to be when they have come away from where they were and they have seen other things there once in a while.

Tom he does then when he does then when he does then Tom he does. Nearly Frank then when he does then when he does then when Frank he does then when Frank he does then when he does and Paul then when he does then when he there then when he does. This makes to be safely have tickets.

She makes them come to have pretty soon all of it as all over it pretty soon as all over it pretty soon.

Will they have plenty of time to answer.

CHAPTER CCII

I think I did.

CHAPTER CCIII

When it is repeated or Bernardine's revenge. When it is repeated is another subject. How it is repeated is another subject.

If it is repeated is another subject. If it is repeated or the revenge of Bernardine. If it is repeated is another subject.

When the same is said of that to be it. To be it when the same is said of that.

Next in place.

When the same is said of that and this is why doing it again is another subject not doing it again is another subject. Need now be.

Doing this again is another subject and need now be.

Explaining why they came is another subject and another subject need now be another subject. Prepare that. Need now be is another subject and need now be is another subject and prepare that. Need now be is another subject and prepare that.

Nineteen makes ninety-four.

The thing that is interesting everyone is that when it looks just like what it is made to look like if it looks just like what it is made to look like Bernardine's revenge or another subject as another subject never losing it as another subject.

Around it.

Imagine it being just like it around it.

If it is just like it around or just like it and a little around it or just like it and as much around it or just like it or more just like it around it just like it or just like it around it.

Can one see sometime that when they are all looking that they are saying just like it or another subject.

Just like it around it or another subject.

Have every one see it every once in a while and another subject see it around it as much around it as little around it as more around it.

Leaving it alone very little.

How does it look like it.

It looks just like it.

How does it look just like it. It looks just like it because as it looks just like it it is smaller or as it looks just like it it is bigger or as it looks just like it it looks just like it as it is just like it. It is just like it.

Supposing everybody looked like it just like it, supposing it looked just like it how many ways would there be then here and

there for them who after looking at it looked at it so that they
might for a change look like it again. Again and again is only
once in a while and so forth.

Be willing to have this part part of the part that makes it be
easy to divide what part it would be if they had had to divide it.
Divide it did they say divide it.

CHAPTER CCIV

Once in a while Ronald knocks and then he says so.

That makes it be more useful then it was.

Believing that they heard about it at that time.

To do and to do not doubt it doubt it may be they do but
they are about to do it.

Tell them that theirs is best.

This is what is said.

She likes it once in a while

He likes to be able to finish he likes to be able to finish it.

She likes to do it when and because they need to prepare it
themselves.

She knew that they would wish it.

Have had better have them.

This is now to be said for them.

It almost looks just like a bird and therefore it is interesting. It
almost looks just like a bird and therefore it is interesting.

How can a novel be about resemblances of what is made to
look like it to what is either another larger altogether.

Another larger that depends upon whether they do have made
it be like it as if when either a smaller or more nearly that and
then there is this difference you can tell them apart.

Might it be interesting for them to be attentive.

It can always be more than half and half and naturally arriving
to naturally and beside.

The way that they make it be make it is that is looks exactly
like it.

Thank you.

The way it looks exactly like it.

This is in consideration of coming coming to see.

Could it be as much as that by then.
Go on.
Could it be as much as that by then go on.
Always to be sure.
They made this and that and do so.
Come to be there were there were and a little like it.
She here they there and then where.
Once more I thank you.

CHAPTER CCV

All ready yet.
They went and made the bet.
Never be disappointed by them time after time.
Back again from there.
They are back again again from there.
They are back again and they are back again from there.
This shows it.
They are back again.
To be a near arrangement of how when it looks as if it looks like it like it as if they were going to be looking as much like it as if they mixed what was it with what is like it. To mix what is it with what is looking like it makes it not only look as like it as it is but makes it comforting to them who are not hesitating.

Speaking of hesitating it makes it a comfort to them who are not hesitating.

Once in a while.

Come to be difficulty once in a while.

When they have this and that to do too comfortingly once in a while.

And he was right, continuous and never angry never angry continuous and never angry and never even never angry. Let all who look be sure to stop and look not because they are to stop and look.

Relieving them every once in a while.

Once when they were just as ready as now they had been very careful.

Thank you so much.

When they were after all partly to blame they were asked how do you feel about it.

Then when they were repeatedly indifferent to their being there at all they might be told anything.

Very well as well.

This is a description of how he could be nervous about not having everything exactly as it was.

Here it is.

They had no doubt about it here it is.

Always to be sure here it is.

That which when it is made smaller is attractive that which when it is made bigger is as attractive that which is made that is attractive is because after a while they will not remember it all the same. All the same they will not remember it.

Perhaps all the same they will not remember it as all the same.

Supposing they told them that they were coming supposing they told them that they had been coming who would be annoyed.

Once every once in a while.

And by and by.

And as they had it.

And when they liked it.

And why they could they no they could not.

Once more to thank you.

They must be always very well to do.

CHAPTER CCVI

Not only by that time but as if at that time they would be interrupted.

They need not have been nor thought about it as much as all that.

Every once in a while and not on their behalf.

To be very pleased.

It is as well to know it all. It is as well to know that he was not affected by it and that he was not likely to be older and that he was not he would not like it by that time. It is just as well to know all that.

Begin again.

It is just as well to know all that.

It is not at all possible to forget fifteen and yet what may they do they may not do that all fifteen may not they may not have done that. Very well they may not have done that.

That makes it more likely that they would be placed there where after each time they would come again. Come again.

Having fastened it with difficulty and so having been thanked very well thanked for it.

CHAPTER CCVII

Once in a while.

Having been as well as they were here and now by this for it with it all. All changes to it now near it near it to be that he thought he would.

You must you must you must you must.

A hundred at a time a hundred of anything.

Let us see what we can do about it.

Blue glass and green glass and red glass and yellow glass.

We must see what we can do about it.

A hundred at a time and we must see what we can do about it.

This is to be now all about it.

A hundred at a time and we must see what we can do about it.

Once upon a time not meaning that it is very apparent that very often they will mean this that after all would they like to be able to do something that has not been done before not only not done before but also not done before that. This cannot be a trouble to anybody this cannot be a trouble to anybody to anybody to anybody this cannot be a trouble because when they have half of it every day nearly every day when they nearly every day beside nearly every day half nearly every day half of it nearly every day half of it nearly every day. It is not at all interesting to be as much as a pigeon pigeon bread when all is said and they do now what they do now to them and always and in their half and in their way and in their time and in their half and in their calling to them to come away.

Has any one told him about how after all even when she did

not want to she could not help having it in her hand having it in her hand having it having it said having it in her hand. Everybody needs to be there when there is more than ever of a difference between what is what.

Nobody knows who is to be told.

And nobody knows who is to be told.

And as nobody knows who is to be told.

And as well as nobody knows who is to be told why when they wish to have them desired to they always need to have it happen that they could be seated seated as seated there.

There can be a chair when they have been as often to the once in a while after all.

Believe me it is not only for my pleasure that I do it.

Nicely told and nicely told and nicely old and nicely old and it may be added nicely told and nicely told.

Why when they are very satisfied.

Like it.

Do you like it.

When it is not only part of the time but as well as all of the time and all of the time and the difference when they need to be as finally as they finally do see.

When it is fairly nearly all in the way and they say remember me and they do not say remember me to them and they do not say who is going to show it to them now then after all when they are very often nearly and by themselves when they are by themselves and change it to by themselves and to change it and to change it by themselves by themselves not only after a while not only for it by their having not found it where they left it.

They might be always here and there.

Might they

They might be always here and there they might be always here and there.

Never asked them how to come to leave it when they had been there every once in a while.

Every once in a while always every once in a while yesterday every once in a while and having waited waited can always be changed to waited.

Do I do I do I see what they came to leave for me.

This makes it their reason.

I will certainly never be remarkable again.

Who hears whom.

I will certainly be as remarkable again as when they had been very nearly by that time who came by that time there is very little doubt that he sees everyone and it is not only this but that for them to be in this way this way make it this way make it this way as this way they made it have be what should it have had it do when it was by that time who makes the third noise. Anybody can cloud that that that winter.

Believe it every little while.

Seriously to be told why.

Why do they like what they like.

Because they are after all very fond of every little while every little while by that time. And he can be be and see and never as prepared for instance.

Leave me leave something to confusion.

And I thank you.

CHAPTER CCVIII

They never said you do but I do not. They never said yes when they had chosen not to give whatever was wanted every once in a while. Forget being ready to be very nearly always more decidedly by this time always established in such a way that there cannot be more than enough there to be left as it could be when they had been obliged to answer yes but after all why did they come to be always half of the time in there as if it were after that better than before.

Not prepared to be more often said to be by this by this who is as much as if it were continuously not more than longer. Who must change to be told that they were finally finally as if as thought to be very nicely as if they could remember that she had said.

Remembering that they talked at all.

How can they decide that they had belied themselves in thoughtfulness for themselves and theirs. By shall they be to be as told. She was and it befell her to be caught when they were could they be when they had never adding as it was having had and very much obliged to them. To them and very much obliged to him. Very much obliged to him can never make of them and of them as if they had been beforehand beforehand makes it as accommodating as they are as they are after all by nearly after all remember me to them.

It must be their afternoon to come and say how do you see about it when there is no need to be more than after once in a while.

After once in a while in conversation to their believing that they might be told.

How many more how old.

She liked it to be about them.

As they liked it to be about them.

As he liked it to be about him as she liked it to be about it what about it.

Every once in a while there are a great many who are a great many who are a great many who are as much as if they had been done with it, done with it to be so to be so to be so and for for for for in as much by it when they had not been angered. Then seeing them sitting sitting is in standing wholly, wholly and in replace replacing stretches stretches by this as that and for that to be with it as a chance a chance when when they had been behind it to be broken broken can be for that when they knew after a time to be so. To be so cannot be before they had it as a better than before by them. So then consider that they will be represented as I said as I said as I said by it it being merely merely to be all to be to be then. How could he think it to be told.

When was he generous.

They forgot lament.

When was she there was she there she was.

They had been could and who could who could and sign. Mr. Henry Lamb was unable to understand that they would and could refuse. He asked why should I be told about it and there was a very great deal of decision in replying yes certainly it might after this nearly once in a while for them.

Should they need it just as much as that.

A way to tell about it is this. They were there and did it too and they were very well to do and they were asked why will you come and then then it was well in advance.

Any one can use a chapter and never recall it at all.

CHAPTER CCIX

Thank you for having arranged it for me thank you for having arranged it for me.

They need to be when they were seen by them too much for them it was much too much and they were left here and it was not what they could do that meant it it was also by this time for them for them can be disturbed by this time can be disturbed and around around can be very likely can be when they are as they were hourly. Hourly and they say so.

Not in their behalf behalf always respected not in their behalf by it for they had seen when when when to be told to help with it help with it and he could be all of it as all of it as well. Very nice and quiet I thank you.

Leaving it to be seen.

It is very nearly precisely their half and half to be sure. To be sure when they not only can but also need to make that do.

Imagine not only their as very likely but when they had left it to be what was mostly artifice artifice by that and be aloud be aloud to do and they can be very nearly when as but it is they need it for what should be sent to them.

Imagine them all selling and often a while all telling and after a while they had left it out and after a while they made them be very likely coming to see me.

That is the way they had it as very likely.

Every little while they must resemble their brother they must resemble they must after all they must resemble their nephew.

It was to be fortune fortune fortune for all it was to be fortune for all it was to be fortune for all. Beginning to be sacs and sacrifice and saleable for all.

There is a reason why when they resemble they do not add once in a while once in a while to two.

Let them see for it.

It happens that not only not when not as if they did look alike look alike makes twenty have more than twenty-five and it is to be sure and it is to be surely their relief. Begin again wedding.

If they look and they see that just as they are about to re-semble they are about to resemble why of course not to be sure why of course when they are sure to thank you. Thank you very much.

Allow it.

When it is meant to be out loud out loud they have their why and my my own for them. Allowing this as they went by.

Never being silly about looking alike.

It is by their use of their use of their praise on account on account of their and they have and when as it is very much the same very much the same as by this when they have been what was it they asked to be to be to say thank you thank you too.

There are two things to do look alike and thank you too.

Thank you very much.

Never having been more troubled than by this. When they had been prepared for it at all not only that they are not a trouble but they are not a trouble they are not a trouble. Leave it alone they are not a trouble leave it alone.

They made them say what they did say to me expect to be when they are as they had it for them for them for themselves to them in two. Believe when.

This is to say that they all succeeded too.

Let me see about success success successful and so forth. When this is by that time by that time can be rediscovered cautiously rediscovered cautiously. Never losing it to be themselves for and forward by that for for it for it and anything else. And questioned quietly.

There is this great difference between apart at that time. When partly when when those who are not very nearly all always al-ways all all in all all in all and then dear to them dear to me dear to me dear to them. When placed when placed where where any where where there is what is never asked for. It is easy to wonder wonder whether wonder whether they did do so and wonder whether they did they did do so and so would be very nearly all the same as when as when can always be repeated. One two and three can always be repeated once two and three and left and right and as much as when they asked me why I liked it can always be repeated can always be repeated can always be repeated.

Listening learning and letting letting me know letting me know and learning letters and learning letters and waiting for it and waiting for it and finding it best and having them say to follow now and see the rest makes it come well from you.

Welcome is one of the things which might be not so very well believed when they did have it come have it come.

I said I liked to look at it.

Never ending for themselves at once at once to be not by that by that time. Was Etta willing that he should keep one out of six leaving her five. She was not.

CHAPTER CCX

That makes it do as well.

Perhaps it is.

This is how they know that perhaps it is. Not very likely that they know that perhaps it is. This is how they know that it is not very likely that perhaps it is.

Letting it pass.

Once in a while letting it pass so that once in a while letting it pass they once in a while letting it pass they letting it pass once in a while how many could let it pass. How many did let it pass once in a while.

Not more easily not more easily and having it as every day.

He never saw her go again. Go again makes it change from so and do they do they keep them away.

Every time that there is this feeling let it be let it alone.

A night in morning and Tom cannot be mentioned that is perfectly left alone when when being exchanged for before. They must be as particularly told so told to have it better than their partly in the way.

Let me tell all about the difference between that and before they could do so.

He did forget she did forget she did forget to do it.

Why are they who are very successful why are they who are very successful not liking to be asked once in a while once in a while they went away.

It does make a difference that they are different that they are different differently and looking like it when at once and then a little a little more than a little more than once in a while a little they they believe it, and it is very true very true that means when she asked in several places have you it, they not only did not have it but were not to have it because at this time it was not at the time it was not one at a time it was not only one at a time it was one and one and one at a time. And now how and how to be excellently addressed and ably ably to be seen and safely arranged arranged one after the other after the other. Always as much as wishes. This may be how four and three and two were implicated in their being alike. Always thank you.

Once in a while and to be pleased once in a while. They made them do what they knew they were to do were to do were to do what they knew they were to do. He says it is very different from anything else.

They might be able to thank him.

And she she might be able to come in in such a way that when it was very likely to be always finally as much as when it was to be as much as they can have it as a moving to and fro to and fro securely. Always to be there by these who make it a last endeavor to be when they are startled and when they are startled. Leaving left it left it to be right. After all thanks are adequate.

A novel of thank you.

Who said that they said that they heard and had known that they would recall it every once in a while. They know that they can be just as willing as they were to read out loud.

Now and then when and then when and they they were here. Always and now and nearly every habit habit being as much a noise as habitual and habitual being in reality what they saw here.

Letting us know this.

A novel of thank you makes it be all mine. Mine at a time, at a time when they use this as a place of advantage advantage to them and they have it left to them. Come to them suddenly it comes to them suddenly.

When everyone is able to say he is a very well placed illustration of that and this they make relatively small preparation for their being alike and very likely and very likely to be sure.

It is very extraordinary that when they begin well they begin well.

CHAPTER

Why did they believe that after all it was just as well after all to change it.

Next to this

Now and then

Easily.

Extra

And by the way. They were to go away.

It has been attributed to thanks thanks for it.

Now and then they they before they had before they had had it had it had it and had it may be they will be once as might they be careful of it.

To arrange how four they knew each other and were there more. Let them be alone with them with them to be alone with them.

Leaving it to be a choice between there this time and there that time and leaving it to be the same all the same to them. Not influence and not be carefully renewed and not be there every once in a while and not be left to do it when it would be most convenient.

How can everybody think of them. George is one name Paul is one name James is one name John is one name and in every language it is just the same all the same as if they had agreed. Listen to who has it. If he is as much allowed for as when they are preferred and left to them for this and theirs to be not not find it at all. Next when she she can never be so much and then who does know who said who said they were they were that time that time to-day. Wonder why he does not come and call come and call makes it be theirs in that way. Making it finally.

How can they never say thank you again all the same.

It is very nearly they did not begin to be not to be not to be theirs theirs have it. It is as many as they came as they came as they came theirs theirs theirs as many as they came and not what they had been for it. And in so much it makes no difference what it was done for. She said supposing they state she said supposing they state they state let it alone they state. So before so before so before so.

It is very easily understood that it will have to go on.

CHAPTER CCXII

Do you hear the little boys at play and what do they say they say they are to be a not yet. Then it can be arranged. Why should one watch two or watch one.

Looking about they chose to be out.

When they have been quickly left it to that.

It is very easily nearly this they have gone to every once in a while.

And now may it be not more than that kind.

It must be when they came to be to see made it start prematurely.

A novel of returned to thank you.

Thank you allows for it she said she was pleased with a plot.

To announce to repair to come pleasantly to accept it in a minute to have lost it and to ask about it. How do they have it be as when she said and do you. No one can be as they said they would.

Having been turned around.

She said I should and I said I did and she said I did and I said when I did and when I did I will not do it again and receive me and hear them say I have never and so when he said he would it gave me a great deal of pleasure.

Always not to be in there in there in there with them with them as if he had said it. This is not to be left in here left and felt and very well I thank you.

Who might be in there when there is question of their passing and repassing and do you believe me easily and does it make you have it have it hear it hear it and capably in that time.

There is no reason to doubt the exactness of Mr. James White's statements concerning me. They are correct and appreciative.

One can but thanks to you thank you.

A novel of thank you and not about it.

It might be allowed.

They should be would they be as much as if left.

Left left left right left and there were little things that made it necessary to change it. I think she must be the one who was to be met here by Mrs. Primrose and not Mrs. Briggs. Every little while not Mrs. Primrose but Mrs. Briggs not by Mrs. Briggs, Mrs. Briggs is not to be met here, Mrs. Primrose is not to meet Mrs. Briggs here. Not helping it all the same not helping it, all the same not helping it all the same.

Once more when they have asked them to come in.

Let us be just as attentive as we were when they asked us to be certain to leave it as it was. Never letting it have it to be here.

Very early they thanked them. They very early thanked them and they very early they very early they thanked them they thanked them very early and they thanked them and very early and as once or twice they thanked them very early. Once it happened that Mr. Edwin Hildebrand who had it in hand meant to please himself as well. Then they had to be prepared and finally just as you say they were very well to do. They need to be to state that after all now after all they do not now after all they do not have it as much as they had it as their repayment. Why do they prefer it when they have it because in that case they can be as easily satisfied. Supposing in everything they succeed. Suppose they succeed in everything. When could they be when they could be and they could be when and at all and after all after all it was just what they did.

She being there could be wishing followed followed it as they liked. Always changing to followed it as they liked.

To often say having the sound of said and said said it as much as when they had no chance to be just as much having it happen to them.

No one in thanking has not had it happen to them that they would that they would be who makes it do.

Not all of it at the time that they had had it by which they mean he the one who was nearly very often in that place could expect it all the time. Come now.

Let me tell you something. In having this to do no one as I once said before no one as I once said before no one.

CHAPTER CCXIII

It is just as well very well just as very nearly as very nearly as well.

Why would ten sent over do no good.

Why would ten sent over do no good.

Why would ten sent over do no good do no good and if it is a satisfaction satisfaction and satisfactory and she could be as she was as she was just as well as she was.

An interest in a which is it to be not there she said it just as much as she had it in themselves they can be quiet.

What do they mean when they say that they do have it as they had it and they do and they have and they will.

Let me be here now.

When in these three days they in these three days not they in these three days not they.

That is one at a time and quite for them too.

And as it was.

When they had been very nearly as they could before. Before is by the way.

Let us see why they meant it just as they did. Let us see why they could and did have it very often when they were not very obliging.

Letting them alone.

Not as nearly and not as nearly and not as she might say carelessly and she might say they would be too much alike. Hand in hand. They would be too much alike. And for it as it was to be left to have it arranged arranged can be as likely as not themselves. Never to be darker if they were never to be darker if they were never to be darker if they were never to be darker how would that do.

For them and mostly they had it when they were to like it.

Let us say how she said yes for that. It pleases them that it is not only why or not but because of that and rain at all. In every way they prefer to lend her.

Now then introducing Esther. Esther was more than once in a while plainly seen and she said he was to be and he was the one who could by being older be persuaded that it was not at all necessary to be loyal could any one be more than have it be there in there in there and was it that they needed to be graceful can be so can be so can be so and so. Not by that time not by that time not by that time at that time. This makes differences imperceptibly imperceptibly used to be used. Every little once in a while and while and while and a while and every once in a while and while. They need always not to be meant to be all that was by this in that and on that account. Excuse me and please please follows follows follows not follows not only follows.

They made it be that much as much as much as all of it for them.

Around.

And they could when they had that as their plan their plan and man man once in a while to them to this to now to always be fortunately. Fortunately is their instance.

Let us believe in please.

Also in that.

Also to be also when we when can they account for it.

Everything happens.

CHAPTER CCXIV

Not as much as twenty more.

Have it.

Not as much as they could be to lend it.

Lend it always means and seen. Seen comes to say so to them.

Anybody can give thanks to them.

So when they mean they mean I mean.

CHAPTER CCXV

When they make it do.

Easily.

When they make it do.

And they had been known to be going to be here and there and to be ready when they had meant it as it was to be. Allowing for it.

One two and three.

He and George George can be either useful or if you like it as well as well.

Paul can be nearly always ready later and to like it as they did not like it here.

John would be met by being younger and would arrange it as they had it heard it heard it here.

James could be so much sustained that when he had well wishers well wishers or well wishers.

And always always makes it by the time that they were when they had it as they had it to be very nearly bent to be.

That makes it that they have again and again.

Let this be all.

Once in a while they had to be can and can be can be found. Can be when he had not been used to have it chosen Thursday.

Let us consider everything.

A novel of say thank you. Thank you.

A novel of the time when they had elected to be plainly cared for plainly cared for and they mean to be left to themselves altogether.

A novel to be used to after all meaning to be forced to be allowed to have it nearly by that time and waiting.

So much has been saved by them. They were more indifferent than they had been and might it be and may it be and would it be left to be likely to be more than that to be as they had it. Let us risk it as they might they might, might could be arranged for by this means and they had to be asked would they do it did they do it do they do it and will I be pleased with the answer.

Supposing everybody thinks of Victor Hugo.

One two three.
Supposing everyone thinks of me.
One two three.

CHAPTER

In the way of asking ask it might they by having to have no possible single and especially by this time very often not at all disliked altogether. That makes it as it was. Was it was it an afternoon. He was not there to have it coming and going and very easily when she was not so much as much as that and by this time.

Let us not change from this I see remember me.

Once in a while when I was there I made it easily at that time differently and when they had to change joining joining it in their mostly when they made it go.

Supposing you stop and say how do you do I hope that you will often do as you are asked to do by those who do not alone ask it but ask it again. This makes them wait almost two years let us say makes them let us say wait let us say almost two years and let us say when they have been waiting almost two years they need not attach themselves to it because it has been said they will not be more than very able to have what they have. He did.

The next thing that happened was this they meant to be almost more than ever nearly able to have it prepared for them. Prepared for them does not do.

CHAPTER

To let it be as if whenever it could be to look at it would be the same.

Supposing I needed it.

They might be and having not had and been arranged that it was when different, different can always be applied as when they have avoided not only by that but with the intention to be and have it arranged. Not that it can be might it be when they have to have theirs also.

Let us imagine illustration.

He said he would like me.

Once or twice they made them give it to them when they had been more than for this alone by this time.

Now have to.

When it is not best to be that they come here unexpectedly.

Suppose it suppose it do suppose it that they will they have had but three in all and compared to that what is it that they could need.

Not if it is as much as they could.

Mr. Edward Harold Howard could be lost to them.

Let it be when they can.

In this be and could it manage it too much. And very clearly very naturally very nearly and and can be identical. It is as it is best for them.

Remaining ready to be theirs every day theirs every day.

Let it be for this.

We made them be what it was not only how they did it but when it was very likely that they had given it up. Be when they could. And hear it. It is not at a time that they could be at their arrangement and returning to identity and their reliance remarkable to be underneath when they have changed. Let us wonder when they will be there. There where they have this in finally at that time. Does it mean that they have undertaken to tell it again when they do not find it as well as that and they do have plenty of time.

The only fault that I can find with it is that they do not happen to be so very well as they said, as they said and as they will. Will they. They can be once when they are and by this time to be sure.

Never losing their importance and so when it is open and closed who can be sure to believe it when it is as well as ever and say to say to thank to thank to have it yes.

They will be there and once again having meant never to fasten it so that when they after all better it can be nearly by it in this way and deliberately. She knew how to send and sign.

It can be to little purpose to always know the name.

CHAPTER

Let us have it told to them by us. Thanks for their being so much as they have.

She gave me three hundred and thirty and he gave me one hundred and eighty and they gave us one hundred and ten and then when.

She made it by this time.

Follow again.

They had been their share.

And their their where where and persuaded makes it by it by it is in their best way for it deliberated. Deliberated can always be exchanged for deliberately. And they may be may be coming back to may be.

If when they begin to be one two. One two to them when they are under under can be admitted as stream and their so very likely to be in the rest of it as much as much can never be changed around.

Need it be theirs to be sure.

Who makes hats.

Who makes heavy shawls.

Who makes window panes and who makes lead pencils.

They do.

They never have been left alone at first. So much for that.

There is a way to be to say I like it.

And not to be therefore.

There is an after all to it by this time.

They have let it be almost better now.

They can be heard.

They can be heard and said it was that best of all by this time. They made them catch themselves by this time.

Is it very easy to be absorbed as much as they had better have it all by themselves readily.

Can Mr. Cornhill have been left alone.

That might be so.

And now how no not to be there this time as she was nearly by their arrangement carefully prepared.

Be careful.

Let us remember how they could be by themselves every once in a while.

Now and naturally.

Let me see.

The reason for this is this they had better not go there.

After that their attention to animation is what they mean by access. Lest they come to be coming in. And when she was not unattentive and she was attentively remembered.

No one can know the difference between why I did and why I did not.

He was one to to be not nearly as leaving it there as they could be arranged around. Not for themselves alone. Not by it to go.

Nicely and near and they have aid as well.

Never succeeding them by their daisies and going to be once in a while carefully and measured which can mean in their esteem. Around me.

This can be a very faithful description of their rearrangement and left and being and when oftener they had attributed shall they be theirs.

One two three times.

There are two groups and sometimes three.

The first group which is included in this novel of thank you very much are those who by this time are not only here but after all very distinguished and very distinguished and they by and by and by it all may be perfectly reasonably and granted that they made the most they made the most for this by even now, and disturbing can never be again out and in when having changed that that makes it shorter by so much.

Leave it to me.

The second group and who may the second group be I ask you who may the second group be.

They not theirs why when they have cares she not be when they have been twofold needed by it can and must he asked he asked the same very and very well.

Now they need is it a weather forecast.

Any four or five who make twenty can when they are left

alone they can be churlish churlish is nicely by them in their I mean. I mean to be early and late.

Thank you.

CHAPTER CCXIX

Why will they sit.

Down and here.

They can be as much as they had planned active and often related.

Come as much as you can and do not be at all inclined to come three at a time, three at a time four at a time two at a time more at a time. When they can be spared who can be much more than their friend.

Esther said that she did and Esther would that is to say Esther would. I cannot forget Esther.

There is this difference between those who came and in this way that they might be called for.

CHAPTER

Let me alone.

After Dorothy after Caroline Carry and Edith after Edith Amelia and the rest left me alone let me alone.

Now and then popular when when will I be popular as you see me.

After all this they made allowances.

In returning a novel of thank you they were returning a novel of thank you.

It is by no manner of means all of it all of it is by no manner of means all of it. They have to have been more nearly having it presented to them in the meantime to oblige themselves to be nearly prepared for anything. Anything can be theirs hurriedly. Let us believe that we know everything hurriedly and that we have to be not only careful but capable not only capable but once in while. And now where they can be previously acknowledged to have them have less less than they had when they were plainly awfully pleased to have been theirs by chance. It is not by themselves that they feel this about it as they neglect it. So much for that when they are told that they like this to be theirs just now. Manage to be for it when they can be chosen. Let me always think about how to pass the time.

Now and then.

It is very nearly often that they have their own that day and please please do you do it just to please do you do it and please why when it is barely for that in their place do they call it out frequently frequently can be arranged for and now I follow them they follow me they will then have this and they see see me. Thank you very much.

Once upon a time there was a wedding and they made coins and coins were in their place and places were better arranged than they had been. They had liked it as well as Liverpool and Liverpool understand Liverpool how do you ask send me and how do you send not lend me not lend me to it to be more than ever utilised as much as they had been. Let us think of their not being obliging not only for it but to it not only when it but why it and not only and not only. Here we meet.

We can easily be very happily quiet and very easily final and very usually appointed and very sweetly in their presence and very unitedly their result. This when they feel anxious may feel anxious may feel anxious when they feel anxious and not only thank you.

Needs be needs be and I do not blame you.

When I come to talk to them I come to talk to them and now and then when I come to when I come to come to be when I come to be naturally to undertake their undertaking which is this why do they like and like it. Supposing everybody had their questions answered.

What does he say.

CHAPTER

Having pleased themselves with themselves having pleased themselves for themselves having pleased themselves as they pleased them please please please.

One two one two one two three they make a mother of you

and me how can you how can I how can they how can it be for them to be for them to be for them as they were very nearly subordinate. Subordinate makes it black and white. If he is not to be payed for it he will not if he is not to be paid for it he will not be what he has had all the time all the time all the time indeed.

Can you be so very much admired by them.

They make it they make it all the time.

Every now and then.

They made them have it be allowed and would they be for that when they had changed it to it for them by and where alone.

Let us explain footstools. Footstools can be such that when they are seen through a window they have almost more than their share of having it around. This makes it please can you see, and when you have gone ahead no one can say impatiently waiting no one can say impatiently waiting all at once now can they.

I have changed to all of it at once.

Now try to be adapted to their being their being and supposing they did plan it and supposing they were every day more or less would it be at all a pleasure and it undoubtedly would.

Not to be relighted three not to be relighted but anyway five if useful can be used again.

This makes it theirs anyway.

It must be seen to be recognised. And now and then thank you.

CHAPTER

Never be the reverse.

Once in a while she in spite of saying how can I be excited she in spite of saying double you for them in spite of her saying they might be generous in spite of my saying I am very glad to see everybody.

Choosing it at first at all.

Let us mean why is it singularly so.

And now as they had been behind with their refusal.

Supposing Ivy was more as she could be when she was very not envious but careful not once more in a wish but once more they need not despair and that makes it different.

Once very likely they had had to have it too and must please themselves very well just as much as they had been to this and found them out. They might be when they pleased and furthermore they do not care and she did recognise it further. Do you hear me have it as well as after all before.

Let us never be afraid of thunder. She might be careful and she might be very well cared for and she might be as much as she could of that very well to be for them as they could and so losing their resemblance.

Come to be once all the time. Here here they come come to see see what they like about it. Very likely they were willing to be better off some where else and so they need to like it every day just that much. Who can be said to be spared.

Let me see about it.

He who who could it be. Who could it be and why why when they go to go there to be with themselves alone and out loud for their having been reached reached when they were. They could not be why they were waiting. This is just like them when they see me and I wonder can they be can they after all be one of those. Very comfortingly.

I cannot see why they have been here.

CHAPTER

Perhaps.

Not having been likely to be when that is mentioned satisfied. One two three.

One two three all about but she she is nearly fairly nearly Sophie.

Sophie will do very well when it is a name.

And now every day and now.

To intend to be after all every little while.

And now.

It is easy to see that it is very well to do what they are very likely to like at the time and it is much as it was when they had been understood to again and again asking of it that it could change and they might by the time that they were likely to repeat they could be for themselves as well as alone here. Let me see to them. Having thought of that and that and that and that and that which is meant to be sustained entirely sustained by this time.

Let me see why let me see and Sophie and let me see why let me see and her mother Caroline and why let me see and let me see her companion Louisa and let me see why let me see that she did not pass it at that time because when she was not thinking she was telling telling them their things so that they might they had that day when they might be there for their own. So they were behind behind with it.

Let us consider the value of thank you the novel of thank you the novel of thank you and the value of the novel of thank you.

Never to be when she and be believe me and be very careful too of leaving it around.

Now this makes theirs at first.

Saying it with this do and do be all right.

Everybody that they know tell them so.

How is it that industrious makes it industrious and every time that they had that and remind remind can never be opposite to and the same as when they mind. They mind it very much when they are always recalled by it. This makes it very different from every time.

Let us tell how often we liked it.

There is very little use in remembering everything and in coming when they ask to see it and in crying when they have not followed it one after the other. Do when they do and say it is coming and do when they do and say. Never to be ready as before.

Let us believe that we have had it very much.

Any many many see them sell it first.

That makes it never better than they had seen why she asked for it first.

Action and reaction are equal and opposite.

CHAPTER

Imagine that they knew copper and windows. Imagine that they knew that they must be more than having theirs as we knew it.

Action and reaction are equal and opposite and so they more

than help it and she is very pleasantly occupied in sewing and she is very pleasantly occupied in coming and she is very pleasantly occupied in their having been more at once and she is very pleasantly occupied in as they were as they made it a refusal and she was pleasantly occupied and to be sure to be sure that it is in their half of all more than they collected. Who makes another go their way who does who does and she was disappointed. Everyone can say that she went away.

When all of it they must be there when she is felt to be there whether it is after all by that time.

And a little later.

They can evenly be sold.

And told.

That they make theirs understated so that they have to please themselves as much.

Once as much twice as much and three times as much.

A little about all day long. Who was he.

They make fortunately for them all of it most and she said no fish and they said yes no fish and he said when there is no fish at this time that means that either everybody is richer or everybody is poorer. Everybody makes it stay stay here. Let me know what she feels about it. What does she feel about it she feels this about it that in describing Elizabeth whose name is Russian she has told that it makes her nervous.

A novel of thank you is historic.

CHAPTER

Not a surprise.

Let those who are interested be in one at a time. Let those who have heard let them listen just as well as they can. Let any one who has been let alone let them be very nearly perfectly as they had been allowed to be this for that as well. One or two.

Now come to be carefully.

When they like pork they like pork and when they like hyacinths they like hyacinths and when they like eggs they like eggs and when they like it to be of glass they like it to be of glass one two three preferably or at most another for them there.

Let me think of how they do please me. They please me by telling exactly how they had to do it not only because they were
once in a while nearly there but because they were by that time
as much as if they had been better than that at all and not only
did not like it.

Who loves roses
They do.
Who gives hers.
We do.
Who must be all alike
They can be had at an interval

Let us have it be that two more than they were certainly not
asking is it his son. So much. And they knew that they had seen
more than always as they had it mine. Mine too. Next. Next
they had been more than if he had heard that they were more
than often once in a while she likes nearly theirs before their
face to be why they must come to be.

Fine again.
Never more in praise.
Not as likely fine they tell let me hear theirs.

As we knew now they could allow she knew the cow and as
he had been given what was as large if it stood there and they
could excuse their allowance as part of it by this means as to
date.

Begin now.
Not at all as why and when they had that as their best, best as
they see and saw it first. First and best, never to be mistaken for
most and best and yet it is when they are part of it for them for
them to be sure that they had agreed leave it alone and say come
to it for they have been theirs and allowed that much.

Why does everybody like it better.
Not for them and having changed it at first as they might as
they might and weddings in every land just as they had been
said they were. Now and they were. Come to and now and they
were and come to and now and they were and as it is to be to-
day. To-day makes it remarkable.

Let me tell of real incidents.
He came and very early had a widow and a child and the

child died and the widow disappeared but was seen later. Later
he had a mother and a condition of being more than much allowed for, for being theirs at once and nearly after then they had
it in mind. Coming to be around could they if not at all like not
at all like it not at all like it.

When they prepared their usefulness.

And not remembered it as well as it was.

Letting them say why they said it.

This is why they went Wednesday.

This is why they have to oblige everyone with being kind to
them and asking them why they did not like it to be as Mexican.
And that makes chocolate of more value than they are when
they have to be there all the best of it as not by this time feeling
it just now.

They arranged it.

To be for a fortune too.

CHAPTER

I meant to say every little while that they were accordingly
encouraged and to be when and why they were hesitating. Not
to be theirs for this Sunday. It is that has been reopened when
they had not made any difference. Believe me.

At the time that they were very likely to have had more than
they wished of what they declared ample and finely said to be
as when they had it for themselves and arranged so very well so
very well when they might be all of it and to decline to face
what they have managed to be and to allow and for it once at a
time. They might be for that and a kind of an enlargement of
their being not only for them and for themselves to be not when
they had for this as witness. They might see and if this is when
and why they must further be more than if there is in exchange
who makes and who can be for them at that time nearly this as
they see and how aloud and when they as further than they went
who comes to be only that might it be an exchange exchange and
instance and do like do alike, so there when there for it as a
deception. They might be theirs charitably.

Let me tell about easter. Easter is a day when they are surprised that it had been yesterday as well. And so more have it days to reappoint and collect when in their being their case to them and he said could he be and wishing and was it because it happened twice. When they pay for their day to their day as they may while they say that they can do this at this time might they when is it. Let me think easter or easter. Can you be when they are might they be if it is of this and coming through too too as well can she be sneezing and asking it as well. Easter and everything easter and everything easter and everything to easter and everything. The next thing, that they find to finish is this. The next thing that they find to finish is what is it when they are idle and to be and for them when they are here now and now. He followed me. She makes of it that they were and change as if they had been heard and might it leave as if they had and marry marry makes what is it when they asked for it alone alone can never be so presupposed as they need call to call to them to them to be and to this kind as if now when they are not to be leaves leaves can be nearly chocolate as a color. If later on they had to do with what they had and were to be as if they might be just as restless when they could be coming to it now as come again and rabbits come again and rabbits and it was a disappointment. He came and we gave it back. This makes it yesterday and obliging and might it be necessary to have a name to a longer nearer best to be for them. And very anxious to see. I will not say very much.

CHAPTER

Meeting thus suddenly, then there were nearly being there where they had left it when they came away and now as they had asked them around. Let us have it in half.

Once in a while each one finds it about and so he could repeat that he did not carefully repeat elephants elephants and theirs by appointment. She was not useful.

We will now gather together.

Once when she was almost believing that they had been interchangeable she was not more than finally as much originally as in a mistake when it might be that it did not make any difference and allowed it and so she said could they be could they have been as they were in arranging as it was arranged. Let me tell about business. Business is a never to be meant that they were when it had come to be that every time when it could they might be as much so to theirs as theirs just the same. Business is as much as it could be that they could be finding their relighting once in a while and street because when and more than believing they can occasionally disturb it too they might coming as it would be for them coming to have it and it and now let me say when they say let them be being being born born left left and ready ready to can it happen to be not only in that and relegating to much more usage to be in there in this in that and time to tell it when they know. Let me tell about business business is nearer than they to me when they when he when they shall be when they can be when they are leaving them to me to me to be why must it mean their reason reason shall always be most of it to be when they and as can it have it in their place. After all any chapter is mine. Thank you very much and never in their bed of forget-me-nots lilacs and painted hyacinths and leave it to me. I wish to state that I have known a great many part of the time and also I have known a great many who can be not only when they have been as much as pleased as much as pleased as much as pleased.

CHAPTER

They had it as it was and they had it as it was and they had it as it was as it was as it was as it was as it was for them. They had it as it was for them. Next time it made a difference.

For themselves and they did have the place to themselves and they could when they asked have the rest leave it now in as much as they were to be sure of it now for the rest of the time that they had been about to be going there any way just as much as they can be leaving it all alone at that time. Now they and then left it to be that as it comes to be fairly as an interchange of leaving it more than often around and by that time not nearly placed to be rightly for it as they can be finally replacing inches to be sure and like it coming to be around when they can call it how do you do as they arranged compared to that finally at this time theirs as well coming thoroughly to be confused with it at a glance and so has to be once in a while in dividing it for them can feel it relieved in their and so in that place where they were as they might fortunately to be touched by it too. I have absolutely forbidden you to give her any money.

CHAPTER

Like that makes it be partially in their happening to be stay-ing easily in the making of theirs once a week all the time so that very much and is what they as using find it do do do it more than that that they were for her sake and for it and that that is why they might be more if it more of it to it to it as they come to be more likely and not putting it there where it is heard about when they wished.

It is just as long as that. Very likely it is just as long as that and they knew that they were eating what they had which was very good and were leaving what they had which was what they had and they were having what they had which was why we hoped not to do it when we came to be very much oftener coming here there and very likely very little has it to do with it when can they sing.

I wish to say that not only was I glad that I had quarreled with them but it was a satisfaction to me in every way to have been here and there and to have allowed for it and they might when they could be joined they would be willing to be very often at any time and for this as their reason because they were joining together in dividing it at once and they might have all of it come to be more nearly as much as it was an instance of it. How very often they wish it. I find that I have in it every satis-faction satisfaction so do you. Let me tell how Tolstoy knew about food. He knew that they were blushing.

CHAPTER

Thank you very much.

CHAPTER

One as they were they will be there and is she best known
as if they came to ask it why could they go when all the same
and theirs by themselves they could be by that on that account
and need it for they have theirs as well as they could if, if she
had done it all in order to have a copy.

Next.

By the time that they were having it having it in place of
many at once for them to believe that they were easily deceived
by their having every little while looked at them come to be
what was it for the rest of the day daylight and should it be the
most in use and union union of opposite to it to it to be to the
same that they were instilled for them in theirs in their as it
changed.

I left it.

This is very often where they have asked them to say to say
do they pay for it as well as when they thank you. Oh so well.

Always more and more may it be if they and can if they can
do they they must be at it be at once. She was disappointed.

I wish to be the first to have the best of it all.

After they made themselves be what it was they could be
theirs as much as they had by this time and I was wondering
could they be foolish.

Now this will be so.

CHAPTER CCXXXIII

It happened to be that they would come here and they would
if they had not only been so much so they would be and theirs
beside because let me see they had it.

When they were anxious they might find it.

Every little bit occasionally.

They were theirs by that time.

It is very customary very habitual very indeed for it as they
and usual very widely and very near very near to be that and
for it when they were theirs would they before it and would

they be more than finally do so. Finally do so and returned returned to their address.

Once when they had been finding do they ever wear it in
just at just at just and just in this way and they might.

She said that they wanted the other first.

Once and then and at a time does not describe does not only
describe grass and what they, were after it makes it very nearly
be theirs before they can say how can never having heard that
they were mistaken when will they be asked to have it by this
and when it is more than ever theirs by choice.

She meant it and it was said.

Once when they were very often needed needed and needless to say it was there by that time.

I always say that it is not at all why they could be where they
can select those having the longest and perhaps if you do you
wait if you do you wait.

CHAPTER

If he does and if she does and he does and a little very much
and which way and so it is better that which we do not say
because it is in their having every care every care is taken.

They meant to come when and where they have to be one at
at time and she was not pleased with it because they might be
as well as what do you do when they might as well have had
it by the time that they were not waiting.

Let me see what it is that she says. He says when you do not
do it and so much is done by theirs being having been and not
so much. Who can say that they are very much obliged.

She will be very well taken care of.

CHAPTER CCXXXV

They might be theirs by the time that when they are so very
likely beside and foremost they have it added in their having
so very nearly come to theirs as by arrangement coming to this
calling it for it so that when it is given they are not behindhand.
Not. Not in exchange and and is resisted lend lend it at most

as if it were theirs occasionally and deceived. He asked if it were necessary as he as going to be as he always did and they knew it as they can be careful of themselves as a reason. Very quickly. And when in the main they have been as nearly prepared to be always every little while as much as they could at their request. Once again. They make it do as much as they make it be theirs really left it out when they came to be having it always.

Let me be easily careful and this has been saved for this not saved for this anything that is not what she had had when she was uneasy was saved because they must be very well pleased in the way of relating it to have been almost the time that theirs was to be joined to the afternoon that was afterwards finally related to it as if they made most. Let us believe that they were influenced by their sister.

CHAPTER CCXXXVI

Finally finally say so.

I wish to know if it is feasible to have it be more than that when it is not best to be left in this way by chance and also I wish to know do they mind if they are more in the place of those that have been able to be here and like it and if also they are not only by that time but also individually likely to be further prepared so that they must be more carefully than ever shown that it is remarkable. After every little while they are widely seen to be really showing it to them and it is nice it is nice and orderly and they are whenever they like having it in a connected and velvety origin and this may be theirs for all the rest and it may be they might who would if they could be only very welcome. No one has forgotten that it was theirs yesterday and they would be very well known and after all they do not press it upon them. When they have been attended by every kind of readiness to say difficulty difficulty might it be very much as much as they can and could and relieve it relieve it in every way from there being any annoyance and so they wish it. Thanks for the message and the time that it has taken.

CHAPTER CCXXXVII

If afterwards they have rested I have rested.

She says every little more is a little more. When they are and had another thing added. At this time. They make it do. Thank you very much when they come. They are there by this time. It is not only convenient but really prepared and they can. Once more and letting it alone.

CHAPTER CCXXXVIII

They are receptive to their lilies of the valley. How many felt it to be theirs to manage to be warned and how may their being theirs made it difficult and difficulty succeeds to be followed by their relieving it as much as if they had not been taken to be in that way and theirs as much and care should be taken of them when they are found as well as gone. Thank you not thanking them. And now on their account.

This made it show this made it be theirs as they came to make it be more known than that relieved to have it anyway and could it be made to be coming coming makes it commendable and she could share that and the same as it for it and very carefully preparing it separately and in their only instance of why they went. They went because they made it do what was very nearly merry. This is not what is ever said settle stable and he quoted me.

Once they have found sixteen to one five to one one to one and he told all he knew of the four and we were very interested.

CHAPTER CCXXXIX

It is easy to see that it is easy to be distinct and shared when they have not all been about and why they must be theirs for it in negligence and around would she be pleased to have it thanked for, thanked for understood. A novel of thank you means that at any time they are as much when it is widened by its being really worn worn out worn less and less worn then and everybody can say should it be what they came to do. When they have left it alone. I am not pleased with it at all.

CHAPTER CCXL

I told him all that I was not only ready but more than there is of seeing it be aloud when they are shared between them and the most they had when they were touched by it in this and for themselves. Listen. When they did not not only hear but see see to it for it in it by it leave it we do not number them as twenty-seven by the way when did you hear about it and this makes it be previously not annoyed by that when she could be as nearly prepared to come and do it. Need it be more than it was after all as they can see by themselves to be left not only but carefully and not joined to it as their meaning. To describe others others came to have it only as if they could have it nearly should it be can they have held in theirs as allowance and when they had faded it was more than many upon them there because let me hear because let me lend it to them in their arrangement of not and by that time. The last time he did not give it and this time he did give it to me.

If every little while is why they came they must. That makes at admired hear and say the same. Let me tell you so shown as that and announcement. Grace Llewlyn Jacott made the most of it she had Fernande. Ellen Israel Lainer made the most of it she had Mrs. Berry, Edmund Minot Andrew had the most of it he had Pauline and what could be the end of by that time in chance chance of their reliance. To rely upon them for it is as much as they can do in this when they have been allowed why should it be that once they can and vipers. Vipers have been waylaid as much as fairly nearly high up on the rest of it as colored. It is easy to understand that a novel and thank you is about at the same time.

Might it be what they said.

Nobody who comes and shows all of it.

It is not only restful but rested.

Having heard that she was new and known to have a hand

to give to those who were to be allowed when they could have
their best to say that she must come and leave it here and now
and when they can be avoided, avoided stopped it. Thank you.

CHAPTER

A very great pleasure.
They might be.
Here it is is it.
If in having that be there while it is find it so much. Not
alone their being so kind as kind not alone their being and kind.
He made triumph triumph be welcome welcome be as well be
as we be as never to be used to it nearly as say so and they quoted
me. Why a while when they come here do they arrange in it
as a Tuesday. Tuesday there things happen. Monsieur Reynaud
Miss Beach and Mr. and Mrs. Hart give a party and on the afternoon of Tuesday and during the afternoon of Tuesday and invited others invited have either meant to make it really do you
believe that they cannot. Let me hear their voices and their very
much better now than either. Thank you Mr. Brooks. The party
of which I have spoken the entertainments of which I have been
told are taking place. She does not need to be away just at this
time. One two three she cherished me. Three four five they
went to think that it was as well to be very glad to see Mr.
House. Five six seven. They might be fortunate in knowing
all the differences between August February and April. Seven
eight nine having asked them to be well and happy.

From this time on they began to be very well able to have built
themselves a house.

At one time at one time it must be theirs where they make
and make it do.

Might have repeated where they make it do and leaving it to
all of it as much as much must be theirs by choice.

Returning to in the rest of it. Once when they had it for them
for them makes a batter batter be she was very likely to have
succeeded.

A conversation.

Was there indeed no likelihood of their being there.

An engagement.

Why when they ask do they mind it at all. If she had known that short and leave it not only on this side but on that side.

They finally did not continue to interest themselves in description.

CHAPTER

Might they have the best of it. Will it be as differently left to them. Shall and might they be desirous of having a whole rest of it be just this and just that.

What.

Why.

Where

When

When

If

Not

Why not.

Suddenly.

Let me believe every one every day.

Thank you.

Let me thank every one every day.

He did not like just the way that he told how it came about.

CHAPTER

Nothing to that Edward Wolfe is nothing to that very easily Edward Wolfe is nothing to that and very easily Edward Wolfe is nothing to that. Edward Wolfe is nothing to that.

Let me like it.

CHAPTER CCXLIV

I said that I did not feel that it would be possible that I would care that I would please be so much as able to be as it is in the way when it was about not to be refused and he would decline and now. Once again.

I said that I did not care to be more than prepared to have it said and not to be like it when it was and could be as thinking and if it was and be there at all not to be richly meant to have nearly followed by that at the time and now, when it is nearly not at all in this very much preferred not by any means at all and like and would not say and you do.

Let me sell it.

Once again and it is not that they are well enough to like it as it is. I said either he was not or would be taken to hear them and afterwards it is meant to be all all alone.

Once more.

When I was angry with him it was because I felt that it had begun anyway and I liked it now I shall be led to be where they are where where is the best way way and went went to be called and hear. Thank you very much as they listened.

Only once

Only twice.

CHAPTER

How do I feel about Paul and James. This is the way I feel about Paul and James. I feel this about Paul. I feel this about Paul and I feel this about James.

CHAPTER CCXLIX

Should not be.

Way away they stay let it alone be there beside hear it with the rest having made it all letting it have been then and they shall be can feel it I meant to have it just as well there it is when left to the rest while it is might it be lost I can be nearly very much of it for me. Now.

It is very well to have it sent to be perceptibly easily formerly and beside when they might supposing they waited for some one to come.

I do not wish to remember just what was said because if I repeat it they will have been and now after all it is not beside that that it has happened let me be the judge.

CHAPTER CCL

Never beside which is it when it and can be tried to be as the rest of the same time is just as well as well as to be disconcerted which is different from the same time. As different from the same time. The less that the one from the other is as soon makes it do.

I exchange it.

I leave well enough alone.

Not at it when it is in and finally reduced to that and there being this is much as it was and failing to be sure of the left it alone.

One

Two

To be sure.

CHAPTER CCLI

Come come coming.

Not as when he went.

Saving it as much.

And it was all along.

Now will you.

CHAPTER CCLII

And how to thank you.

It was nearly very carefully in plenty of time.

CHAPTER CCLIII

If one had not known Emmet Addis one would not enjoy it as much.

When it was better left alone then it might be very well attended.

If it could be arranged better arranged it would be as satisfactory.

As it must be as much enjoyed it is more easily left there

then and because of it being left nearly very often as it was to be followed. Thank you very much.

When it is very well done and when it is not very much more than asked for when it is most and best when is it to be allowed. Thank you.

It is by this time very much to be wanted and also as it is mostly there and prepared may it not be wondered about and as it is usual strange as it can seem to be left there regulated. Again thanks.

It is mainly because of this that it is fortunately what when there is no negligence it is as when it is as a right a right to be asked and answered and it is now an occasion for an expression of gratitude in the form of thank you very much.

It is this that is desirable that it is nevertheless undertaken and if it is better to be ready to come to go might it be just as much if replaced by just as well suddenly and find finally is as the mention of it so to be registered. In this way it is to be called away. This needed and needs the introduction of more if not of it and left if not of that and held if now and when is it to be nicely comforted. Thanking them for the intelligence and good will that has been displayed. Their satisfaction.

CHAPTER CCLV

Whenever it happens there must be a change.

It is not in this way nor by that attention that it is directed and feeling it weaken if in their arrangement there is having ended such such security.

CHAPTER

Her father said if you must do it do it graciously her father said if you must do it do it graciously and her father said if you must do it do it graciously.

CHAPTER CCLVII

Let me see pansies smell very sweetly.

CHAPTER CCLVIII

Leave it to me that pansies do smell very sweetly whether they are yellow with black centers or yellow with yellow centers either kind any kind of pansies smell very sweetly.

Leaving it alone.

Then they can be very much indeed when they were.

And they might have been as much as that.

When they were as if it had been sent.

Why they could and left it to them then.

If it is as much as if they had.

And why are they left to it because they could never come to be all told. Thank you for them.

It is not why and as much as they have come to be always used coming to be best at all and now they hear and leave it when they must be forced to have a considerable difference just so much of the time and thanked and left it and coming fortunately as they did.

They thanked him for theirs.

The next time to consider it and let it alone let it be in the place of arrangement and theirs by as well as if they could could relieved by well and having. Thanks.

CHAPTER CCLIX

Would you like to.

CHAPTER CCLX

Always knowing it.

It happened that he did not like it any better.

Theirs as well.

It would be best to have it heard at first as well as at last.

Just as well.

They might be once or twice finally to be sure of it.

Much and once more

And thanks to you

Thank you

Thank you very much

It is not best to call it all of it as it is when it is more than in praise. Praise and leave leave and let it come to first and find it come by chance.

Very nice and please and thanks.

It is in its way not might it change not might it come to have it here when as it comes out more it is in and alike when finds it to be more than as it was in case of change. They make no mistake.

CHAPTER

It is very well known.

It can be where it is felt as it in place of and in that at once as place. A place is situated on or between the most and best and find it. One can think. Not it to say. Let me see why. Not at all left to and sound and not at in by and for rent and not as it came and was seen seen to it change and left it to be next to the same when counted. Never thinking it well enough alone.

Does she invent a stitch.

CHAPTER CCL

It is their hope.

Thank you.

They make it theirs.

They feel that they know. They can be rested. They enjoy this. They do not like to do it. They leave it as they must when they are ready. They find it as they have every opportunity to originate what they find highly desirable. They must be partly very well prepared to allow them and themselves as well to manage to do it. They must be fortunately by this time left alone when they had the time to do it. Thank you for the pleasure you have brought and for the pleasant walk and entertainment and for the satisfaction of their being allowed to remain partly here and partly there and also for its being very well understood that she being a godmother would if she were able be pleased to come. This may be a part of it when it is nearly placed in such a position that it troubles them and that it troubles them as well and might it be not only in their interest but because of it being desirable that they must be finally author- ised to insist that there should be more than was at all necessary and if it were meant to be about to be changed they might be what they could if they understood it at the time and after- wards they feel that they must. At this time depend upon it.

They when they nearly are to be as seen telling very much as much and pleasing them insomuch that it is never question- able do they find them do they cease to make it be more than enough and have they had it as they very fortunately expected and with this as their arrangement.

Once more.

They need to be nearly perfectly and finally settling them- selves in such fashion that they must never mind it at all.

She was mistaken.

CHAPTER

Let me happen to have theirs as often as they do and might they and letting it be theirs come to be and as it came to be for their leaving as arranged. Let me listen to them. They need it fortunately coming to be through their obligation to the best that has been made where it is intended to let them have it there and so they might a little at a time. And I think so too.

They must be having it when they need it. Thank you for that. And they must by this time know it as theirs and do you think it right. I feel myself to have every need of it. She must have been very likely to have been left at the time and they they could be to be sure theirs very sincerely.

CHAPTER

When this is left what is it that is aid and also when do they commence theirs. She said that they might have been two. Two and now there will be every reason altogether.

Near by and by as it could be left as much alone and if it is largely that it is all of it not by that as it is to be left to be all of it made reckless. Gradually. It is to be that when it is felt as much as it is by that in it as a chance it is left here and being almost then to be why it must as it can be shall and fairly might it come to that instead by that time really and this that makes it as an extra having it to leave it come to that in its being more than enough to be appointed for it with it and alone and left to it for the best of that to them and for instance who did come in.

I am very much ashamed of having left it not out but around in the middle where there is part of the place that is arranged for it by this time as the way to be not having had it interrupted by the time apple orange grapes and learning and the place if it had been not only by that as it is in leaving more than is not as an announcement and nearly find it to be in exchange by to be left in the place of leaving it as what was not a connection between understood and understanding that is what is meant by their nearly shipping it to the nearly larger and after all who could put it in this place. Not as if it was the kind of difference that there is at that time. May it be known just how much it has varied.

CHAPTER

Never minding what is seen what is seen to be seen to be said what is said what is said to be seen to be seen to be said to be said what is seen what is seen what is seen to be said to following as much as they followed it by this time thoroughly and needing it as a mistake mistaken as around around and resting very nearly twenty times in relation to having found it. It is very pleasant to have them living as they do when they do. Very foolish to be very often left to themselves. Might be by this time. Let it be stated that a sentence does not begin and thank you very much.

Leave it to mislead and they will never say that they will go to the time when finding it very different indeed to a larger one. Never having been left to them it never having been left to them. Let me see that it is so.

A novel of thank you makes it be theirs too.

CHAPTER

Let it be left to them.
They might be just as well.
It might be all or more.
Can it be left.
When they are nearly there.
They must be always told.
Must and shall then be asked.
When it is best.
Let me never think about it again.

CHAPTER

After they came did they they came after they came did they
after they came did they after did they after they came did they
after they came did they after they came after they came did
they after they came she was very interested in saying did they
after they came he and she were very interested after they came
did they after they came they were very interested after they
came did they being interested after they came they did after
they were very interested after they came after they did did
they after they came they were very interested after they came
did they they did after they came they were very interested
after they came they had theirs as they had liked the best and
they had been if they had these as they were leaving it to them
after they did leave it to them did they and not to like it very
much very much and thanking thanking very much and they very
much as they were as they did very much and very well I thank
you. It is very useful to have a blue flower and a green stem.

CHAPTER

She made it do and so after a while it was an afterthought
after it was theirs to be left alone and have it as if they minded
that it was not very likely to be shared with them for them with
them all right and theirs were known as much as if they could

be seen and if they must when they and leave it due to them that they had been compelled compelled compelled to have it meaning that they should by that and leave it more than this with that and they can find it might be told just when when they were more than always right. They were more than always right. Leaving Saturday free.

It might be best to have it publicly known that the way that it is not at all related to their having thought it as a prize a prize which in between to-day and after to-morrow makes it leave that choosing the leaves which have been heard about might they be there to see. They might. It is very easy to predict. After that they make very little be all prepared for its renewal as they came left it might it be mine. Be mine as I said I do not understand if we were able and she was coming to the lest it be having had it not for that. It is something to be able to say that it was very likely at a time a day. It might be just as well.

Why can it be not so much as that. Because it is very well arranged. Do that like that is said that is be what he said and after all it was in a way that way. No one thinks thanks. She was not pleased in just the same way as Mrs. Stindast. Supposing there was no nuisance.

CHAPTER

Never have believe me so definitely they said that apart from it it was not nearly that they must be so so say thank you for for it is a very well known fact to me that it is not what they say but what they say what they did but what was done why they came but why they are coming and it is all a pleasure if I thank them very much and so having meant to be naturally please be there now will make invitations come once in a while every time when they are theirs by choice if indeed not as it is left alone to change it so often that it makes it be very well understood as to their advantage and at noon. To be accounted for by its being merely more detained and in a way by that in time with them as here by leaving it out now and as it is very well known to have many recollections which are not merely in this way but in that way for them. Let me have it at once.

Not and now around. Thank you very much for having introduced me to your mother.

CHAPTER

If Dorothy Niece and Eldred Leland meant to be united today how can there be very much more expected of Genevieve Clay and Milton Nome and if they had been there very often it might be that after a while being of the same size it could be distinguished as theirs at once and might they be very often very nearly morbid and blushing blushing makes imitation of Celestine doubly pleasant to them if it is not an inviting of Henrietta. Supposing she swallowed rapidly very rapidly and supposing she did not go did not go to the christening of her godchild would I be bound to imitate her. I might not be bound to imitate her but I might imitate her. If she says thank you at all she says thank you very much this makes it very well known. Thank you very much.

CHAPTER

Fluently
She makes it be theirs when she is not only as she was but as she is.

CHAPTER CCLXXXII

Always well to have it.

It is very likely it is not disliked it is not to be the same as here for them and now relieve me.

They make the same that is when night and beside as much as theirs to be and two can see it that it is beside the same for them and very likely used to be nearly as much as understood in time more leave it in the better of it can be not included as the day and daytime called when theirs is lately fairly well disturbed. Disturbed is used because theirs might be for instance. Once in a while.

Once in a while please me. Oh no theirs is why they have it left out and come to hide it as if in that month they were all together.

It is the method in the best leaving it alone should it fortunately this and there as a piece divided by re-stretching and leaving it announced and please can no one leave it have it and around.

I have made a mistake.

Not at a time.

Once it happened that they were very well about it and could be easily prepared to re-arrange their voices. This makes it that I have found it.

Re-arrange this makes it that it is found to be allowed fortunately theirs originally intended and but is it when they thank you.

I have told her about this at once.

Once more they came coming leaving it by that time.

Could they know if he were only three years old.

CHAPTER CCLXXXIII

Once they came to stay and shortly once they came to be asked why is there more than there was if you had three sons and a daughter.

Begin jealously to arrange the leaves where they are in tulips where they are in tulips where they are where they are in tulips.

This will if you please this will if you please if you please this will this will this will if you please please if you please this will this will if you please.

Might it be theirs by choice.

CHAPTER

I wish it to be remembered that I have to have have to have to to go to the leaving it alone for them. For them in this way. In this way as annoyance. As annoyance believing this readily this should never be allowed to be left more nearly next to it becoming to foreseen arrange it for the leaving theirs yesterday.

Yesterday makes it every day an Easter.

Thank you very much.

CHAPTER

Having met someone I can be had to leave it hoping theirs is as well known and should it be nearly called that. Anyone can thank them thank and thank you. To thank you.

CHAPTER CCLXXXVI

Leave it to me.

After it is very desirable to be attended as if it had been left there not to be called to have it heard that it is changed leaving it be securely managed arranged having a garden to be seen not by the time it comes happily happily at a time by leaving it for as it makes use of in change and more more than it might have been in the best way of reply. Replying to it. It might be nearly more when it is appointed come to be here need it leaving that alone surely in the place and quietly gained it most of all not leaving it about. It made the rest of it change places too. Leave me to see to it.

Needing theirs all right left it in that on that account this that the most of it when it should have have it not only there left it when it is not by it to be more in that case near and now. Leave it to me as I said.

The rest of the minding it in leaving in it by it being near nearly not not nearly only to be this at all when it is followed.

Very well I thank you.

CHAPTER

This makes it be as much as it is held held to it by the time this time is theirs when they may be may be to be lost. How can it be said about it about it being said being said it is lost it is lost at that time at that time faintly faintly they never matter it never matters to us at all does it now.

He was very displeased that they were not willing to dispose of it. Not now and not at all not at all and might they be easily pleased with it. Very well too to be sure. Not only by the time that they had been around. And to continue.

CHAPTER CCLXXXVIII

And to continue.

And they leave three at a time.

And they might be offered it now only only now as nearly as they know.

He said to thank him.

Merely not at once.

Whenever it is by the time every intention to be theirs too leave it to be shown when they came to more easily easily and nearly too. To remark it.

CHAPTER

I follow them blindly.

CHAPTER CCXC

Makes it partly.

Never needs to make it partly and never needs to make it partly and never needs to make it partly to have this to use it for that and deny it to the best of their arrangement.

I feel a really anxious moment coming.

This which is the way that it is placed so that it is added when it is alike and this around and liking not because of having asked at least their own alike. Thank you as much.

To feel leaving it to be sweet.

Sweet when you like.

When it is not only around but always meant at last to leave. Leave it to them it is not why or when it is not known allowed allowed and coming here by its own half and half of it can be. Can be could she ask how did they feel.

Once in a while.

I wish to know do you think that there is any difference between days and admire and leaving and coming to be careful and not as much as they could and having heard it before. I am not very well pleased.

I wish to know why I am anxious if I am anxious to be sure. I wish to know who can be left to take care of it. I wish to know how by this time it is not better than they liked. I wish to know might it not be that they were laughing.

One at once and two who makes you, I easily change makes to made and made to might and might to might it and might it might it be theirs just as well when they have been careful of it all of it all to will and leave it here. We are going to invite Mrs. Clermont-Tonnerre and Mrs. Brooks and Miss Hylan and Miss Arthur at the same time that we are going to invite Mr. McBride and Mr. Regan and Mr. Martin and Mr. Thomson and Mr. Talcott and Mr. Milton. We are also going to invite them as they are here. Having asked it of them we are certain that it is something that no one should ask of any one.

You are not pleased to be here and I am pleased to be here and I am pleased to be here and you are pleased to be here and you are pleased to be here and you are pleased to be here and you are pleased to be here and we are pleased that I am pleased to be here.

Thank you very much for that and for everything.

CHAPTER

Mr. Taylor Mr. Fletcher and Mr. Bradley.
Unconsciously.
Renewed makes renewed renewed.

They must be second and scarcely scarcely leaving it leaving it alone. Always thanking for that which has been this and theirs and theirs and then and then and let me know about it.

It was a mistake to eat strawberries after dinner.

The time when and the time in and the time then and they in a minute they be theirs next and and they had to meet to need to leave and second second to it at not leaving this in that case, in case may be as much as if they had to like what it is very

very compulsorily in the liking which makes not very nearly ever and ever so can they see that it is not in changing leaving it much as much as if they could from left to right and right to left satisfactorily.

She put it away perhaps it is gone if it is gone if he should come would I be at all likely to remember what I intended had intended to put in and if I do not what do I do. If he thinks to thank me. I have known that I have to have written written to have left left it in the way that I have not only not ever done before but also remember to remind it of me. And then as much as much in theirs in a minute severally leaving it by this in theirs coming to be through and recognising thoroughly the difference between a tomato and an apple from a distance as well as from a distance and well and from a distance and well why when both are beautifully red. Thank you very much for this distinction.

Can you be and when they mean to leave it all alone.

It came to be compared to it.

Now.

And then.

I have not a feeling that at any rate it should be having exchanged they and theirs to be sure as if in leaving having shall it coming reasonably and different as that as a little while theirs thoroughly. Should it just as if in this and their intelligence. All right around.

It might be that she resembled had it in the way of told to have reinstigated made it left to be and it was was it could it if they liked it much. She added butter to meat. Meet and leave the very nearly when they mend. It was very attractive.

CHAPTER

Leaving it to leaves leaves are as much and and is registered. Rely on this and that to make it mine. Mine any day.

One two three we went one two three one two three we went we went one two three we went. Leaving it alone.

There are two things to be considered thank you and there are two things to be considered and I have changed my mind.

It is by by and by by being certain by and by by being certain

by and by that they mean it. Thanking them alike. After all
and thanking them alike and it is just when it is might it be left
alone nearly and not not can be told at all when there is this
and increase to be left around and should it do would they be
having loaned makes it be once in a while after all mainly with
them.

Now I will tell it.

It is very remarkable but I do not know anyone whom I have
I had known at that time and it is very remarkable that at one
time it was not at all for this reason that they exchanged con-
fidences. I will never mean this.

Letting me have it.

CHAPTER

It was very well known that he and she had come and had
not stayed.

They had not stayed very likely because at this time they
were able to carry out the intention which they had had when
circumstances seemed to be possibly going to make it seem
more possible to do something else than that which they were
in every likelihood going to be doing. This makes it very much
more satisfactory to those endeavoring to decide not only upon
the exact situation but also upon everything in any way connected with it. Everyone anticipating that they had been very
much disturbed could be comforted. It is very likely that at
some time at some time and changing as it were more and more.

We as well.

I have not been at all disturbed by not doing it as it was hoped
that I would do it if I continued to return to it and I am doing
so. I promise that.

CHAPTER CCXCV

Little a little silver silver does get washed alike. When they
make them need it be that it was left to be as well as they had
said if they must.

CHAPTER CCXCVI

This makes it too yes you do.

Who makes what makes it makes it let it makes it do as it is to do and is to do. It is very well intentionally to make it come very well I thank you very well I thank you.

Now let me tell just how it can be left entirely by itself for them and it might. One two three just as sweet as she just as sweet as she she is just as sweet as when she as she must be seen to be known as just as well never to be left their entirely as seen to be. Now and then.

If Mr. and Mrs. Hardy and Mrs. Hardy's brother come at the same time as Paul Chantier is here is there any awkwardness in the meeting. There is because if it had been that they intended they would have been much more perfectly prepared to be not what is it when it could be theirs. Also if it is not by this time a mistake did it need to be found where it was when in describing it managed to allow this to be that in half leaving it so that it would be coming to be less than more also is in that chance by its being to be scare and nicely when it is and there is more. More can be left. May we ask her to make it for us.

CHAPTER

It is beginning to commence again which is why they must be sure to do it do it do it to be sure to do it do it to be sure to be sure to do it.

CHAPTER

This is what is what is what is not as much as this around.

Having been and leaving leaving and having been and not as much as when it is finished left to it like that.

Once twice and once more. They might have theirs as if it were as strange.

It is very likely that it can be can be that it is like that and this this might and might that when that can and that is left. Left left he had a good job and he left, left left left right left,

he had a good job and he left. From left to right and from right
to left satisfactorily.

This is what I told them.

It is never advisable to think that it is best to do so nor is it
advisable to have it be that then then and like it as it is as much
when it is not as it is not liking this to be the rest as known. Feel
it to be not amounting not that to is it leave and can it be the
best and have it have it should it should it when they recommence the most. Recommence the most is added.

CHAPTER

Once they came to say let it be that and this and twice first
and not as she could do knowing it too. Made it as much and
leaving it she never had been more than theirs at most. Let me
tell you just how I feel about it.

Please say the same and leave it be left to the same that when
it hindered that for this in this peculiarly peculiarly from left
to right and from right to left not peculiarly to be. Did he say
that he was left as old as that as old as that might it. It is very
easy to turn an old hotel into a new hotel. It is very easy to turn
a new hotel into a new hotel. It is very easy to turn a new hotel
and an old hotel into a new hotel and an old hotel. It is very easy
to turn an old hotel into an old hotel and into a new hotel. It is also
very easy to have a man who has as an occupation to sprinkle
something so that there is no great likelihood of it happening again
having the pair he has of shoes nearly newly nearly newly made.
Every once in a while. They stopped it stopped not that it stopped,
I stopped to say thank you very much. Always meaning which
it is. As it was left to them.

CHAPTER CCCI

Leaving again.

It is very difficult to be certain if it is or if it is not very likely
to remind and be reminded of it, it shall not be continued nearly
nearly really never to be left alone.

It is never to be left alone.

As I like it.
It is all.
Might it be.
Shall and have.
There is nothing to be regretted about having been born.

CHAPTER

He is certain that I will have satisfaction.

CHAPTER CCCIII

Not at any time need it be hoped that it will continue to be what they say as they passed and they passed in order to be not only very much but very likely theirs as well. What did he feel when he knew it. He felt that he could not but express this and that and also they might be very careful to be ready to go anywhere. They can be just as kind.

Let me describe Beverly Nichols. Beverly Nichols is as it is when they can let it ask again to-day or to say and not alone not when if that and in and change the most. It is very remarkable that although it is not by any means the case we she and he being and be obliged to make it and increase let me find you. Beverly Nichols is by the way just be so and it is remarkably there and all when this you see and letting letting it be more. Letting it be led and leading. It is this more than all. Beverly Nichols has been leading more than in the middle of the change and choice choice makes it choose and choose when the time soon and at best. Best and most when they may. Overly this looks in use of the reason why this is the rest. It is very nearly that now it can and it can and be and told and thank you as much.

CHAPTER CCCIV

To return to it.
When he was alone for me.
Every little while and come.

Leaving all.

Having that.

Shall it be splendid too.

He needed it at that time.

Letting it be charged at most.

At most and best.

They might be theirs.

Let it not be more than it was when they were they were
always where where it can join in with it leave most of it as it
is after all not mine.

They had been there.

CHAPTER

She had and they must be as well as when they can be heard
in the way that it is known to be finally left alone. Finally left
alone.

This is to tell that it is very well partly when they were waiting and beside when they agree to it for all of it by this time
that it can shall it be known. They liked it. Nearer when it is
nearly nearly by this time by this time it might be just as well
just as well known in time in time to go and it is not only best
and better than why is it when they prefer it. Make it do so.
Let it not be that only alone it is very likely why it is liked. Why
it is liked makes it not be all of it nearly as it is not by that time
as it is not as much as if it could be be called Marguerite Package.

There is no difference between Mildred Aldrich and Edith
Willow nor is there any difference between Elmer Harden and
John Fountain nor is there any difference between Bernard
Nichols and Philip Regan nor is there any difference between
Ellen Placing and Janet Bullen. Every little while they do. It
would be of use to them. They can be not at all very likely when
it is necessary. Show it to them now.

CHAPTER CCCVI

Please say it now when it is left as when they can and nearly
by this time all of it and now and likened to it be now. Be now
very careful of everything.

How differently do they make it do that do that do that in between what he knew that she was to to be sure that is to leave it alone. This makes theirs extra wishes.

Let it be why they went went to leave it leave it after it was it was partly when it was left there by the time they knew that they could be just like and liking liking it. Did he know why I came and left.

CHAPTER CCCVII

Describing how they asked and had it separated and then left it alone and after all how could it be followed about leaving it here.

Left it about and leaving it here and nearly not only perfectly but this not by this as it had been as it was being left alone by this time. It changed it to two. Do they like it. It might be what it was to be when it was known. There is always this having having having having having having having left it. What is the name of it when it is left.

Following follow me disappointing disappoint with it leaving it leaving it here having it all at once. Every time it was known that he knew it he knew it to be all left left to it. Why did it mean that when five five made it two and two divided by one. One must be what it meant meant so. Let it be liked that in two days more she is to be ready and up to that time fishes up to that time and after up to that time very like it up to that time how do they do that that is this that this is what this is as to like it. Thank you very much.

CHAPTER

That is about all.

Let it be very let it be who knows let it be who knows that when there is an answer to the let it be left where it is. Making it around to-day.

Who knows this is that.

To wish to say that they they let it be that it was let it be who knows. Let it be who knows how how to be let it be let it be who knows let it be.

This is how to be at last, at last most and best best and most.

Sincerely Beverly Nichols Avery Hopwood Allan Michaels and Rene Felicity also how many apricots are there to a pound.

That is one way to be all and wall if it met with the best that it was known would it be known to be utilised.

There can be no beginning in beginning a voice to let it have it alone that it is not by this time theirs to please. Every time in different different to be in the way. To wonder if she is right.

All right they admire them as they made it do and admired them as they did it because after that left it to them see said and might become that.

It cannot be felt that they describe rather they describe rather describe rather this as left left to them immediately. How do you do can you say that you know this as well that as more than it is by the time in which way can be left out. Left about makes it nearly not to change.

It has been a great pleasure that we have liked it.

CHAPTER

Make it much as it is never left alone by this to mean that never having thought of it to be that it would as much as the same that it had had in time. As this. If it is when the leaving it alone is not entitled to unison, left at once leave it as it was when it was where was it by the time it was to be like that entirely. Relieving it immeasurably. It is not as it is if it is when it is not as it is by door by door or just the same. It is as if in it and by the left and left it too and two make more. This is the time to do or say so. Having neglected it as thanks and thanking for this this and just as much. If it is not as it is in it as if it in the best and nearly nearly very very well let it alone now let it now let it alone. To be certain of the might and having what is by it as in place place of this as it and in and obliged. It was obligatory.

Can it be finally this and noon by this and if it is not which is theirs and he and all. Can it be continued to be now.

It might find this.

Can you be nearly ready.

Leaving and theirs is here.

Why did she do or do or do so. Thank you as much.
Having heard and said of Eddy, Eddy is his name sir.
Every letting it be mine to-day.
And I do.
Sharing it is principally as it should.
She did not believe I did. He did not believe I did. He did not
believe I did and she did not believe I did.
Wishing to ask another and mother and brother and as this
and as which and as well and as for this and for this and for this
and for this and for another. Separated just exactly so.
So and so is more than readily.
Does he really want to see me too.

CHAPTER

Having stated that it could not be thought of.

CHAPTER

She does.
When this you did she would she saw she might, just she was
the same and the same very much as much as felt and had and
could be left to that. Now then now and then.
Now to estimate what they do. They say and as it were to
turn and as it were to have and as it were to be and as it were
letting it not be this to stemming. In what respect did it have
that not to be the same as now when it is by this to that and leave
it hers and come to be and would if it could be as agreeably
agreeably means just as much as substance for it with it with it
while it is and even as and with it be the best that is it in the
time that it is left alone. Very well left alone. Letting it be all of
it once before.
Once every little while it was and drew.
That makes this be leaving, leave it to me.
First a piece of land being property having lilacs and snow-
balls and needing to be needed never to more than believe that
this is mine. In every way I avoid talking to and drew. Need it
in it by it with and west west directly four and four and out loud

and might might can connect with it by this and fortunes have been saved. Save is the same as saved and drew for you is the same as that and drew. Drew makes it be what is it.

What is it.

I wish never to neglect lamps and a spoon and spoons and this as well and as well and it might be likely likely for the nicest of it nearly be for two. How many can nearly be for two. To wish to be certain that neither inch being inches or like that being like that will be theirs again.

To thank you to think of it as it is to be thank you and I thank you.

CHAPTER CCCXI

Zucheville Dupoint Gavotte, a cheese.

These they a and neglect, these theirs this the distance and in place of every day that this is theirs. Shall it be what is it when when makes it leaves and leaves and leaves and leave it alone.

This in their way.

To very much prefer forests to fruit trees and fruit trees to marguerites and marguerites to follow and follow to arrange around. Let it be theirs instead of theirs instead of leave instead of white instead of white instead of is it why they did it as if it it was to be sure what it was as if it were meant. Is Fontainebleau open or closed is Fontainebleau open or closed is it open or closed is Fontainebleau open or closed.

CHAPTER

An instance of their expectation.

A relief to be a relief to sink or swim to be nicely and seem to have near it what it was. Let us be seated.

Near and nearly makes it stay makes it stay either way they might if they might who has to go around.

Thank you very much in English.

CHAPTER CCCXIII

It is very easy and easily it is very easily, it is easy it is nearly near it by the time that if in speaking he had a Greek mother and an Armenian father and he thanked in thinking thanking for a duck if they say duck if we say duck and a hen a hen and a dog and often all Scotland has been known to be divided into Lowland and Highland. What is the difference between this and why they meant meant to be all.

CHAPTER

Once more and they think to thank you.

CHAPTER

Thank you very much.

CHAPTER

It is very easy to be without doubt undoubtedly and they met it then. First they were and second they were and third they were and fourth they were and fifth they were, fifth they were.

Made it be very likely that after all let us hope that she will not regret it regret having decided to give up Lucy having decided to give up Lucy having decided to give up Lucy.

Theirs and this who had it called to mind.

Win and she very well and quite as I think and thank you.

Up and down introduces a nightingale.

Very well, I thank you.

She made it be returned to that it was what is to be there most and might it it is not with it who makes theirs be last.

Just as you say.

To hope that she will not regret having kept Robert.

And to hope that she will not regret to hope that she will not regret hope that she will not regret having kept if only as it

is as increasingly difficult having kept having not to be left to be
adding to be keeping to be hoping, hope to keep Robert in that
way.
   If it is mine whose is it.
   Thank you for this resemblance.
   And if it is better that it is why they say mixed it with a very
louder one what might it have if it is attended to. I never do like
it as you say I never do as you I never do like it as you say I
never do like it. This makes the most of it happen very often that
they do decide about the sun.

                              CHAPTER CCCXV

As say.
Say and settle
Settle and seal
Sealskin has value

                                 CHAPTER
   Leaving it as much as they could make it be rather very well
then how does it have it be left to this.
   To what it is.
   Not asked what is it.
   Not asked what is it because it is it, it is it, what is it it is it,
oh yes.
   Now one day and fifty away what do we say we say we will
say a little every day. What kind of a novel will I write. When
one day and one day and one and a day away what is there to
say nearly met it. It is remarkable remarkably so remarkable that
there is something that coming between where the sun is setting
and where we are sitting makes it be the same as there taking
and would it make any difference if every one of them had one
child.
   It is very extraordinary that as long ago as three hundred
years that they had second-hand chimney pieces put into their
houses. It is undoubtedly true and just as if it were repeated to
them repeated to this then to be sure. To very much regret not

having waited to have that with this. After all one can enjoy meaning, I mean to be let alone and not to tell her that now there is no need for it. Thank you very much and thank you very much is not forgotten.

How has it left it here to be this nearly. This how they were not to be disappointed. Thank you very much.

Commencing leaving it have it have that.

This is there when having changed where to why and why to waiting and waiting to be always might it be just now.

Having much to do to-day.

Letting this be told to them by now.

PART TWO

CHAPTER I

Christening.

Having hindered christening by all of them follow following to be by this time who can be happening to be leaving it for this. Thank you very much for christening.

Is it at all likely to keep on.

A great many are helped by this that it does not at all make it possible and said and thank you.

Beginning to be left to christening.

Jews do not like the country, yes thank you, christians do not all like the city. Yes and thank you. There are no differences between the city and the country and very likely every one can be daily daily and by that timely. Do be and to be and to be christened to be christened this makes pushing and pushing what there is in front of them. Then might it be what they might what they might what they might what they might what they might and change. We have left the pagoda behind us.

CHAPTER

It makes a difference if they say it say it that it is above and below and above and below. Thanked for thanking and pleasure

for pleasure and white by white and most and best. Having entirely satisfied entirely. Does it look like it. When the door is
open and in and the gate is open and in and always open and
the gate is always open and the gate is always open and in.
Always open and in means and flustered. Flustered is theirs
by and because it was connected.
In what way can it be not really leaving it alone. Yes and to
please please in the use and use and use of using. This not this
might and needed now. Let me make believe that I have seen it
and then. I will describe it.

CHAPTER III

Nineteen sixteen comes before nineteen eighteen and after
nineteen thirteen and very likely as soon as nineteen seventeen
and so forth.
A man who has been after what seemed to be twenty-six and
thirty-six years after that kept it as much as he could kept it as
much as if it was what she wanted. What did he do when he did
it. Does it make you more or less curious and is it what is it and
does it seem as if there was nearly likely to be what is it.
Need it be that she liked it. This is to describe how having
lost a pencil and regained it flowers were added not added afterwards but added before. This brings us back to this christening.
What is it.

PART THREE

If it were to be called Bedlington would it have to have the
name changed if it had another name or might one not more
easily do as it had often been done simply disregard the name
that is no longer being used in which case Bedlington will become its name. Moreover there is every reason to be thoroughly
content that this name not only was not given but will not be
attached to the place which it is now not any longer at all

desirable should be bought. The reasons why there is every reason to remember that there who made money in sufficiently large quantities either by the sale of their work or other work would in buying choose not only what was desired but what is no longer desirable no longer desirable means no change means indeed only an unnecessarily complete error. After all we have not had it nor do we intend to have it. We are now entirely occupying ourselves with an entirely different matter. A novel returns at once.

Never needing to be adding a novel never needing to be adding to a novel never needing to be adding to a novel at least never needing to be adding to a novel at least never needing to be adding to a novel. Never needing to be adding to a novel.

A novel of thank you and really they might do so too. What is a novel when it is not to do so too. A novel is not needed and so a novel and to do so too is not needed and a novel is not needed. There is a novel that is not needed the novel that is not needed is the novel never needing the novel that is not only not needed but also very well needed after having for this time liked theirs as well. To own a piece of be change be changed. The way to own a piece of be changed is to have supplied with a bell. To have supplied it with a bell as a request for supplying it with a bell makes it be that in this way it is to own a piece of it and in owning a piece of it it will be not occasionally that it is found to be a bell. To own a piece of it by owning all of the thing which was bought for it. Owning all the thing which was bought for it own a piece of it, anybody would know that that was that not by what was said but by what was bought, by what was bought and by what was bought, if it is in question.

In this way we have bought what is what is bought. In this way not only now but also just before going away quite a little while before going away, having given it to them at all not at all.

In this way a novel does not only begin but might it be what it is that they ask them. They asked them to stay but not yesterday.

What might it be by this and where, where it would be very undesirable and might it not be due to having wanted it for that.

It might. Having placed their arrangements all around how often can one one and two be deceived by architecture. Twice certainly. After that should there be any active arousing of their being very nearly left alone very nearly left alone. A man may not be there at the time. This is the difference between this and that.

THREE MORAL TALES

THREE MORAL TALES

One Two Three Four Five Six seven, all good children go to heaven some are good and some are bad. One Two Three Four five six seven.

Water is cruel, war is cruel, weather is cruel weddings are cruel, windows are cruel and accounts accounts are regulated.

When I went to England I met a man. I said to him what do you think of bathers. He replied bathers are deep in water. Not all of them, I said. No not all of them he replied. In a way it is not terrifying to hear an elaborate reply. All the forms that substitutes take are pitiful.

It has been often said of London that there is not nearly as much distance to be covered in wandering about Paris as in wandering about London. We have found this to be a fact. We have also noticed that one more readily walks long distances in London than in Paris. In fact it is almost certain that the same conditions keep the flowers fresh and of an extraordinarily brilliant color. And yet light is not as light as violence. No one pushes violently. Because in sincerely addressing one another one certainly means to be an advantage. These are moral tales.

I fled. I fled from the vehemence of speech action and elaboration. In violent actions there is no elaboration.

Please me by pleasing me.

Can you consistently wonder why you wear red yellow blue and mauve.

The detail is this.

A man of a certain age met a girl. He said to her why do you wonder about navies. She replied in no uncertain voice. I do not wonder. He earnestly said. I believe in speech in thought in action and in gestures. She replied I cannot be unconscious. He was worried. He said I have not pursued my intention. She replied. I have not belief in masterpieces. And he said earnestly. I am not patient and earnestness is jeopardised by reproaches. Do not reproach me, said the girl. I do not reproach you he answered, but I regret that you do not see your way to analysing reproaches. I do not fear reproaches said the girl and then she withdrew with her mother. It is certainly very easy to hope that health will improve and that all women have a mother. Really we have almost questioned the truth of all these reflections.

We said of someone how do you mean to flatter. He replied by losing my three sons and their mother. And wealth, we asked. No not wealth. I am wealthier than ever. Do you regret anything we kept asking him. I regret nothing, I regret that responsibility is not lacking.

A young man is in a position of great responsibility. He can decide about men and women. He has nothing to do with children. Work does not agree with him. What can we do to make him realise that work does not agree with him. I am afraid, nothing.

I am afraid of nothing. I am nervous when I am irreligious, I am querulous when I have substitutes and I do not delight in cures. Cure me of seasons. Please cure me of seasons.

Raymond Ferguson was easily imprisoned. He felt that he hoped that he intended to banish everything and to commence by idling. He said let there be war and there was war. He lost his three sons, his wife, his china and his dishes. He kept his glass and his wealth. He grew steadily richer. He died an old man. In blossoming he said I have a daughter. He had no daughter.

In reasoning he said I do not recognise war as slaughter. There was no war, there was no daughter, there was belligerency as he had taught her. In this way he called out every day. Swim to-day, oh you little fairy swim to-day. Silver and glass. Who knows more about silver and glass than some do. Silver and glass birds and dishes, climate and ferocity, fog, and irreligion, an old man has a great deal of air. He likes to publish his wishes. There are many aids to wishes.

I climb to a fight. When the ball is all wet, can a dog's mouth wet a ball, when a dog is all wet, why do you worry a kitten. No one is a kitten. Alas, the beginning of eating is soup and after that, after that fish, and after that, after that, meat, and after that, and after that, salad and after that, and after that, savory, and after that and after that and after that, after that fruit.

II

Birthdays are honored.

Intelligence for intelligence how can you believe in betterment. They are not typical.

Did you explain to me why you felt that about it. Let us listen. Women as readily as anyone have certain songs. Men and other members of the human family urge us to do better. We can say that pearls are pearls and we can also regret that amber is amber color. We can also reason about whether it is especially noticeable that actions lead to war. Do actions lead to war, does war lead to action does menace lead to kindness does alarm lead to calm.

We have a story to tell.

In the midst of the many people at the end of the street, when we say top we mean where we are when we say bottom we mean the bottom, in the midst of the many people who were standing there together there were some who spoke English. English is a pleasant language. One can explain that.

They were all standing and no one stands a long time without moving without training. They were not trained. There were a great many standing at the end of the street and among them were those we admired. We found them very beautiful. We recognise beauty by disagreement. This may simply mean that I am not interested. Do you need necessarily to turn your head in looking sharply from left to right and from right to left.

I can feel the beauty.

How do you do I forgive you everything and there is nothing to forgive.

I explained sentence by sentence just exactly what I mean. I mean to convey the impression that reflection upon moral themes is so attractive because we learn by this means to spend money freely to earn to lose, to enhance the illustration of parade. How easily we ride the loss. How uneasy we are when we are pained. In these days we are not easily pained. We cease to tranquilise ourselves.

I very recently met a man who said, how do you do.

A splendid story.

William who was employed as a gardener married the only virgin in Pansy. Pansy is a pretty name. He said he would not remain in Pansy unless he earned a good living and so he raised his prices from one dollar and twenty cents an hour. Imagine what pleasure everyone had in registering the name of men and women in the Pansy meeting. How curious everyone was and what a long time there is for blooming every season. Lilacs and hawthorn and marigold and spirillum.

Another evidence of creation. He had heard of my cousin. She had heard that I had lost something. She wrote mysteriously that it had been found that it had been found by little Aileen Louise's little girl who had not known what it was and it was a miracle because a great many wagons had passed all morning. I had missed nothing.

A long way to go it is a long way to go if you go all the way to the South from all the way north. It may be cold, it may not, it may not be very cold.

A story of sculpture. Bend down, look up, trust a chair, and read a dove. A dove and a pigeon and a merry-go-round of pigs saturate a drunken man. I do not believe in drunkenness. Can you meddle with me.

Sculpture. Sculpture is made with two instruments and some supports and pretty air. Air is so pretty. Air is so very pretty. There is such very pretty air there. We are not in contact with millions of posies. Posies and poses. Wretched roses and wretched willows. Why do weddings sleep. Because the oranges were frozen. We are going to see. We are going when they have invited us to be.

I am discouraged with sculpture.

I do understand Cynthia. Grace calls her Cynthia. I do understand her. What did you say I did not say anything. Where shall I put it. Put it nowhere. He replied.

Loving birthday wishes to my husband. All that is fairest
brightest and best. On this your birthday dear Husband be your
guest. Birthday greeting to my dear wife. My darling wife may
all that's good in life be yours to-day and lasting happiness be
yours that shall not pass away and as the years roll onward all
gladness may you find and every hour be lighter than the one
you leave behind.

III

Individual wrongs. To be right. Women are usually right. To
be always right. Men are almost always right. To be very much
in the right. Women and children and men are almost always in
the right.

Mrs. Edward Malay, Mrs. Edward Malay had a friend. This
friend travelled with her and then she wrote of her travels. They
were both timid. They did separate. And the lamp. We do not
use lamps in Paris.

When the sun shines there is no reason to be nervous. We hope
that the sun will shine.

This is a description this is to be a description of the success of
making fun of your country.

Mrs. Gainsborough had been moderately successful. She lived
she met people whom she interested. She blushed, not as we
might say from shyness or from awkwardness or from irritation.
How can you blush.

She was friendly. We were not friendly. Do not listen to us.
I often ask myself what would we do if we were together.
Where. In our home.

Oh dear home.

I exclaim.

A moral tale of Russia.

My cousin is not a Russian.

He was not born a Russian. He has not become a Russian.

Moral tales of yesterday. To-morrow we are going to be led.
Led where, led away. To-morrow he is going. Early. Yes we
hope quite early.

Moral tales for every day.

Hungarians why are Hungarians hungry.
Why are Englishmen sad.
Why are Belgians notorious.
Why are Americans slow.
Why are Indians neglected.
And why are Negroes stale.
Bread is stale.
Moral tales for Negroes.
Negroes are blessed when they receive.
And was that a pretty compliment.
Who honors a birthday. How do you know when you were born.
Stern measures of reform.
Language was reformed. Language is reformed, nectarines, cake and sandwiches and a great deal of veal.
Let me tell what happened to Kitty Lodenstall. Kitty was the wife of a professor. His name was Royal South Lodenstall. She had succeeded all their lives in everything. One son was killed in the war, so was another, so was their daughter. This left them two sons and a daughter. One of these sons was killed in the war.
A long story to finish.
I could not wish anyone to expect me. There is a lack of frankness in this arrangement. And everybody smiled.
A story.
A daughter of the armistice. They were poor they expected to be poorer.
I need not care I need not despair.
Often I think about another.
Emil Favre was a young gentlemen who had been educated to be the son of a school teacher. He thought very well of himself. Most unexpectedly he went to the war. It was not unexpected in one sense because he was actively in service in the army when the war broke out and the war was not unexpected.
He was wounded but not seriously and his heart did not trouble him. How easily all men are equal. A great many people talk readily.
In this way Emil Favre was wonderful. He was not insistent. Very well.

Very well.

I hear very well.

And his eardrum.

And his eardrum had been, his eardrum had been it was not all right.

Emil Favre was not at liberty.

He was older than the purse.

How can you call him.

Emil.

Emil.

He and his brother and his father.

Arose. He arose in the morning and whistled.

A handsome state a handsome estate is one in which windows burn in the sun, balconies are little and tender, houses are rose color and doorways have curtains. I am genuinely astonished by my experience. And is he. He has not had the experience. And eggs. He does not fancy eggs. And breathe. He breathes very well.

Splendid little pastime. And names. How old are names. Emil Favre was born in the mountains. His home was the home of thunder his village a village of lightning and his passion his passion was for bicycles for balconies and for seasons. For four seasons. All four seasons look alike, that is if you travel. How pleasantly were painters published. They publish them in sets.

How easily are gifts received and returned. How easily.

Emil Favre was anxious that history should repeat itself. He says I so often hear praises.

Emil Favre cannot say that he is pleased with the result.

A door should be a door must be a door should and must be open or closed. Close the door and draw the shades. Close the shutter and open the window. Open the window and open the door.

Anybody can make that song.

Thank you very much.

PRUDENCE CAUTION AND FORESIGHT

A STORY OF AVIGNON

PRUDENCE CAUTION AND FORESIGHT

A STORY OF AVIGNON

It is just what they would do eventually.

Leon was married. He had a wife. He had four children. He had four girls.

He has come

Who has come.

That does not attract the attention of anyone.

Who has come

He has come

He has not come.

Leon was married, he had a wife, he had four children he had four girls. They were all young. Leon had been told, he told that it was better to be nervous than to be neglectful. He was not nervous and when he received a reward he was rewarded.

In varying religion he did not mean to write for them. Nor did he. Nor did he die fighting. Nor did he differ from the men who sang. They did not sing to be told that they were singing. They did not sing in order that they would prefer tears. How can you cry and not die.

Prepare to be a little astray. Do not prepare to describe to-day. He described how he saw all he saw and he had not seen bridges and water and climbs. He never climbed there because his friend had not been there before he had not been there before or after he had been there. He told us what was more important than this to him.

When he had not been left alone and could you be really prepared in a mine or in a ditch or in a room when he had really never been left alone he rarely felt that he had forgotten to mention the matter. And regularly when there was danger he could recollect that he could see before him his four children who were four girls. He never thought then of calling the littlest one a one languaged butterfly, nor did he speak to us of heredity. He felt that his wife had had sisters and brothers. And where were they please.

If you please.

Leon was necessarily dead not necessarily dead.

Leon had not been perfectly immune. Nor had he chosen to see to be.

He had indeed followed advantageously. And in following he had not felt very nervous nor very timid nor very aggressive nor very dangerous. He had indeed felt that he was to be spared. And was he. He was.

He collected readily he recollected readily and more easily than not he was angry. And when he was angry what did he say. He said he had not neglected his own affairs. But he had. And then the contradiction was made and he contented himself with work for himself and others. In coming to addition he again added that he was no immune. That he did not know this and that he had not neglected to add in addition.

We see opposite to us another older and we hear opposite to us a calendar. Leon did not mean to be more assiduous.

Can you have their adventures with a mother. With their mother. Their mother later arranged a little writing table for herself.

Leon did not prepare pleasantly. Oh yes he did.

Leon very nearly entered in here and he very nearly entered in here again.

From this there was no appeal. And in reality catch as catch can is not a plan.

There is a bridge at Avignon can you believe that it is a suspension bridge when you see it or when you walk on it.

I arrive.

I arrive here and I leave here after I have arrived here.

Expenses color me in a way.

PRUDENCE.

Leon neglected no fanaticism. He did not neglect any fanaticism. Nor did he fear to consider that he had escaped the rest. He was not nearly so easily restored not nearly and he undertook nothing else. He was not extraordinarily circumspect. He was not more cautious than he was prudent and in a manner of speaking he had slept well.

CAUTION.

When I was connected and caution was said to be more meaningful than patience I remembered that I had meant what I said.

Leon was not more cautious than he was patient. Prudence and caution do not mean being prudent and being cautious. In Avignon every other day is every other day. In this way they separate night from day. This did not concern Leon who was not readily adaptable. How can you please to see. You do not deny any occasion to preach repetition to me.

Leon was useful and necessarily satisfied. How can he visit this on himself. And where does he prepare to stay. Leon was not more cautious more patient nor more prudent than in war and in peace.

FORESIGHT.

To foresee changing places. If you foresee changing places do you change Avignon for Marseilles and Marseilles for Avignon. If you foresee do you foresee what there is to foresee. Do you foresee that you will be pleased and not seen when you no longer care to see to it.

Leon died.

And this made it easy to foresee that he would have been better pleased if he had been very well.

It was easily felt to have been left to remember there was plenty of foresight.

Prudence caution and foresight, and she foresees and he foresees and there are a great many hills in Marseilles and none in
Avignon. There are hills around Avignon. Avignon is a walled
city and the river is close to it. Marseilles is built on hills and the
river runs into the Mediterranean and Marseilles is on the
Mediterranean and the Mediterranean is close to it.

Prudence caution and foresight.

Leon had a wife he had four children all of them girls.

Foresight.

Leon was nearly as well attended to as if he had been married
and had had the attention of his wife and he did not have necessarily to have pleasure in repeating this to them.

I foresee that he will see to this and to them. Now it is all
changed. If you change you change that and if you change that
you change this and if they change this they are not more than
changed.

He did not die to cry. No indeed nor did they hurry. You
hurry where they hurry, and they hurry where he hurries. He
does not hurry here and there. He did not hurry.

And yet in his movements in his movements he was very hurried in his movements and in his ways he was hurried in his ways
and in his way there was nothing in his way. In his way he was
very useful and proud and decisive.

Ring again.

Pleasurable.

How pleasurable.

I foresee an added alarm.

What did Leon see.

He saw just the same and he did renounce his attention to
pursue himself adequately. Do be gloomy to-day and do say
that Leon went away. He did not go away in that manner of
speaking.

Hear him express himself readily, hear him recount and recount and yet he and yet he had seen the same when at the same
time violence was all the same. Is violence all the same and is his
attention the same and is his intention the same and is his attention the same and does he answer the same answer and does he
answer and does he deserve and does he serve and does he ob-

serve and does he quiet them and is he quiet then and did he answer and did they ring and did they ring and did he answer and did he address and did he have address and did he come to say what did he come to stay and did he stay there where did he say. Do say were you interested in what he did say. He said well he was conversing then he said he understood very well and naturally he was not neglectful.

Foresight means going to Rome. A frenchman does not roam. No indeed. Leon was a frenchman. And his wife. Did I say his wife. And why was she faithful and why were there four children. The four children were little girls. In the meantime cheerfulness can be me met and so can energy and economy and foresight and administrative ability and too great abstention. And in the meanwhile were we sorry. We were very sorry when we heard of it. And the way to place a name there his name there her name there, she placed her name there his name there not their name there.

Not the name there. Naturally not the name there.

She stayed there.

A LITTLE NOVEL

Fourteen people have been known to come again. One came. They asked her name. One after one another. Fourteen is not very many and fourteen came. One after another. Six were known to be at once. Welcomed. How do you do. Who is pleasant. How often do they think kindly. May they be earnest.

What is the wish.

They have fourteen. One is in a way troubled may he succeed. They asked his name. It is very often a habit in mentioning a name to mention his name. He mentioned his name.

Earnest is partly their habit.

She is without doubt welcome.

Once or twice four or five there are many which is admirable.

May I ask politely that they are well and wishes.

Cleanly and orderly.

Benjamin Charles may amount to it he is wounded by their doubt.

Or for or fortunately.

No blame is a blemish.

Once upon a time a dog intended to be mended. He would be vainly thought to be pleasant. Or just or join or clearly. Or with or mind or flowery. Or should or be a value.

Benjamin James was troubled. He had been certain. He had perused. He had learned. To labor and to wait.

Or why should he be rich. He was. He was lamentable and discovered. He had tried to sin. Or with perplexity.

She may be judicious.

Many will be led in hope.

He was conveniently placed for observation. They will. They may well

Be happy.

Any and every one is an authority.

Does it make any difference who comes first.

She neglected to ask it of him. Will he like gardening. She neglected to ask her to be very often. Made pleasantly happy. They were never strange. It is unnecessary never to know them. And they

Be happy.
Any and every place an authority.
Those at court any difference who comes first.
She returned to say it is real. Will he like the gardening. She
departed to call her home very warm. Made pleasantly happy.
They were never strange. It is much easier never to know them.
And they